The Journey Prize Stories

Winners of the $10,000 Journey Prize

1989
Holley Rubinsky for "Rapid Transits"

1990
Cynthia Flood for "My Father Took a Cake to France"

1991
Yann Martel for "The Facts Behind the Helsinki Roccamatios"

1992
Rozena Maart for "No Rosa, No District Six"

1993
Gayla Reid for "Sister Doyle's Men"

1994
Melissa Hardy for "Long Man the River"

1995
Kathryn Woodward for "Of Marranos and Gilded Angels"

1996
Elyse Gasco for "Can You Wave Bye Bye, Baby?"

1997 (shared)
Gabriella Goliger for "Maladies of the Inner Ear"
Anne Simpson for "Dreaming Snow"

1998
John Brooke for "The Finer Points of Apples"

1999
Alissa York for "The Back of the Bear's Mouth"

2000
Timothy Taylor for "Doves of Townsend"

2001
Kevin Armstrong for "The Cane Field"

2002
Jocelyn Brown for "Miss Canada"

2003
Jessica Grant for "My Husband's Jump"

The Journey Prize Stories

From the Best of
Canada's New Writers

Selected by
Elizabeth Hay, Lisa Moore, and Michael Redhill

National Library of Canada Cataloguing in Publication

Library and Archives Canada has catalogued this publication as follows:

The Journey Prize stories.

"From the best of Canada's new writers".
Annual.
15-
Continues: The Journey Prize anthology.
ISSN 1707-9640
ISBN 0-7710-4393-7 (volume 16)

1. Short stories, Canadian (English).
2. Canadian fiction (English) – 21st century.

PS8329.J68 C813'.010806 C2003-904912-4

We acknowledge the financial support of the Government of Canada through the Book Publishing Industry Development Program and that of the Government of Ontario through the Ontario Media Development Corporation's Ontario Book Initiative. We further acknowledge the support of the Canada Council for the Arts and the Ontario Arts Council for our publishing program.

For "The Uses of the Neckerchief": The quotations about scouting are taken from "Scouting with a Neckerchief" by W. E. Longfellow (The Boy Scout Service Library, Series B, Number 6, Boy Scouts of America, 1927). The geological material is taken from an article by Peter Russell in *Wat on Earth* (vol. 14:2, spring 2001).

Typeset in Trump Mediaeval by M&S, Toronto
Printed and bound in Canada

This book is printed on acid-free paper that is 100% recycled, ancient-forest friendly (100% post-consumer recycled).

McClelland & Stewart Ltd.
The Canadian Publishers
481 University Avenue
Toronto, Ontario
M5G 2E9
www.mcclelland.com/jps

1 2 3 4 5 08 07 06 05 04

About The Journey Prize Stories

The $10,000 Journey Prize is awarded annually to a new and developing writer of distinction. This award, now in its sixteenth year, and given for the fourth time in association with the Writers' Trust of Canada as the Writers' Trust of Canada/McClelland & Stewart Journey Prize, is made possible by James A. Michener's generous donation of his Canadian royalty earnings from his novel *Journey*, published by McClelland & Stewart in 1988. The winner of this year's Journey Prize will be selected from among the thirteen stories in this book.

The Journey Prize Stories comprises a selection from submissions made by literary journals across Canada, and, in recognition of the vital role journals play in discovering new writers, McClelland & Stewart makes its own award of $2,000 to the journal that has submitted the winning entry.

This year the selection jury comprises three acclaimed authors: Elizabeth Hay is the author of two novels, *A Student of Weather*, winner of the CAA MOSAID Technologies Inc. Award for Fiction and a finalist for The Giller Prize, and *Garbo Laughs*, which was shortlisted for the Governor General's Award and won the Ottawa Book Award. Her short story collection *Small Change* was a finalist for the Governor General's Award, the Trillium Award, and the Rogers Communications Writers' Trust Fiction Prize. In 2002, she received the prestigious Marian Engel Award. She lives in Ottawa. Lisa Moore is the author of two short story collections, *Degrees of Nakedness* and *Open*, winner of the Canadian Authors Association's Jubilee Award for Short Stories and a finalist for The Giller Prize and the Winterset Award. Her work has appeared in Canada's most prestigious literary magazines and has been anthologized in *Coming Attractions*, *Best Canadian Stories*, and The Journey Prize anthology. She writes a biweekly column for the *Globe and Mail* and lives in St. John's. Michael Redhill is an award-winning poet, playwright, and novelist. His first novel, *Martin Sloane*, won the Commonwealth Writers Prize for Best First Book (Caribbean and Canada region) as well as the 2001 Amazon.ca/Books in Canada First Novel Award. It was shortlisted for The

Giller Prize, the Trillium Award, and the City of Toronto Book Award. His most recent book of fiction is *Fidelity*, a collection of short stories. He is the publisher and one of the editors of *Brick*, a journal of literary non-fiction. He lives in Toronto with his partner and their two sons.

The Journey Prize Stories has established itself as one of the most prestigious anthologies in the country. It has become a who's who of up-and-coming writers, and many of the authors whose early work has appeared in the anthology's pages have gone on to single themselves out with collections of short stories, novels, and literary awards. The Journey Prize itself is the most significant monetary award given in Canada to a writer at the beginning of his or her career for a short story or excerpt from a fiction work in progress.

McClelland & Stewart would like to acknowledge the continuing enthusiastic support of writers, literary journal editors, and the public in the common celebration of the emergence of new voices in Canadian fiction.

For more information about *The Journey Prize Stories*, please consult our Web site: www.mcclelland.com/jps

Contents

INTRODUCTION

In reading through the eighty-one stories gathered for consideration for *The Journey Prize Stories* this year, we were looking for nerve-scraping suspense and bone-deep pleasure. We wanted to read stories that were heartbreaking or hilarious, or stylistically brazen. Gorgeous, emotionally driven writing, shot through with wit. We wanted to find what we half-suspected, and what we could not have previously conceived. We were looking for moral complexity, questions with no easy answers, all the answers. We wanted stories that made us squirm with discomfort when we came upon a character with whom we could completely empathize and who was about to make a very bad, life-altering step. We wanted to be jarred. We wanted sensuality. Pyrotechnics. Bold, steely confidence. Surety. We wanted our curiosity inflamed and satisfied. The brand spanking new. We wanted all of that.

And we were thrilled whenever we came across these elements of the story. We were thrilled by glimpses into new worlds thoroughly realized and ultra-fresh. We found stories in which every word was in the right place; words with no choice but to be exactly where they were.

Short stories can do everything a novel does, only faster. The stories we chose for inclusion in The Journey Prize anthology are fast-paced – stories that engage the engines of thought and emotion and make them rev, so that time flies past while we read. These are stories that charge toward a nascent, inevitable conclusion, one that we didn't see coming.

However short a short story, it has the ability to allude to not only the entire life of a character, but the social and political terrain of the nations and histories which formed those characters. Think of the gesture drawing that can capture, in a matter of minutes and a few scrawled lines, the model's shape and mood, the tension in her body, where she aches and feels good, how the light falls over her. A short story can encapsulate a similar wealth of detail just as succinctly – with a well-placed line of dialogue or a small domestic moment a whole life unfolds before the reader.

The stories we pounced on with excitement were the ones that showed a vast imaginative scope and some or all of the elements of fiction mentioned above.

Patricia Rose Young's "Up the Clyde on a Bike" is a character-driven story, with pitch-perfect dialogue and an uncanny ability to suggest the complexity of a past barely hinted at.

Kenneth Bonert's "Packers and Movers" shows, convincingly, the paralyzing apathy of a young man, hopelessly defined by the bitter racial tensions of South Africa. The seemingly unavoidable, subtle hatreds and impotence Bonert articulates in this story will unsettle any reader for a long time.

The story "Benny and the Jets" by Jennifer Clouter is beautifully imagistic. Take, for example, the moment when Clouter's protagonist, a boy on a camping trip with his family, puts his eye to the opening of a gas can to watch what happens after he has dropped a lit match inside. What happens is an elegantly constructed, artful building of suspense and horror which, naturally, explodes.

Or the humour and bathos in Devin Krukoff's "The Last Spark" that makes each moment bright and fierce, however ordinary the occasion, in this case, a small gathering of friends who have come together to have a few drinks at the boss's house.

Reading these stories was an honour and a pleasure. The best part of our job was seeing the short story stretch and morph and redefine itself to articulate the diversity of truth writers in Canada are compelled by and obsessed with, the many different truths that are shaping the short story form anew.

We would like to thank McClelland & Stewart for their support of new writers through The Journey Prize, and the editors and staff of the literary magazines for showcasing the work of Canadian writers. *The Journey Prize Stories* is a celebration of the best short fiction in the country, and Canadians are recognized around the world for their advances with this art form because of such endeavours.

Elizabeth Hay
Lisa Moore
Michael Redhill
Toronto, June 2004

The Journey Prize Stories

MICHAEL KISSINGER

Invest in the North

My father was not an intelligent man. He lacked what most people would consider an adequate and proper education, having left school by the time he was eleven when his father killed himself in the family kitchen. His father had come home early from work after being laid off, had locked my father and my father's mother in a broom closet – they were both small people – and shot himself in the stomach with a deer rifle. He finally died four hours later. Two hours after that a neighbour, quite by accident, discovered the body and removed the chair that had been wedged under the doorknob of the closet.

It should be said, on the other hand, that my father was not dumb. In fact, he seemed to appreciate the fact that I possessed a certain sensitivity that allowed me to make such distinctions. Unlike my older brothers, who had only come to the same conclusion after years of getting it beaten into them – although I suspect that their opinion of him had merely shifted to where they no longer thought him dumb but mean. Actually, my father was not a particularly mean person either. He just knew that there were things that needed doing, regardless if anyone, including himself, liked the outcome or not – whether things ended pleasantly or something less.

He once said that an intelligent person and a dumb person were essentially one and the same. If you were to ask the intelligent person or the dumb person why they had gotten to where they were in life, they would both say it had either had something to do with the choices they'd made, or plain luck – whether good luck or bad luck or just dumb luck. Although the way he saw it, a person's situation – the way they had come into it and the way they would leave – was governed by something significantly less forgiving.

It was near the end of a particularly mild August, a few weeks before I was supposed to start my last year of high school and then graduate and then go on to who knows what. But since the spring, I had made it abundantly clear to my father that I had no intentions of going back. It had been an unpleasant year.

What's out there for a boy like you? he said on more than one occasion. But deep down I think he knew there was little sense in arguing – that a person of my persuasion would never be given an easy ride through school, if anywhere. My schoolyard fights and suspensions had been more or less expected – they had been going on ever since I first went to school – but when I'd started hanging around a certain bar near the fish docks and cavorting around town with a group of college boys and not caring who knew about it, things had become uncomfortable.

At the time, my father worked for a man named Douglas. A man who, like most things in my father's life, existed out of sight and was rarely, if ever, talked about.

Those who knew of Douglas referred to him as the Mayor, although our town already had a mayor – a drunk who had made his fortune in waterfront real estate and dressed as a pirate whenever attending public functions. I remember once when I was quite young and had to march in some parade for cadets, he had walked alongside me for a while, wearing his pirate costume. Invest in the North, he'd said, rapping his blotchy knuckle on the drum that I was supposed to be playing. He even had a sword with him, tucked through the belt loop of his white knee-length pants. Invest in the North, where the land is ripe and the water is ready. Invest in the North and you can never go wrong.

Although my father never talked of Douglas, I knew that he was a man my father respected a great deal. Whether he liked him as a person or not, I do not know. Douglas was not someone you showed disrespect to. Years back there had been some trouble on Douglas's property. The police had made some visits. A restaurant that he owned had to be shut down for a few days. People who were known acquaintances of his suddenly had their special permits and licences revoked by the city. But later that year when the police and city officials had their annual fundraiser ball, no one in town purchased tickets or attended. That same night there was a small fire at the back of the police station that damaged a fleet of cruisers beyond repair. After that no one had problems applying for special permits or licences from the city, whether you were an acquaintance of Douglas or not. And no one set foot on his property any more unless they were invited.

By this time my mother was long gone and my brothers already up in the interior working on the pipeline. And although my father did not condone my ways, he did accept the fact that I was not going to be changing them any time soon. Then again, maybe he thought that getting a job like the one he had working for Douglas might change things. Maybe if I worked for Douglas and people knew about it, they'd be less likely to cause me the kind of trouble I had been getting into – such as ending up in the hospital for three days that spring with a punctured lung, among other things.

Me, I just wanted the money. Some of the college boys were planning a trip down the coast. I hoped to go with them and, with any luck, not have to come back.

One of the few things I knew of my father's job was that he did not have to work very often. I knew that sometimes he did security for parties at Douglas's house. But most often he would get a call in the night, no matter what time, and have to leave right then and there, without any explanation to us, though he was always home when we woke up. I had always assumed his job had something to do with drugs, delivering or picking up drugs for Douglas. For some reason it was something I could see my father doing – not that I had ever seen him so much as have a drink – it just struck me as something he would be good at.

It isn't anything like that, my brother Donnie said to me once when he was still living at home. And don't even think about asking him unless you want to get your ass kicked into next week.

My father was a small, quiet man. There was an exactness to everything he did. An efficiency and decisiveness not only in his size, but also his speech, his movement. I had heard bits of stories here and there, never from my father, of him levelling men twice his size with a single punch to the throat or by cupping their ears in such a way that they would lose their balance and not be able to stand for a good while.

When my father mentioned the possibility of me working for Douglas he brought it up as if he was continuing a conversation that in reality we had never had.

Douglas says it would be all right to go with me on a job, he said. It was six o'clock in the evening and he was eating a bowl of cereal, sitting in his chair that divided the living room from the kitchen. Just to see what's what, see if it's something you'd be interested in doing.

What would I be doing? I said cautiously.

Don't be a smart ass, he said. Then he got up and put his bowl in the sink with a loud crash. Be ready at eight. That is, unless you have a sock-hop to go to.

We sat in the car for a good minute before we backed out of the driveway. It was as if he was mulling something over, working out an equation that I would never be privy to. His eyes were a dark blue, and he had a clean-shaven face that looked like its skin was a half size too small – especially when he clenched his jaw in thought. *The Pitbull,* I had heard his friends call him from time to time.

We cut through the centre of town via the old highway that hardly anyone used any more on account of the new bypass that had opened up the year before. Our town's mayor had been there in his pirate costume to cut the ribbon and hand out bumper stickers to the first five hundred drivers – most of whom had lined up overnight to be the first ones to drive over the new road.

Before long we turned down a street of furniture warehouses and sign shops and a parking lot where school buses were kept when not in use.

When I was your age, I was sent to live with my grandfather, my father said out of the blue.

I nodded slowly, not knowing where any of this was going, but thankful for some conversation to take my mind off the drive. My father did not like the radio. He said it lacked a certain calmness and reminded him of things he'd rather forget.

My mother had gotten remarried to a business man, he continued, and decided it would be best to leave me with my father's father rather than on my own.

I knew that, I said, because I did. I knew lots of things about my father, although I was not sure how this had happened. He was not one for divulging information. Our eyes met in the reflection of the rear-view mirror, and I looked away.

This was when he had gotten sick, and he couldn't take care of himself any more, he said.

What did you do?

I had to feed him and clean him and carry him around the house.

Was that right before he died?

Yes, he said, checking over his shoulder. I would take scalding showers for hours at a time and still never feel clean.

I wanted to ask him about his own father, about what he and his mother said to each other in the dark of the cramped broom closet, about so many things that filled my head at that moment, but then we turned up a narrow driveway made of gravel and came to a stop in front of a small yellow and white house with an empty hummingbird feeder hanging from the low roof. It was an old motel cabin. There were similar cabins on either side of it forming what must have been a courtyard at one time. The one in front of which we stopped looked especially old and vacant except for a large television set that I could see was on.

Once again we sat in the car without speaking. My father's jaw was clenched up as if he was grinding his back teeth.

You can get out of the car with me, he said finally. But I want you to stay a ways off. And don't say a goddamn thing, or I'll make you wish you'd never opened your mouth. He walked around the car and pulled a piece of rebar out of the trunk. The door of the cabin opened, and a man in grey jogging pants and an Extra Old Stock T-shirt came out with a cigarette in his hand.

Terry, he called out to my father. How about a beer? I was not used to hearing someone call my father by his first name. For some reason, one that was not immediately clear to me, the man's voice sounded strangely familiar. I squinted my eyes to get a better look at him since it was almost dusk and my eyes had not yet adjusted.

Norman, my father said, nodding slightly. It was then that I noticed the tinted prescription glasses the man was wearing and realized who he was. The man's name was Norman Wheeler. He had been my English teacher in middle school after our regular teacher had gone on maternity leave. Our class had been his first teaching assignment, which struck everyone as a little odd since he was well into his forties at the time. He would later tell our class that he had gotten his teaching certificate through a university program for adults who had been out of the workforce for some time.

A few seconds went by, and I could tell he was looking me over. Perhaps he was trying to figure out why I was there, standing beside the car. I had heard that he had gotten a permanent job after he taught us, but was fired a few years later and was no longer teaching. Someone had seen him driving a cab.

I watched him twist the stub of his cigarette into the wooden railing and turn back towards my father. His face had shown no sign of recognition. I was merely someone who worked for Douglas.

I looked past him into his living room. I could see one of those talk shows on the television. The kind where boyfriends and girlfriends or husbands and wives reveal to each other some horrible thing that they did or were continuing to do – like sleeping with a prostitute or having an affair with a relative or a midget.

You know, Terry, it's a funny thing you should show up here. I was just talking with Douglas. About an hour ago, as a matter of fact.

Even I could tell that he was lying.

Don't get me wrong, I appreciate the house call. His voice sounded rushed and nervous, like he'd been drinking. But me and Douglas have got things all squared up. We've worked out a little arrangement for the time being. So there's no need to worry.

My father did not say a word. He just stared blankly at Wheeler, who had to have noticed the rebar dirtying up my father's left hand.

The two of them were now only feet apart. So if you don't want to sit down for a friendly beer, he said. I could tell something was working its way through Wheeler, maybe a thought or a feeling or something altogether different. That is, if you don't want to sit down and shoot the shit over a drink or two, then maybe you should both just fuck right off.

I looked at my father, who remained still. I thought back to middle school when Wheeler had been my teacher. There was not a whole lot I remembered about that time, except that there had been a boy who sat at the back of my row named Albert, though that was not his real name. It was a nickname he had been given after an incident that was not his fault when we were no longer in the same class together – although I wasn't sure how the name related precisely to the incident, or what his real name was.

I remember it had started with Kyle Bartlett, a loudmouth at our school who was too big for his age and liked causing trouble. He had come running out of the boys' washroom saying he had just seen someone jerking off in one of the urinals. A crowd gathered around Bartlett as he retold the story to anyone who had missed it the first time around. A minute later the boy who had sat in the back of my row in Wheeler's class walked out of the washroom. A roar rang through the hallway as people started clapping and howling and calling the boy all sorts of names. That's when Bartlett started chanting, Albert, Albert, Albert, and before long everyone in the hallway joined in, including me I'm not proud to say. For the rest of the year the boy was known as Albert, and not a day went by that he didn't get reminded of this. Until then he had been a nondescript, almost anonymous student. As far as I could tell he had a few friends, passed all his classes, didn't stand out too much – kind of what most of us hoped for. But after that day he became the most recognized kid at school. He started getting into fights, his friends no longer wanted to be seen with him, and he eventually transferred to another school – even after Bartlett admitted he had made up the entire story just for a laugh.

The boy in the back row and what happened to him was what I remembered most about Wheeler's class. Wheeler, himself, had seemed like an all-right guy. A bit disorganized. A bit nervous. A bit unkempt for a normal teacher. But nothing that might have hinted at where he was headed.

A distasteful look spread across my father's tightened face. One that could have been mistaken for a smile. In fact, his entire body was vibrating, and I was sure that Wheeler was not aware of it because if he had been, he most certainly would not have done what he did next.

By now the sun had almost completely gone down, but I could still see both men clearly due to a motion light attached to Wheeler's cabin that kept tripping off and on.

After clearing his throat, Wheeler puckered his lips and made a kissing noise toward my father. Then he turned around and started walking toward his cabin. This is such bullshit, he muttered, and I remember thinking that maybe that was it. Maybe there was nothing more to be said or done, and we would just get back in the car and drive away. But as soon as I thought this, my father was gone. He moved swiftly across the yard, taking no more than a second to catch up to Wheeler, who was unaware that my father was now behind him.

My father reached back and swung the rebar, striking the back of Wheeler's legs with a dull popping sound. Wheeler yelped and fell forward onto his knees while my father, with his free hand, grabbed the back of his hair and dragged him away from the house.

Fucker, Wheeler hissed. Mother fucker. Father swung the rebar down on the side of his neck, bruising it instantly. Wheeler let out a loud, exasperated sob as he tried to protect his head with his arms and shoulders, which took the brunt of the blows. His attempts to defend himself only increased my father's determination, who was by now circling Wheeler's folded-up body and hitting him wherever he wasn't covered up.

I noticed that there were people standing at the front windows of some of the other cabins. Some of them looked at me, instead of at what was going on in the middle of the yard. But none of them dared go outside. I glanced over at Wheeler's contorted face for a second before looking away.

What do you think about when you watch your father beat a man who used to be your English teacher? Do you think about this man and wonder just how he could have gotten to the point in his life where a situation like this was possible? Or do you think about your father and ask the same thing? Or do you think about yourself?

I thought none of these things. Standing beside the car with the motion light from the cabin flashing on and off like prolonged snapshots, I remember thinking about our mayor and his pirate outfit and what he would look like sitting on the bottom of the ocean, drunk and happy and warm. I remember thinking about the softness of my mother's breathing, and the size of a broom closet, and the sound of a rifle. And I remember thinking about the pickup truck that had just pulled up behind us.

There were four men I did not recognize crammed into the cab. The expression on their faces was both scared and wild – the worst kind of combination, my brothers had told me on a number of occasions. And I could tell by the look on my father's face that he did not recognize these men either.

NEIL SMITH

Isolettes

Blue tube, green tube, clear tube, fat tube. A Dr. Seuss rhyme. The tubes run from robotic Magi gathered around the incubator, snake through portholes in the clear plastic box, then burrow into the baby's pinkish grey skin. One tube up her left nostril. One tube down her throat. One tube into an arm no wider than a Popsicle stick. One tube tunnels into her chest. The skin of her chest seems so thin. The baby's mother can almost see the tiny organs beneath, the way shrimp is visible under the rice paper of a spring roll. The baby doesn't move. Doesn't cry. To the mother, the baby, with its blue-black eyes, is an extraterrestrial crash-landed on her planet. Hidden away and kept alive by G-men while they assess what threat this tiny alien might pose.

"What kind of mother will you be?" Jacob asked. He and An sat side by side on a braided rug watching a flickering candle on An's coffee table. An said, "I won't be a mommy who bores people with the trials and tribulations of teething." Jacob disagreed: "You'll be like those TV-commercial moms who fret over whether to buy two-ply or three-ply toilet paper." From the coffee table, An picked up a blue ceramic cup, the kind used for espresso, and handed it to Jacob. "Real traditional," she said, "real Norman Rockwell." Jacob grinned and stood. He had long coltish legs. While he was in the bathroom, An dropped a jazz CD into her player and then went into her bedroom and lay on her bed. Before the first song ended, Jacob came out of the bathroom.

"You were fast this time," An said. Jacob replied he'd been practising at home. He handed her the espresso cup and kissed her forehead. "I don't love you," he said. An replied, "I don't love you, too." After he'd let himself out of the apartment, An drew Jacob's semen into a syringe. She hiked up her peasant skirt and slid off her underwear. Then she lay on her bed, two pillows propped beneath her rear. It was the first time with the pillows: gravity, she reasoned, would help.

Neonatal Intensive Care Unit. Otherwise known as N.I.C.U. The doctors pronounce it NICK U, as if it were a university. "Our kid is studying at NICK U," Jacob jokes with a nurse, who stares at him blankly. An thinks of NICK U as a baby hatchery, one that smells like the stuff dentists use to clean teeth. The incubators, a dozen aquariums, are not in neat rows, but here and there the way progressive school teachers arrange desks. Ventilators hum, monitors flash, alarms sound, a baby makes a noise like a gobbling turkey. Meanwhile, neonatologists complete their rounds. Some spill a hot alphabet-soup of acronyms – ROP, BPD, C-PAP – in An's lap. Others say with a hand on her shoulder: "We realize how stressful this must be." To them all, An wants to yell: "Nick you!" Better yet: "Nick off and die!"

Four months into An's pregnancy, Jacob moved into a top-floor apartment in her building. He called the place the *pent-up* suite, because according to An, the former tenants, a sulky husband and wife, were passive-aggressives. To exorcise the couple's demons, Jacob wandered around his stacks of moving boxes spritzing a citrus deodorizer. "If marriage is an institution," he said, "married people should be institutionalized." An wondered if this was a veiled reminder: that she and Jacob were not a couple, that they weren't bookends propping up *Dr. Spock's Baby and Childcare*. Still, the move into her building was Jacob's idea. An concurred, though. Proximity without intimacy: it sounded good to her. She had no desire to actually live with Jacob or any other man. Men's bathroom habits, the Q-Tips caked with earwax they left on the sink, depressed her. "Maybe more marriages would last if couples didn't live together," she said to Jacob as he unpacked a food processor the size of a space probe. "Maybe couples should buy a semi-detached and each live on either side," she added. Jacob laughed his nose-honking laugh. "That's why you always strike out at love, An," he said. "You're so semi-detached."

Between the twenty-third and twenty-fourth week of An's pregnancy, the placenta began to separate from the uterine wall. Semi-detached, An thought, when the doctor told her. By this time, she was lying under a spotlight in the emergency ward of the Royal Victoria Hospital. Her contractions were a minute apart. A nurse, the one who'd injected her with antibiotics earlier, yelled out, "Cervix fully effaced!" The warm amniotic fluid trickled over An's thighs and the obstetrician soon announced, "She's crowning," as if An herself were Queen Victoria. Then came the huge irresistible urge to push. When the neonatologist lifted her newborn daughter, An saw the tiny baby bat the air with one arm as if to clear everyone away, the doctors, the nurses – even her exhausted, terrified mother.

Though An hadn't wanted a baby shower, Jacob gave her one anyway. The theme, fittingly, was showers. The weather co-operated by drizzling. First, they took in the stage musical *Les Parapluies de Cherbourg* co-starring An's mother, Lise, who played an umbrella-shop owner in Normandy who meddled in her daughter's affair with a kind-hearted mechanic. The daughter got pregnant by the mechanic but ended up marrying a diamond importer she didn't love but grew to respect. During the standing ovation, Jacob whispered, "Only the French can make a *comédie musicale* depressing." Backstage, Lise pulled An into her dressing room and shut the door. Her stage makeup was as cracked as a Rembrandt. Lise sat at her vanity, pulled bobby pins from her soufflé of a wig, and talked to An's reflection about the play's theme. "Not only passion and true love, but more subtle kinds of love and devotion and attachment." She talked loudly as if she were still on stage. "You want me to marry a diamond importer?" An joked. Lise tossed her wig at An. "What I'm saying is I'm trying to understand." An thanked her mother for making an effort – an effort that deflated when An opened the dressing-room door. In the hall, Jacob was talking to the mechanic, his hand on the actor's thigh. "Watch out for that one," Lise yelled to the mechanic. "He'll ejaculate into anything."

"What's your baby's name, honey?" the big woman asks. She has crinkly permed hair and fleshy arms like hams. "Haven't thought of one yet," An mumbles. The woman sits down beside An in the lounge outside NICK U. The chair creaks under her weight. Sheila's her name. She delivered a twenty-nine-weeker. "We wanted to call our son Alek," she explains, "but he was born all pink and mewing and tiny like a newborn kangaroo, so we named him Joey." An has seen the sign taped to his incubator: HI EVERYONE, MY NAME'S JOEY. Many of the incubators are personalized with signs. You can even stick stuffed animals through an incubator's porthole the way you'd place a treasure chest at the bottom of a fish tank. An tells Sheila she's afraid to name her baby, that naming her might be a jinx. An is surprised at herself: for saying such a thing (she's not superstitious) and for revealing something to a stranger. It must be exhaustion, or too many peanut-butter cups from the vending machine. Sheila grabs An's hand and squeezes. "No, no, no," she insists. "Naming your baby will encourage her to live." Above Sheila's head is a poster of a baker frosting a cake with the letter B. The pattycake, pattycake man. "What about B?" An says. "Bea!" Sheila squeals and then adds: "Short for Beatrice. Like Beatrix Potter – nothing bad ever happens in Beatrix Potter!"

An's own name started as Anne Brouillette-Kappelhoff, the last name a coupling of her French-Canadian mother's and her German father's. When Anne was in high school, she often signed her papers Anne B-K to rein in her unwieldy name. By the time she hit university, she'd also sliced two letters off her first name. "A N," she'd spell. "Like the indefinite article." It got people's attention. Made them think her eccentric, and at twenty-one, looking fourteen, that's what she wanted. While her friends dressed in black, she wore flowery Laura Ashley dresses, accented with green Doc Martens lace-up boots. In her creative writing class, she handed in "Gee Your Hair Smells Terrific," a story about a crazed Avon lady who drowned a suburban housewife in a bubble bath. A boy in the class, who wore a spiked dog collar and an alligator polo shirt, liked the story very much. It was different, he said, from the "ethereal lyrical namby-pamby schlock" that the other girls handed in. The other girls began to hate this boy, whose name was Jacob.

Jacob sings "Supercalifragilisticexpialidocious" to B because he says she's so precocious. He waves to her through the plastic. She is four days old and weighs five hundred and twenty grams, about the weight of the two sweet potatoes An bought for supper last night. Every day B gains the weight of a penny. "She's got your wrinkly forehead," Jacob says to An, who sits in a moulded plastic chair next to the incubator, smoothing out the yellow robe all the parents wear and twiddling the plastic bracelet that reads MOTHER 87308. Across from them, Sheila sits with her robe open and her blouse lifted. Joey, who's now two months old, cuddles against her stomach, skin-to-skin contact that the nurses call kangaroo care. Sheila is humming "You Are the Sunshine of My Life" because Stevie Wonder was a preemie. An gets up and paces the room. She goes out the door of NICK U and into the elevator and down to the lobby and out the front door. A pregnant woman is waddling in. Little head, huge belly, like an upside-down question mark: ¿. A single sob jumps from An's throat, and the woman throws her a startled look. An goes over to the bike rack in the hospital's parking lot and sits on a purple ten-speed with a banana seat. It's not hers but it looks like the bike she had as a kid. It's a spring day, sunny but chilly. She breathes slowly and deeply through her nose as in her yoga class. After a half-hour, she feels almost serene. She goes back up to NICK U where FATHER 87308 has become a thespian. "To B or not to B," he drones to his daughter.

On stage was a stripper dressed in a fireman's yellow coat and rubber boots. The costume made dancing difficult, but he tried, shuffling back and forth to a rap song whose refrain went: "Don't blame me if your mental age is three." An's librarian friend Catou screwed up her face and said, "How could you have agreed to this?" She meant Part II of An's shower, which was held in a strip club called Wet. In the middle of the stage was a see-through shower stall where the fireman, now naked, was soaping his chest as water drizzled over him. Jacob had reserved a spot to one side of the stage. There, gathered around two tables pushed together, were eight of An's friends, a couple of translators and a few academics from the university where Jacob taught Russian lit. In the middle of the table was a stack of baby gifts: teething rings, pyjamas with the feet in, a duckie mobile. Jacob held his gift over his head: a clown doll the size of a ventriloquist's dummy with a bulbous nose and a wreath of rainbow hair. Mr. Pinkelton was his name. Jacob pressed the doll's belly, and Mr. Pinkelton emitted a phlegmy smoker's hack. Catou told An that she had met a real clown that week, a social worker who dressed as Bozo to read to children at the library. "He's single and he loves kids," Catou said. "I could set you up." An replied, "I'm six months' pregnant, for Christ's sake." Up on stage, the stripper wagged his genitals like a clown twisting a dachshund out of party balloons.

When An agreed to Catou's blind dates in the past, she would often see something in the man's eyes. Not passion but more a yearning for passion. She, however, could never drum up the same enthusiasm. The whole scene always smacked of play-acting, like those histrionic *téléromans* her mother starred in. The dates made her want to laugh; she did laugh in a few men's faces. One called her a cold fish, which made her laugh harder. So she'd given up on relationships, although she'd never really given *in* to them. Jacob said she was like a two-cigarette-a-day smoker who'd kicked the habit.

One of these dates, a Korean immigrant still struggling with idiom, asked An, "What do you do for the living?" With a stranger, small talk often kicks off with your job. So that's where An begins when she eventually leans over the incubator to introduce herself to B. "My name's An and I'm a translator," she whispers. She admits to B that she'd always hoped to work at something creative. "Drawing, writing, acting – I have some talent," she says. "But sometimes no talent is better. It saves you from expending so much energy when the best you can hope for is above average." She explains that, in university, she majored first in English lit. But the professors were so fiercely intelligent their IQs left scratch marks on her ego, and so she switched over to translation. She now works freelance from home, mostly subtitling television documentaries. In her job, she shrinks people's words down to a pithy sentence that fits on the screen. "But B, who am I to put words in their mouths," she whispers, "when most of the time, I barely understand what *I'm* trying to say?" Across the room, Sheila spies An talking to B and gives a thumbs-up. Translation: Finally!

Sheila is not the type of woman An usually befriends. Not once in her life has Sheila uttered the word "paradigm." Sheila lives in a suburban bungalow. She shows photos of this bungalow to An before taping them to Joey's incubator, picture side against the plastic. "So he'll feel at home," she tells An. To her skinny marsupial baby, she promises, "Someday you'll have your father's beer belly and my fat ass." Like the neonatologists, she makes her rounds, visiting the other parents, asking questions. In the Pattycake Lounge (as An has dubbed it), she calls Jacob An's "hubby." And so An explains. Sheila's eyes grow even rounder behind her fishbowl glasses. A father who is sitting nearby and who calls the mother of his child "the wife" mutters, "That doesn't sound very natural." An is too weary to argue, but not Sheila. She gets up and throws open the door to NICK U, exposing the battery of machines keeping their children alive. "Show me one thing in there that's natural!"

Natural air is about 21-per-cent oxygen. That's what Dr. Amelios, the neonatologist, is telling An and Jacob. B lies in her incubator, a tiny stocking cap wiggled onto her head to help conserve body heat. The clear tube down her throat is her air tube. B wrenches her head sideways as if to free herself. "This baby is state-of-the-art," Dr. Amelios says, and till he pats a hand against the ventilator contraption, An thinks he's referring to B. "It oscillates fast so it does little damage to the lungs," he says. An says, "Little damage?" The doctor explains that oxygen is dangerous for preemies given their underdeveloped lungs. Too much oxygen can dilate the blood vessels, detach retinas. An says, a bit impatiently, "I've always suspected oxygen of getting off easy. Sure, we blame greenhouse gases, but maybe it's the oxygen killing us all." Dr. Amelios looks perplexed. Jacob looks embarrassed. For the third time in three days, Jacob says, "An, it's not your fault." She snaps, "I never thought it was." She's getting the paranoid feeling that he's speaking ironically, that he's secretly angry with her for belly-flopping in his gene pool. She stalks off to the vending machine to buy more peanut-butter cups.

At twenty-four weeks, a newborn's chances of survival are 70 per cent. Severe disabilities occur at a rate of 20 per cent. At twenty-three weeks, survival drops to 40 per cent and disabilities jump to 60. An tries memorizing these figures the way she once studied for math tests. She thinks: Which is older? A baby born at twenty-three weeks who's lived two and a half weeks out of the womb? Or a baby delivered three days ago at twenty-five weeks? Sitting in her plastic chair, she watches a nurse spread Vaseline goo on a baby's skin to keep it moist. Across from An, Joey is being fitted with a breathing apparatus that resembles scuba gear. It's called a C-PAP. An tries to recall what the letters stand for; if she can just figure out this acronym everything will be fine. Her head is a playpen strewn with new words. Extremely premature babies are called micro-preemies: a fusion of science talk and baby talk. Micro-peepee, micro-poopoo. The incubators here are called isolettes. Then there's the litany of new words An has learned for what can go wrong: bradycardia, apnea, bronchopulmonary dysplasia, desatting, spastic diplegia, tracheotomy, retinopathy of prematurity.

Jacob brings An a *caffè latte* from a nearby coffee shop. With her hands wrapped around the warm Styrofoam cup, she mutters, "I don't want this." Jacob replies that it's decaf. "The bells and whistles, the tubes, the deadly oxygen," An says. "I don't want any of this." Jacob sighs, looks up at the fluorescent lights, looks down at B, who's wearing a mask over her eyes, like those that flight attendants hand out to passengers. Jacob mumbles, "She'll die without them." An says calmly, "If my womb rejected her, maybe she was meant to." As a child, she'd thought people were saying "youth in Asia": she'd pictured newborn Chinese girls swaddled in blankets and left on mountainsides to die.

An's mother is entertaining the troops. That's how An sees it. Lise is standing in the middle of NICK U with the other parents crowded around. They recognized her, of course. Her presence here is lucky, they must think. In the seventies, Lise played the Black Mouse in the children's television show *Les Souris dansent*. The part became her bête noire because, when the show ended, she struggled to get acting jobs in programs for adults. Lise is telling the parents about a miscarriage she had in her late thirties. An, her two younger sisters and her parents had been driving through Chicoutimi when her mother started bleeding. "After I lost the baby, I couldn't stop crying," Lise says. "The nurse wheeled me back to the waiting room, took a look at my three little girls and said, 'Why all the fuss? You don't have enough kids as it is?'" The parents tsk-tsk, and Sheila touches Lise's arm in commiseration. An recalls that, when her mother was pregnant, she'd flick the heads of dandelions into An's face and say, "Mommy had a baby and her head popped off." Now An looks at her mother, wet-eyed and basking in the attention. She was a good mother, An thinks. She really was. Though at times, when Lise played with An and her sisters, dressed them all up in wigs and costumes for Little Red Riding Hood or Heidi, An had the uneasy feeling her mother was rehearsing for a part.

The blue espresso cup, the one Jacob had masturbated into, sat on the concrete wall of An's balcony. By this time, An was two months' pregnant, already spitting up every morning in the kitchen sink. Jacob decided that, for luck, they had to break the cup. Toss it ten storeys to smash in the parking lot below. They were talking about parenthood, and Jacob was describing his own parents, who lived out west. His father was a constant complainer prone to tantrums. When he'd discovered Jacob's stash of stolen Barbie dolls, he took them to his tool shed and decapitated them. "I remember screaming at him to at least spare the black one. She was unique – she was Afro Barbie." An mentioned her own parents, how her father and mother were so much in love they still took bubble baths together, with scented candles atop the toilet tank. Jacob joked, "Their profound love has set expectations that no boyfriend of yours can match." An replied, "Thank you, Dr. Kitchensink," and then pushed the blue cup off the edge.

An is telling B about Jacob. She talks about his feigned cynicism, his pretence at unconventionality with his dyed blue-black hair, the lizard tattooed on his hipbone. He's threatened to spike the lounge's water cooler with Ecstasy. Play some trance music over the PA system. A rave in NICK U! Strung-out fathers unfrazzled. Moms dancing with their kid's ventilator. "But really, B, Jacob is more dewy-eyed than my sisters and girlfriends. On an errand to pick up his dry cleaning, he'll fall in love twice." The unconventional one, An admits, is herself. "I don't fall in love, but I do fall in *like*. I could probably fall deeply in like." She looks at B's face, distorted by the air tube jammed into her mouth. She recalls Jacob kidding with her mother, asking why the French language doesn't distinguish between like and love. Why *aimer* is enough. Lise said that, for French people, to like is to love. "What do you think, B?" An asks her baby. She sticks a hand through the porthole and, with her index finger, touches B's elbow.

When An opens the front door to her apartment, she still smells taupe. That's the colour she painted her bedroom two weeks earlier. In the entrance hall are the bags of baby-shower gifts she got the night her contractions started. Sticking out the top of one bag is Mr. Pinkelton's malicious clown face. Her fantasy of tossing the gifts down the garbage chute is interrupted by the phone. She doesn't answer. All week she's spent talking to friends and family, repeating to everyone her Cole Porter refrain: "It's just one of those things." On her balcony, she pops open a bottle of Cabernet Sauvignon, thinking that at least now she can drink. As she sips, she sees the greenhouses atop McGill University's agriculture building a few blocks away. All that greenery so far off the ground is miraculous and consoling. In the apartment tower kitty-corner from hers, a woman carries a chair onto her balcony and steps onto it. For a dizzying instant, An thinks she's going to jump, but the woman simply hangs a pot of ivy.

An walks back to the hospital. The sun beats hot on her head. She's still dabbing sweat from her forehead as she enters the Pattycake Lounge. There, Sheila lurches out of her seat and flings herself at An. An feels the drag of the woman's weight, her body heat; she smells the oiliness of Sheila's scalp. Sheila begins sobbing, the sound resembling Mr. Pinkelton's phlegmy cough. An tries to pat the woman's back and pull away at the same time. "Joey?" An asks.

Jacob is in a private room down the hall from NICK U, in a plastic chair, cradling B in a tiny handmade quilt of green and yellow squares. Only B's face is visible. An sees that, without the air tube, the baby's mouth has the same rosebud lips as Jacob. He is singing now. Softly, slowly, as if his song were a lullaby, singing about the biggest word he's ever heard. She chose him as the father, thinking he wouldn't get attached. Yet here he is – cradling and crooning to his daughter. An sits on a trundle bed next to him. She fingers the quilt. The hospital gives these to parents as mementos: quilts and locks of hair and footprints of their dead babies. She wonders if, under the quilt, B's feet are already black with ink. Jacob says, "Would you like to hold her?" But An simply touches B's head, the soft spot where you can feel a baby's heartbeat but where she feels nothing. Jacob resumes his song, almost in a whisper now. An stares at B in his arms; she recalls the baby pushing everyone away in the delivery room. After a moment, she says, "I don't love you." She waits for Jacob's usual "I don't love you, too," but when he looks at her, his face is ashen. He has understood what she meant. "Why?" he says, with a look of pain and puzzlement. "Oh, but I liked her," An says, almost pleadingly. "I liked her so much." Jacob starts crying. Soundlessly. When he finishes, he murmurs, "Well, that's something." And An, her arms wrapped around herself, holding herself together, hopes that it is.

ADAM LEWIS SCHROEDER

Burning the Cattle at Both Ends

Me and Liam Jr. in rubber boots in the office off the milking room, with the old green filing cabinet, breeding charts on the wall and lists on the wall of Liam Sr.'s highest producers for milk-fat percentage and just plain quantity of milk, milk-fat be damned. Liam Jr. runs through the broken glass, out past the milking carousel, around the corner so the dogs lift sleeping heads, he doubles past the end of the barn heading for the house so I just step out the front door of the office and there he is. I'd catch him right then but he's got up some good speed – he's thirteen years old so his legs are grown-person length now but his head, neck, arms, trunk might just as well be eight years old or nine, that age, he runs for the house up the driveway and rubber boots flap around his calves. It all goes in a circle coming back to this point of him running.

He still has a quarter-mile before he gets to the house, stubble grass up the middle of the driveway, smooth from Liam Sr.'s half-ton wiping the dirt clean and even more the gigantic milk tanker once a week. Liam Jr. sees every step to the front step and porch and front door and Mom – looking for her but not sure he ought to find her because if I never get to him it'll be him in trouble instead of me, right then he's in the wrong. But I hop on tractor, turn the key hanging in the ignition, pull out the choke, throw it up into eight, top speed – always tried to think what each speed was worth, if speed one was five miles an hour then is eight really forty, something like that, I even think that now, at this idiot moment – aim the tractor at him like a big slow bullet that turns the corner at the house and at the last instant turns his ankle for him in that rubber boot so he tumbles on the lawn right in front of the steps. I ride on the bullet and I'm the brass, the primer, the box the bullets came in, all along thinking he was going to hop the fence, cross the pasture, tie me up completely. But the stupid kid never did. Even over the roar of the tractor his ankle made the sound like you'd expect – kindling breaking over your knee.

Ambulance went out of the farm with no lights going or anything, quiet up the dirt road, dogs barking and happy running under the fence then alongside it. Cop that had me in back of his car was pretty nice all in all, probably took some workshop one time that said these yokels come in off their tractors can only be pushed so far. We talked about the Canucks and everything, how it didn't matter if they made the playoffs now they had so many injuries and about the thing on the news where the goalie's throat got cut when the guy slid into his net with skates in the air. Laughed. Then he put me in the cell and spat on the floor. I told him again it was because of the penicillin everything had gone so bad. Suddenly it seemed if I said it one more time everybody'd change their minds about me, but the big door just closed behind him with a long hiss from that device that pulls doors shut after people.

When I was, say, eleven, I did screw up. Never enough to get to jail like this, it was leaving sprinklers on, not giving the dog water, not coiling the firehose, smoking early, staying underwater too long so people got scared, sneaking out so people got scared, letting the dog out, breaking the expensives, not pulling every weed, setting up cans by the road and shooting a friend's air rifle and hitting a guy in the knee when he rode by on his bike. A lot of that was scaring people, that's where the hell came from.

Then you reach a point, age, where they don't give much of a damn any more, you screw up, let yourself in people's houses, break kindling under a tractor and that's your trouble, Bed, you're your own man with your own rattle-brain to boot. But as far as I know I've no bigger a brain than I did when I was seven or eight only the trouble now is bigger and the public concern that much less. Let the idiot drown they say. Which is good. I wouldn't want any of them, no Kathleen, no pretty cousin Tina even and definitely not Phil, no no never Phil, coming down here to the station and talking to me in a cell. Let me hold my breath underwater here on my own, let me hold it hold it hold it.

It's a long time I'm up on the tractor, fiddling with the key in the ignition and the dangly key chain, a white plastic bottle opener that says Hawaii, deciding to turn it off or not, Liam Jr. laying on the grass between the big wheel and small. In the house, Liam Sr. in his black Finning cap and with hardly any eyebrows he'll come up from the cold-room with a watermelon before long, set it on the chopping block, go over to get the knife and see the blue of his tractor past the window blind, pull it up and see me and Liam Jr. out there, realize the noise wasn't a calf in the paddock at all. His son holding his leg, eyes looking up at me, eyes rolling back at the house and just hollering.

He's thirteen and I'm seventeen.

Liam Sr. brought me out to the farm to help him with the cattle after my foster-dad Phil was sent down to Matsqui 'cause he hit a guy with a baseball bat, some big trouble, anyhow finances in our house were shaky. Powdered milk and all of that. The girl Phil was fighting over called up, Kathleen, she called me up said if things were tough financially this guy Liam Sr. was looking for somebody. You could hear Kathleen's earring against the phone on her end. She said Liam Sr. didn't mind if I'd been in trouble and with talk like that I figured them for born-again Christians, but really he just couldn't find anybody else who'd drive all the way out to the farm. So I hopped in Phil's fishbowl-booking Pacer and went out there and Liam's wife came on the porch to see who was stirring the dogs up. She stood there with batter dripping off her spatula and a bit of stomach hanging under her shirt, told me to park on the exact piece of lawn where one day the Liam Jr. business would go on.

Liam Sr. had three dogs, Roy, Snow, Beer, and they all liked me right away, leaning against my knee for a good ear-rub, happy old tongues, so that did a lot as far as Liam Sr. was concerned. I went out in the field and we walked all the cattle in for milking, 240 of them and number 117 always the first to the drafting pen rain or shine, she's a funny old girl. I got the run-down on it all. These are Friesian-Jerseys, mixed because one has quality milk but not much of it and the other has lots of milk but thin, I can't remember which was which. Their green shit sat all around in slick piles, Roy's white feet scampering through them. Three dogs ran in big circles around the cows, but if I snapped my fingers a little, clickety snap they'd come straight around to me better than whistling. Dogs with long tongues tilt their heads to listen.

Here's the important bit, says Liam Sr., we got to watch out if they're sick, crusty eyes, skinny, shining all over themselves more than usual, because then we've got to lock them up on their own and jab them full of antibiotics and such. I nodded my head, of course that made a lot of sense. But he said don't worry about the long snots hanging off their noses, they got that always. We got in the milking barn and he let the girls all wait in the drafting pen and he showed off his big silver 7,000-litre milk tanks, 14,000 ruddy litres of milk pumped from them during peak but only 5,000 before the November dry-off, you get this? If the truck from the Dairy Board comes and picks up all this milk and there's one molecule of penicillin in there, or whatever, bovine virus number 12, the whole batch is off, plus the batch the truck unloads into at headquarters because they don't do their tests until later, the driver takes a sample so they can track the guilty party down, all right? Have I impressed this upon you? says Liam Sr. They track the poor sod down and the fine is $10,000.

I say, how does the medicine end up in the milk? Anything in their bloodstream ends up in the milk, he says. Then in my head I start working on some plan where you can separate the bloodstream and the milkstream inside the cows, I see these tubes and wires inside them, all these little schematics, so we all can be saved all this trouble.

At 9:30 at night the cop lets my cousin Tina in to see me, she's the number I gave to call and she's eight months' pregnant. I remember that Tina had a broken ankle once too, just like I do, then I remember it's not me with the broken ankle at all, it's Liam Jr.

Tina puts her hand through the bars and grabs on to mine. Hey, Tina, I say. She says, hiya Bed. Then she says, well?

I say it's a stupid story, but probably everybody in jail thinks their story's the stupidest, right?

She says, when did you think up that to say?

I say about an hour ago.

She says Phil's proud of his story, hitting that guy with the bat.

I say that is a good story.

I haven't seen her for a while so she starts in, glad to be pregnant and new life inside her, happy home, women's support, blah blah blah. Then I hear myself thinking this ungrateful stuff, about Tina, the world's only Tina, and I think what's happened?

I was in the swing of things after a couple weeks so Liam Sr. let me go it alone on the 5 p.m. milkings. I didn't worry so much about the sick cows, I mean I did, but it didn't eat me up like I thought it was going to because the healthy girls are all the same every day, number 117 always first up the ramp and into her stall on the machine, day after day same for each, and it was only sick ones that fought you and didn't go along. So they pointed themselves out, almost every time. You'd put them in their own field, tell Liam Sr. about it on the way by the house, or tell his wife or Liam Jr. if Liam Sr. was at the liquor store or getting a new fuel pump or something.

But after I moved the sickie and before I went home I'd do the milking, of course, I'd be in there with the apron on, pulling the chain across the back of their legs, starting the suction, pulling out the cups and let them suck up each teat in a split-second and milk rumbles up the clear hose, then pull the rope and off they go, whole big wheel rotates and next old cow steps up. They'd go around the whole circle and if their milk had stopped by then, the chain would drop automatic and Mrs. Cow would back out into the chute. Me by the end, crusted in their green shit, arms, hair, forehead, grass swallowed that day drying, flaking, falling off as I drove home in the Pacer with the window wide open and radio on.

Kathleen'd call up, how's it all going? She still had a thing for Phil if she was calling talking to me, even if she and the guy Phil'd smacked, Dennis, she and Dennis were going to get married. She'd always talk about Phil's trial, a kangaroo court she called it, always confused which side she was on since really it'd been Dennis against Phil. I'd thought about her a lot at the time since the guys I used to hang out with were in high school trying out for the ping-pong team and such and I hadn't had a whole lot else going on.

Kathleen's favourite from the trial was the social worker who'd said that Phil was a stand-up guy and the thing with Dennis was isolated, and the way he'd raised me and Tina proved what a good heart he had. But then the Crown said he wanted to question that, pointed out how Tina's whereabouts were unknown at the time and I'd taken a bunch of Walkmans from the school cafeteria. I figured Phil would flash me a look when they said that but he never did.

Me and Kathleen cursed out the Crown to high heaven all the time afterwards. At the lunch break in the trial Kathleen took me out to Burger King two blocks down from the courthouse and said how under section 267 of the Criminal Code, Phil could get ten years maximum, isn't that awful, of course Dennis says he should get life. In the end they only gave him two years less a day so instead of going to federal prison he got to go to a provincial one, which was supposed to be nicer.

He wrote me a letter one time saying half the time when he wanted to watch hockey on prison TV the more long-term guys would say they were watching some idiot sitcom, so that's what they'd watch. He said when he got home he was going to put his ball cap on and light a cigar and watch the hockey and how everything would be grand. I read that and thought, poor old Phil, missing his hockey, but I was forgetting about the time I'd left the garbage bags out where the dog could get to them and Phil came and found me in the kitchen.

When Liam Sr. was showing me around in that first while Liam Jr. was always hanging around, holding onto his dad's fingers, bawling about he had a sore wee-wee or something, and I'd be thinking eleven's not as young as all that, is it? So once I was doing the milking on my own and he was hanging around trying to bat the cow's tails with his little tennis racket, I gave him a kick in the ass, hard, with my rubber boot. He didn't cry, he put his hands on his ass and ran for it to the house.

Me and Liam Sr. went hunting gophers a few times on the rocky patch. He had a box of these .22 shells called zingers. What was different in them mechanically I don't know, but we took turns shooting one with zingers and one with regular, and boy, one gopher'd just have a hole in him and the other'd be in one piece over here and the other over there.

Liam Sr. and I spent about twenty minutes one Sunday looking for the back half of one, a lot of laughs, Liam Sr.'s funny face all crinkled up with no eyebrows to speak of. Liam Jr. would always be there beside the truck when we pulled back in, sulking, saying he wished he could've come along but when we'd been setting out to go he'd been in his room playing Monopoly by himself with a bad stomach, some load of crap. We'd be taking the warm guns back in the house, he'd look all sad and stick his finger in his nose. Old Liam said I had a way with the cows, and I said it was just I had a way with the dogs that had a way with the cows, and he said Liam Jr. didn't have a way with either.

Tina's drinking coffee out of a paper cup, the hand that's not holding mine's got it, cup decorated with spiralling lines of happy faces, lines alternating one pink and the next purple on the cup. I sit and look at them spiral behind her fingers while her other hand in mine she fidgets every now and then, gets it more comfortable. How many times did a line circle around the cup? Two? Three? When a line spiralled around enough to hit the top of the cup, was that it for it? Or did it keep going along into the next cup that was still at the top of the cup-stack across from that cop's desk? Was Tina really still talking? The world's own Tina?

Because the cups all in their spiral stop me thinking about the office off the milking barn, when Liam Jr. with his big bottle of pop said it didn't matter what I said to anybody, it was too late for anybody to think it was anybody but me and sure he'd admit he left the gate open. Maybe he said it 'cause he could feel his legs growing big under him, his balls dropping into place, he could say anything do anything, he was Liam Jr! Liam Jr. there let me know now on my last day it was him that was the boss around here all along, him that was the boss of cows and milking and lording it over me, him already thirteen years old.

I'd been good, too, with a way with the dogs, quick with the suction cups, the shit drying on my face, my wet hands all over their udders fat with milk but painted green with shit. Tina lets go of my hand and puts her hand on top of her belly, her blue flower dress.

Liam Jr. told me. He was drinking a bottle of A&W root beer and while he was in the office talking half the time he was holding the bottle up to his face, looking at me through it with one eye, hiding behind it, sees the world more clearly, he went on talking, got armpit hair now, said he let the cow out on purpose so I'd get hell. But I didn't believe that really. I figured he did it by accident and wanted to try looking extra-tough. He said, you know, you really acted like you were great all the time. All along when Liam Jr. was talking he wanted me to say it's all right, kid, we'll let it slide, I'll take the idiot fall for you. Like I had for the two weeks since the Dairy Board man pulled up in his station wagon.

But I decided deep down I would take his idea that he really had let the cow out to do me in, which neither of us thought was true, and run with it. Because why not get mad? It's fun to get mad. I'd seen it done. The best part is when the kid's trying to make up for it like Liam Jr. was, trying to do the stand-up thing so it doesn't haunt him later on to think of me, but I still got mad, and I let him see it in my eyes, you do something with the lids and the pupils so there's no doubt how much the kid's screwed up.

Phil gets mad like that. Everybody gets mad.

Liam Jr. saw the eyelids as I got up from the ground where I was pulling bits of hay out of my wool socks, slowly. I took a long time standing up so he'd see the mad eyes from different angles, and it hit him then that the stand-up thing hadn't worked out for him. The A&W root beer slid out of his hand, smashed to bits, and he went out of the room and past the milking machine, the cows all gone from it and back out to the pasture. Roy got up from where he was lying outside and came in across the concrete to see me, clickety clack his nails.

This my last day milking. The $10,000 can be made faster as a mechanic, something like that. No hard feelings, Liam Sr. says, when we talk it out when the word on the tainted milk comes down, but I don't have that kind of money any more than you do, he says, only it's your fault and it isn't mine. And I get a flicker of me pulling up in a limousine, handing over the $10,000 in this rhinestone briefcase but after the flicker everything was sadder still.

I decided not to go after the kid, went out the office door, opposite direction to what he'd run. But sure enough he was right there six feet from me, circling past, and he was so stupid in that moment, running right back where I was going to be, I decided to see this thing through after all. Climbed up on the tractor. Was near at hand.

As he left our house foster-dad Phil grabbed the old aluminum baseball bat that was by our back door, and when Dennis opened up the door of Kathleen's trailer to see who was knocking, he got it in the ribs and fell down in the driveway and his glasses came off. He reached over for them but Phil nailed him a few times in the knee, like chopping wood, and Phil only stopped because Dennis was hollering so loud. And I guess Phil probably thought for a second then too, maybe like I did, maybe just the same, what the heck is going on out here. Before Kathleen with her earrings came out on the step wearing her cleats and shorts on her way to soccer, and Dennis dancing around down there on the ground.

Through her dress Tina's rubbing the baby pretty good. Little idiot in there, imagine him. Him born and three years old, looking up at you, straight brown hair, his big eyes, verge of tears for some reason or other. Do your fists bunch up at the thought of it? Are you looking after him or aren't you?

Tina says I hope you and Phil can help with the new one.

PATRICIA ROSE YOUNG

Up the Clyde on a Bike

Before Dad left I talked about nothing except how much I wanted a horse. I said how miserable my life was and would continue to be without a horse of my own. The sixties were boom years and Dad, a welder, started going away every few weeks to work on construction. The first time he went Mum accused him of accepting the job to get away from her.

"You think I'm bammy," she said.

"Don't talk that way," he said. "Say things like that you'll have me as daft as you."

They were sitting at the kitchen table and I was cantering around on an imaginary horse. Between them, an ashtray, a white porcelain swan with a thin curved neck.

"The money's too good to pass up," Dad said. "They're saying lots of overtime. Double, triple pay."

Mum smoked and flicked ash into the swan's back. If he took advantage of all the work up-island, Dad said, they could pay off the car, put a few bucks down on the mortgage. We could take a week's holiday, rent a beach cabin in Parksville. When he said that Mum looked at him as though he'd just said we could rent a rocket and go to the moon. She stabbed her cigarette in the cavity between the swan's outstretched wings and went to the broom closet. A door slammed and Mum returned with a mop. I stopped cantering to watch her fill the sink with soap and water. Dad ignored her and picked up the ashtray.

"Will you look at this?" he said. "The poor wee birdie's lost an eye." On one side of the swan's head was a black bead; the other bead was missing. Mum started splashing the mop's stringy head around on the linoleum. "Bloody hell, woman," Dad said, lifting up his feet. "Are you going to drown us out of house and home?"

Was he the crazy one? I wondered, wading out of the kitchen in wet socks. How could we stay at a beach cabin? Had he forgotten that on her good days Mum didn't leave the house? On her bad days she didn't leave her bed?

Before Dad left Mum broke things – platters, ornaments, lamps. Pushing the vacuum, she was a rampaging thing bashing its way into corners of rooms and down hallways. Sometimes I'd sit on a stool in the kitchen watching her chop vegetables for dinner, imagining myself the calm centre of the world. Three whacks with the big knife and she'd hurl chunks of cabbage into a pot; boiling water would spill over, extinguishing the gas element. Mum would bring down the lid as though bringing down a cymbal.

Before Dad left Ella and I would walk to Quan Lee's grocery after school, hating the metal cart because as far as we could see only humpbacked old women pushed metal carts. Inside the entrance of the store we'd take turns bouncing up and down on the mechanical horse, trying to coax life into its hard fixed saddle. At seven Ella was small with ears that poked through her straight hair. She wore thick glasses. Sometimes a man waiting for his wife at the checkout would take pity on Ella, and put a dime in the metal box. For three minutes my sister would buck and holler *atta girl, giddy up* with such wholehearted joy it was embarrassing to watch.

Before Dad left we'd always forget something on Mum's shopping list. It might be steel wool or toilet paper or bobby pins. That day it was cigarettes. We watched her pull porridge oats and cans of evaporated milk out of grocery bags. "Where's the fags? Jesus Christ, lassies, did I no tell you to buy me a packet of fags?"

While Mum searched desperately for a packet of Matinée at the bottom of a bag, I looked past her head at the tobacco tin on top of the fridge. It was full of buttons. Wooden buttons, pearl buttons, glass buttons that rubbed against each other like flat shiny stones. The longer I stared at the tin the farther away it became. Blue speck at the wrong end of a telescope.

"You'll have to go back," Mum said. "That's all there is to it."

Ella groaned and kicked a kitchen chair. "Martha can go."

"Why should I? I always go."

Without taking her eyes off us, Mum raised her mug of tea to her mouth. "No fags," she said. "I'm fair disgusted with the pair of you."

Ella picked up the box of Tide and inhaled. "Mmm, lemon flavoured." And then she sneezed, dropping the box. Ella stuck her fingers in her ears and walked around the kitchen, head jerking, making clucking noises in her throat. She looked like a crazed rooster.

"I know what you want," Mum said, drawing in her breath and letting it out slowly. "You want me in the nut house. Well, I'll be climbing the walls soon enough and then you'll see."

We'll see what?

By the time Dad came home from work we were exhausted, battle worn. We ate in silence. Afterwards, he leaned back in his sleeveless undershirt and khaki work pants, patting his stomach. "You're a right connoisseur of spuds, so you are," he said to Mum. "Now where's dessert?"

"Up my jumper," Mum said.

And they laughed. Every night the same dumb joke.

Before Dad left we'd climb the apple tree in the back yard, swinging down from the branches. We did this so many times, blisters formed on our palms. "Garden gloves," I said one afternoon, charging ahead of Ella into the shed. Back in the tree, I reached for a branch but had no grip. When I came to, I was lying on the couch and Mum was shouting into the phone.

"Three one three five Blackwood Street. Can you no understand King's English?"

Ella was standing in the doorway holding an enormous leek. I glanced at my arm propped on a pillow. Arm the shape of an S.

The taxi arrived and Mum said: "I'm awful sorry, hen, I cannee go with you."

"I know," I said, not knowing what I knew or why she could only stand on the top step waving goodbye while the taxi driver carried me to the car.

At the hospital I sailed down the hallway in a bed that eventually slid through swinging doors into a room with blinding lights.

"Count backwards from ten," a nurse said, placing a black toilet plunger over my mouth.

Later, when Dad walked past my room I wondered what he was doing in the children's ward of St. Joseph's Hospital. Each time he passed the door I thought how handsome he looked with his hair combed back, but it didn't occur to me to call out. Finally, he came into my room and sat on a chair beside the bed. I'd never seen him in a sports jacket and tie.

It had been a short fall but I'd broken two bones and cracked two more. The first doctor straightened the arm and set it in an L-shaped cast but, after looking at an X-ray, the second doctor decided the first doctor had done a poor job. "Shoddy work," he said, rapping his knuckles on my plaster. The next day he broke and reset the bones.

Sandra Parsons, the girl in the bed beside me, talked non-stop about all the Jell-O and ice cream she was going to get after her tonsils came out. I had never met such a jabber-box.

"Will your mother be coming up, dear?" Mrs. Parsons asked the day of Sandra's operation. She was sitting on the edge of her daughter's bed, long legs crossed at the ankles, and I could feel her watching me as I tried to colour a picture of a boy pushing a girl on a swing. Using my right hand required all my concentration.

"Maybe tomorrow," I said.

After her operation Sandra's face was bruised and swollen, and that night she lay facing the wall, sobbing. When she went home, a shadow of her former self, I was alone in room 303, except for a baby who slept all the time. And then the baby was taken away and a nurse pushed his crib down the hall, one gimpy wheel hobbling all the way to the elevator. I decided the baby had died. Now I lived in dread of the eight o'clock juice cart. When the lights went out I lay awake, heart pounding, convinced that I too would die in the night and my bed would be removed as unceremoniously.

Before Dad left he'd bring home news of the outside world. Women's magazines, religious literature, library books with titles like *How to Stop Worrying and Start Living*. He'd bring home newspapers and political pamphlets handed out in the street. One day he came home with a paperback he'd picked up from a drugstore rack: *Apple Cider Vinegar and Honey: Good Health the Natural Way*.

Now Mum would greet him at five o'clock with a tall glass of amber liquid. They'd sit on the back steps, smoking Matinées, and sipping slowly just as Cyril Watson, the author and a preacher from Minnesota, advised.

"Och," Dad would say, "it's bloody vile."

"Bloody revolting," Mum would answer.

Before Dad left my right eye twitched but with the vinegar and honey Mum insisted this tic could be cured once and for all. To keep the peace I held my breath and gulped down a morning and evening tonic. Ella, however, was not interested in the peace. The first time Mum insisted she drink vinegar and honey for her allergies we were waiting for a ride to the matinee of *National Velvet*.

"I won't," Ella said. "It's cruelty to children."

"Och away you go," Mum said. "It'll no kill you."

Ella refused.

"You'd make a saint swear, so you would."

Ella said she couldn't drink it. The smell alone made her sick.

"You'll no be leaving this house until you've taken that drink. Every drop."

As though from a distance I watched Ella and Mum, the mauve tumbler between them. Their hands and mouths were moving in an exaggerated way and their voices came from a long way off. It was like watching cartoon characters work themselves into a frenzy, the volume turned low. The phone rang in the front hall. Mum left the kitchen and Ella leapt up, pouring most of the vinegar and honey down the sink. When Mum came back she looked at the tumbler.

"Do you think I came up the Clyde on a bike? Answer me. Do you?"

Ella squinted, glasses on the end of her nose.

"I drank mine," I said, quietly.

Ella turned to me – incredulous, betrayed – but she lifted the tumbler to her lips. She took a sip, and then doubled over, making retching sounds.

"You can quit your antics right now," Mum said.

A car honked in front of the house and Mum picked Ella up off the chair and shook her by the shoulders. "You're a bad stick," she said. "A bad, bad stick."

I walked dizzily out to the car and slid into the front seat beside Lorraine O'Connor. For two hours I sucked on lemon gumdrops in a kind of delirious sweat, watching a girl named Violet win a national horse race, dressed as a boy.

Before Dad left Mum would sing as she washed the dishes. *I belong to Glasgow, dear old Glasgow too-oon.* I'd stand beside her, holding a towel, waiting for the water to drain from the plates in the rack.

"Where's Glasgow?" I asked once, and Mum said it was on the River Clyde, the wonderful, wonderful Clyde.

Glasgow was also the hometown of the radio talk show host she listened to each afternoon at one o'clock. Jack Webster's voice penetrated every corner of the house. If he agreed with a guest or wanted to sum up a point, he'd say "Pree-cisely," in a loud and exacting way. If he disagreed, he'd say, "Och away you go and dinnee be daft." Just like Mum. The same fierce language.

Before Dad left she cut out a picture of Jack from a magazine and put it in a little frame above the fridge so she could look at it while he was talking. His face was as gruff as his voice, but Mum liked Jack because, she said, he didn't back down from anyone, no matter how high and mighty they were. He scrapped with union leaders, members of Parliament, even premiers, calling them rogues and scoundrels, the bloody lot of them. At least once during each program he'd quote Robert Burns, "A Man's a Man for a' that."

Before Dad left Mum canned and froze and pickled all the vegetables growing in the garden. One afternoon I was at the sink, scrubbing beets, hacking off the leaves, when Jack interviewed Christine Dove, a woman who'd written a book, *Twenty-Three Years Locked Inside*. Apparently, Christine suffered from a psychological condition that no one, not even psychiatrists, fully understood. She spoke of all the occasions she'd missed because of her condition: picnics and family gatherings, her sons' lacrosse games, her daughter's wedding in Nanaimo. And the little things she couldn't do: walk to the corner to mail a letter, take a bus into town to buy a new dress. Mum stopped slicing beets into a Mason jar and pulled up a chair. She sat and listened to Christine describe thc symptoms she experienced whenever she tried to leave her house – racing heart, panic, sweating, nausea, indescribable dread. My blouse and shorts were sticking to my skin. The air was thick the way it is before thunder.

"People think you're crazy," Christine was saying to Jack. "All the lies and secrecy. The shame." Until recently even her husband hadn't known what was wrong with her.

"At least prisoners have company," Mum said.

"What?" I said.

"Whisht."

Christine was telling Jack that she'd tried explaining her symptoms to her family doctor but he told her she was a worrywart and prescribed Valium. "Relax," he'd said. "If you're going to be raped, you might as well lie back and enjoy it."

"Daft bugger," Mum said.

I looked at the beets on the floor. Dirty bouquets wrapped in newspaper. "How many more do I have to wash?"

Mum leaned closer to the transistor. Christine said she drank to deal with the anxiety and depression, paying her sons to buy her liquor. She even paid them to not tell their father. Jack, who normally barked questions at his guests, was quiet as Christine related her story of insomnia and dread and wine bottles stashed beneath dirty laundry. Only once did he speak: "You're all right, love, I'm listening."

Standing at the kitchen sink, I turned to look at Mum. Tears were running down her face. When she saw me looking she brought her hand up to her mouth. "I didnee know," she said.

"Know what?"

"I'm no mad."

"Mad?"

"Bammy."

"So."

"Did you no hear? There's a name for it. It's got a name." And she pronounced the word properly, without an accent. The way she might have if she were imitating London toffs. "Agoraphobia."

A scream ripped the heavy afternoon air and Mum snapped upright. Ella hopped into the kitchen on one foot, crying. "I stepped in a wasp's nest, I stepped on a zillion wasps." Mum moved across the room, slowly, as though over spongy ground. She opened the fridge and took out an onion.

"There now," she said, "a poultice. To draw out the poison." She took Ella's foot in her lap and rubbed the sliced onion on the swelling skin. A local newscaster was now announcing the opening of the Woodward's mall that coming Saturday. Everyone was invited. There'd be balloons, soft drinks, and free samples for all. Not only that, The Junk Yard Beats would be playing rock hits from two till four.

"The Junk Yard Beats," Ella said, leaping up, forgetting her pain. "Can we go? Can we?"

Mum didn't say yes but for the first time she didn't give an outright no.

Before Dad left, I wrote to him constantly.

Dear Dad:

How's construction going? Ella and I got scalped at the barber's. Nothing exciting has happened except Mr. Gartrell put the perfect spelling tests (three) on the wall under a sign that says *We Tried Hard*. He put all the other tests under a sign that says *We Will Try Harder*. Ha ha! Mum yelled at Ella for stealing money from her purse. She bought licorice gum. It looks like you're chewing black tar. Don't forget to bring me home a present.

Love from your adorable daughter, Martha.

p.s. The present starts with H.

Before Dad left he came home with a horse, or, rather, a horse's head on the end of a pole. I named it Gondola. Now, at every opportunity, Ella and I played farmyard in the spare lot beside the house. As the farmer and the oldest, I'd give the orders but Ella wouldn't pick dandelion heads to feed the ducks. The sheep would be dying of thirst but she wouldn't fill the metal bucket at the outdoor tap. She'd just stamp her feet and wail for her turn to ride my horse. One morning she wailed until Mum stuck her head out a window and shouted, "Is there no rest for the wicked?"

"I hate being the wife," Ella screamed, but Mum had already gone inside and shut the window.

"Okay," I said, "but first you have to milk the cows."

And Ella went berserk, running through the thistles, stomping the fallen plums with the heels of her gumboots.

That night I couldn't sleep. Mosquitoes buzzed around my head, dive bombing for my ears and eyes. Earlier, I'd gone into the kitchen to ask Mum to sew my pant leg; it had ripped on a nail. I went through the house, calling. When she didn't answer, Dad and Ella and I searched all the rooms, checking behind curtains and under beds.

"Well, she keeps saying she's going to head for the Sooke Hills," Dad said, trying to be funny. Ella began to cry. "I'm no serious," he said. "Your mum's just playing a game. You wait and see, we'll find her."

I didn't know where the Sooke Hills were though I did know members of a religious cult had recently gone there to wait for the end of the world. Mum had read in the newspaper that hundreds of people were camped on the highest hill, believing it would be easier for God to lift them into heaven. I imagined her standing on a hilltop surrounded by people in white gowns, a huge hand reaching down from the clouds.

I rushed around the kitchen, even looking inside the fridge and flour canister. My mouth was dry; it felt like my heart was stuck in my throat. When I opened the broom closet I hadn't expected to find Mum but there she was huddled in a small space with room for only a few mops, the bag of rags, the Hoover. Knees pulled up to her chest, she looked frightened, the way the rabbits looked, their nostrils quivering.

"For the love of the wee man," Dad said quietly.

"Away you go," Mum said.

We didn't move, just stood looking at her.

"Can you no see I'm trying to get a moment's peace," she said.

Dad closed the door and we stood in silence. I tried to imagine other adults – Dad, Mr. Gartrell, Lorraine's mum – sitting on a Hoover in the dark. And then I wondered if I'd just imagined it. Maybe there was no one on the other side of the cupboard door.

Later, Ella and I stood in front of the bathroom's little vanity mirror brushing our teeth. Toothpaste foamed over her face and hands, right up to her elbows. Blobs of toothpaste dripped on the floor.

"Why do you have to make a big production out of everything?" I said.

Ella's eyes were bright behind smudged glasses. "It's none of your bloody business," she spat through a beard of white froth.

In bed I kept seeing Mum huddled in the broom closet, Dad's pot room socks loose around her ankles. The more I thought about it, the farther away the image slid, but still I lay awake. The house was quiet when I stole down the stairs and through the kitchen, carrying Gondola. As I passed Dad's sunflowers growing against the house I noticed several had been ripped out. The gaps in the dirt looked like spaces in a mouth where teeth had been pulled. The McKeechie boys, I thought. They couldn't wait.

The sky was pale blue, and everything – the pears hanging from the branches, the tall grass, my own moving legs – seemed shockingly alive, much more alive than they were in the glare of day. For a while I cantered around the edge of the lot, whinnying softly, the breeze ruffling my hair. And then the strange light seemed to fill my bones; I could feel it lifting me up.

Before Dad left I imagined fantastic things. That Gondola and I would take to the air; we'd fly above the rooftops, girl and horse, and look down on the sleeping city. The few people walking their dogs would look up, amazed, pointing, shaking their heads.

Mum, too, would wake and peer out her bedroom window – from my perspective, small as a prison cell – and see me soaring above the willow tree, the compost heap, the rabbits who mated day and night, and she'd gasp, and say, "Och aye, there goes Martha, my own brave lassie."

And then Dad left. He left on an ordinary Saturday, on one of those long golden days at the end of September. He left after making pancakes and crispy bacon, after drinking three cups of cowboy coffee.

Living with Mum, he said, was no kind of life. He was sorry for it, he was truly sorry. He'd hoped it would never come to this, but he didn't know which way to turn. At first he'd thought Mum was just high-strung, that she had a bad case of nerves, but it was obviously more than that. And she refused to get help, refused even to go to the doctor despite the fact she knew what ailed her. If it had a name, for Christ's sake, surely it had a cure. Dad said he felt like he was suffocating or losing his mind, often both. Maybe Mum was better off without him. He said all this while Ella and I sat at the table putting small pieces of pancake into our mouths.

After Dad left Ella and I would put tea and toast beside Mum's bed before going to school. For months she stayed inside her room with the transistor radio, the blinds shut. She was like someone hunkered down behind the Iron Curtain and Jack Webster was the voice of the free world. On weekends we'd spend whole days at other people's houses, and beyond, where Blackwood Street tapered off into wild swampy places, we fished with baking sieves, catching things in jars, fluttery things, things that looked back at us with tiny O-shaped mouths and bulging eyes.

After Dad left the garden turned to weeds and the rabbits ate their young. We learned to negotiate Mum's darkness. And then one day when I was thirteen and Ella was eleven, we came home to find her slicing apples and rolling out pastry. There were ten pie plates lined up on the counter. With the help of no one, Mum gradually began to ease herself back into some kind of light.

After Dad left she must have cursed her pride and the terrible cage her body had become, but that morning as he stood on the porch, unshaven, hands at his sides, waiting for something – a sign that Mum needed him to stay? – she just slid her fist inside one of Ella's shoes and began to paint the scuffed toe with whitener.

"No one's holding you," Mum said. "You'd better be off if you're going."

She brought the shoe to her lips and blew. For a moment she might have been someone whose world extended beyond a gouged table and scrape of a clothesline. She might have been someone with somewhere to go, a woman who, having just applied nail polish, was blowing it dry.

DEVIN KRUKOFF

The Last Spark

To those stray geese, winged banjos in the Nebraska sky, the house would not seem so large. There are twenty like it in Lockwood Heights, lining a crescent-canal that allows a few fortunate residents direct access to Gift Lake. On the opposite bank lies a golf course, whose patrons mainly drive up from Little Sahara, a trailer court the size of a small town not far from Lockwood's front gate, in a neighbourhood commonly referred to as "the hood." But Lockwood is a fortress, walled on three sides and moated on the fourth, and "the hood" is more of an abstraction to be navigated in daylight with car doors locked. Or avoided completely via a recently constructed byway – one small branch in the swift vascular system pumping traffic into the heart of the city.

Up close, the house is a grounded ship, leaning down to catch its reflection in the water. Four levels topped by a multi-skylit roof. Twin wraparound patios joined by a wooden staircase. A backyard sloping deeply to the shore, where an aerodynamic boat is moored to a private dock. On the house's uppermost deck, three men sit on well-padded chairs, the glass-topped table before them crowded with drinks and potato chips heaped in ceramic bowls.

"Here, let me," Karl says, eyes rimmed with pink, "let me fill you up."

Lakeman pulls the T-shirt from his belly fanning himself, while Karl pours equal parts Jamaican rum and discount cola into his wet tumbler.

"It'll be dark soon," Lakeman says, considering the steep lawn. Before taking the house a year ago he tested every horizontal surface with a level: floors, countertops, cupboards, and was impressed by how consistently the caught bubble found its liquid centre.

Across the water, a retiree in plaid shorts swats at his tee. A short woman in a wide-brimmed hat, presumably his wife, claps like a seal, while the man leans on his club and squints seriously after the ball.

"Beautiful," Karl says.

Lakeman looks at his wrist with contempt. "What time did Judy say? Eight?"

"That was my understanding, yes."

"Well it's eight-fucking-thirty now."

"Maybe she got caught in traffic."

The couple across the way follow their balls in a rented golf cart. Halfway to the green the woman stops and trots over to the rough. The man sits in the cart, waiting.

Lakeman checks his watch again. "I hate this! I'm hungry. Are you hungry? Hey, Paco!" He fires an ice cube at Gabriel. "How about you get started with those tacos? Those . . . ha ha . . . wake up, Paco!"

Gabriel, who had lapsed into semi-consciousness, rears up, waving at the wasp that just bit him. "What the – Jesus . . . what? What?" Visually grounded by the two men, he shuts his eyes again. "I told you about that, man. Didn't I tell you? How, what, hurtful it is when you call me that?"

"When I call you what?"

"I don't need the a-buse, okay? Pick on the Swede, he's the whatdoyoucall. The immigrant."

"I said tacos. Ta-cos. We're hungry."

"Shit. Okay." Gabriel stands with effort and makes for the sliding glass doors.

"Obedient fucker, I'll give him that," Lakeman says when he's gone.

Karl considers this while the man across the water taps in a long putt for birdie and pumps his fist in the air. The woman takes three strokes to cross a similar distance. "So, ah, what's the situation with Judy?"

Lakeman yawns and stretches his tanned legs out on the deck. Coarse dark hair carpets the knuckles of his toes. He's noticing this for the first time, though it can't possibly be new.

"Because I've seen her," Karl continues, "at the office, how she responds to you. Her body language."

"What?" Lakeman looks up at his blond colleague, face like a stewed tomato topped by that thin down.

"Judy."

"What about her?"

"I'm just saying I think she's interested."

"Oh – that." He turns back to the hairs. There's something about them that makes him think of houseflies, rubbing their little hands together. "The thing about Judy," he says, transfixed by the hair, its sheer length, "is that sometimes she can look pretty good. When she's all done up say. Or when we're out boating and her hair's wet and everything's hanging out." He curls his toes and the hairs stand up, quill-like. "But most of the time" – he stands, compelled to deal with the problem immediately – "she's just butt ugly." He leaves Karl without explanation, pushing into the air-conditioned house.

Inside. Gabriel is hunched over the stove, pots and pans going on all the elements, spatula in one hand, spoon in the other. The ground beef goes from pink to brown, emitting a high-pitched note, which he unconsciously echoes.

"Deeeee," he sings. "Beeeee."

"'Atta boy, Paco!"

By the time Gabriel can lift his head, Lakeman has passed. Where the voice came from there's a painting of an African woman with a great pile of fabric wound about her head. The painting is more cartoon or caricature and Gabriel wonders if he should be offended. The marijuana is leaning heavily on him, pushing him down. Suddenly, the woman has become Consuela: her heavy-lidded eyes, her angular, tapering face.

"It isn't my fault," he tells her, and looks around for someone to corroborate. Out on the patio Karl is alone, looking in through the closed door. The sky is deep indigo and magenta, a few stars beginning to push through. The Swede continues to stare into the house, right at him. The longer they lock eyes, the angrier Gabriel becomes.

A man enters the canal on a Jet Ski, and Karl acknowledges him with a raised hand before turning back to study his reflection in the patio doors. He has the face of a great, aging child. Angels that cluster around saints in Renaissance art all seem to have his face, that serene blandness, at once infantile and ancient. There was a time when women found him disarming, charmingly impudent. Now, in his mid-thirties, he's noticing a gradual shift. The young ones are difficult to sway and women more his age, like Judy, seem wise to him from the start, as if looking deep into his soul and dismissing what they find there.

In the middle of this reverie, the door slides open and Lakeman emerges with Judy and a plain-faced but athletic girl Karl doesn't know. She wears the uniform of youth – halter top, low-cut shorts – much more honestly than Judy. Between her belt line and the hem of her shirt, an inch of teenaged belly winks at him.

"And this," Judy says, taking the lead, spreading her arms with game-show-hostess flair, "is the upper deck."

"There's two?" the girl says, still recovering from the shock of the house they just passed through. Gymnasium ceilings, expensive-looking sculptures, a television the size of a wall. "Open concept" was what the man had called it, the way the entire level connected into one vast room. She couldn't imagine having a place so large to herself. It echoed.

"Yes, but this one" – Judy leans over the balcony, arching her back, lifting one sandalled foot into the air – "gets more sun."

Karl clears his throat, having stood for the new guests. His pose is carefully relaxed. He feels the hair clinging to his skull like damp fabric, yet offers his most winning, cherubic smile.

"Oh, and that's Karl," Judy says, flitting her fingers in his direction. "Are they starting? Come see, Manny!"

Lakeman wanders over to look at the sporadic fireworks leaping up from the horizon. His toes are freshly naked and itching. He's veiled pleasantly by the encroaching darkness and the liquor's warmth as he approaches Judy. He can't see the blue veins on the back of her legs, the deep creases fanning from her eyes and mouth, the greyish hue of her teeth. She's surrounded in the fruity aura of some hair or skin product.

"Those are just private fireworks," he says, unscrewing a wine cooler on his T-shirt. "The real show'll be much bigger." When Judy turns, Lakeman is closer than she had anticipated. Heat rushes to her face as the bottle passes hands and his touch lingers. In the water below a dark, moving shape glides past.

"I'm Judy's cousin," the girl tells Karl, trying to not be daunted by the relative age and money, and the odd sitcom dynamics of the group. "Amelia."

"Is that right?" Karl pads over to the girl. "Something to drink? I assume you're old enough . . ."

"Not here, I guess. Back home I'm legal."

"Ah. And home is . . . ?"

"Ontario. In Canada."

"And you came just to visit Judy?"

"Not really. My parents and I – they're back at the Ramada – we're going down to, well, this is more like a family, you know, holiday. . . . Sure, a drink would be good." She tries to sound casual, but it comes out false after the reference to her parents.

"What would you like?" Karl asks.

She looks to Judy for help, but her cousin is standing on the opposite side of the deck, laughing at something the tallish man is saying. He's handsome, but kind of old. They're all kind of old. "Rum?"

The patio doors rumble open and Gabriel emerges from the house. He's carrying a portable stereo that bangs against the wall of the house. The drugs have crested and eased off and he feels more drunk than anything, which is familiar at least. He bends to try to get at the wall socket, plastic covers snapping shut on the plug before he can fit it in. Karl's voice seems excessively loud, asking the girl if they have this and that in Canada, making a great show of being alternately surprised and fascinated by her monosyllabic replies.

"So you have Wal-Mart but not Walgreens. Hah. Isn't that funny."

"I guess." The drink Karl made tastes awful to Amelia, who has never had spiced rum before. She drinks quickly to be rid of it sooner, feeling abandoned.

Judy is already on her second wine cooler, playing catch-up. Lakeman alternately rubs the toes of one foot with the heel of the other and focuses on her more positive parts, her mouth, for example, which has potential.

"SHOW WILL BE GETTING UNDERWAY IN JUST A MINUTE BUT FIRST THAT WORLD-RECORD-BREAKING RENDITION OF 'TAKE ME OUT TO THE BALL GAME.'"

"Paco! Volume!"

"GOING FOR THE WORLD RECORD HERE, FOLKS. THREE MINUTES STRAIGHT ON TEN THOUSAND KAZOOS! JUST LISTEN TO THEM WARMING UP IN THE STANDS!"

Gabriel has slumped into a patio chair beside the stereo, eyes shut, and Lakeman thumps across the deck to swat him on the back of the head before twisting the knob down. It feels good, to give him that little sting. He'd like to hit him again, but can't think of any justification.

"A bit loud," he says instead. "Grab another beer, buddy."

Gabriel begins to formulate a slow answer, but Judy cuts him off.

"Hey, I forgot! We brought Roman candles!"

"No!" Lakeman is sincerely excited by the prospect. "Bring 'em out!"

"They were in my bag. Where . . . shit!"

"Come on, Judy! Joo-dee! Judy Judy Joo-Joo!" He rushes over and dances around her, seizing the opportunity to frisk and touch. "Give, Judy! Give!"

"No! Ah! The car! They must be in the car!"

They race off through the open patio doors.

Amelia is struck by this juvenile turn of behaviour. Her glass is empty and she takes advantage of the break in Karl's barrage of questions to ask where the washroom is, feeling tipsy already. The men offer conflicting directions, arguing about whether to turn left or right at the nsai tree. When she's gone they sit in silence for a moment, Karl at the table, Gabriel against the wall. It is now fully dark, the golf course a suggestion of forest across the way.

"OKAY, HERE WE GO FOR THE WORLD RECORD. AH-ONE AND AH-TWO –"

The frizzy nasal drone of thousands of kazoos blowing the same familiar tune seeps from the muted radio, solemn and nostalgic.

"So I heard about your latest pitch," Gabriel finally says. "Frozen pancakes?"

Karl ignores him. He's thinking about the girl, how not long ago she would have been a more likely prospect. But now her eyes are devoid of interest, the barest glimmer. He's a eunuch to her. A non-sexual being. A sweaty balding oaf.

"We've had frozen waffles forever for a reason. People like waffles. Because they're designed for the toaster, right? But pancakes?"

Karl whistles through his teeth, looking everywhere but at Gabriel. "What did Judy say was in the car? Something Roman?"

"And it's not even original. Kellogg's has them on the shelf right now, as we speak, so what's new?"

"Is that them by the water? They must have gone around the house. Hey, what are you two doing down there!"

"Do people want more frozen pancakes? You've got to ask yourself that question. Because we're not all in Lakeman's position. Next weekend, when that axe falls? He's about the only one in the division I'd say whose position is totally, what, secure."

"Wait, what are you saying?"

"And why is that. Because he's got pull. Connections. He doesn't have to worry about the viability of frozen pancakes or whatever."

"Wait, Gabriel. Next weekend? Where did you hear this?"

"He could pitch frozen dog shit if he wanted. Not like the rest of us. We've got to produce or be reduced and blah blah blah –"

There's a sudden shout from the water below and three balls of coloured light punch up at the house. Two tear past, and one hammers the vinyl siding beside Gabriel, showering him with sparks.

"Jesus Christ! Holy Jesus I'm on fire!" He jumps up, flailing at the embers on his shirt, in his hair. The firework spins and fizzles on the deck.

"That was close, wasn't it?" Karl says mildly, as Lakeman's laughter drifts up from below.

"Did we get you?"

"Get us? Jesus! Yes, you fucking got us!"

Six more balls arc over the house, at higher angles this time.

Flinching and swearing with each one, Gabriel looks for something to hurl back down, hand settling on a full bottle of imported beer.

"I think it would be in your best interest," Karl says as three more sail out over the golf course, illuminating the tops of trees, "to calm down."

Gabriel weighs the bottle and listens to Lakeman haw-hawing in the darkness below. The Swede is right. He contents himself with kicking the cooler and returns to his chair on the wall, resolving to get as drunk as possible as quickly as possible.

Karl lights a cigarette and the flame jitters in his hand. "You know," he says, "we're in a similar boat right now. Rock too hard we might both fall in. Especially now, if what you're saying is true."

"How was that for a light show kids?" Lakeman asks, taking the stairs up in twos.

Judy slips past him and makes for the drinks. "Hey, what did Karl do with Amelia?"

"THERE YOU HAVE IT, FOLKS, A WORLD RECORD! NOW TURN UP THE VOLUME AND ENJOY THIS FOURTH OF JULY EXTRAVAGANZA, FIREWORKS SYNCHRONIZED TO SOME OF YOUR FAVOURITE –"

"For your information, I –"

"It's starting! Amelia!" Judy rolls open the patio door. "Something's burning!" she calls back brightly.

With a shout Gabriel is on his feet and racing after her. Lakeman chuckles at the volley of profanities coming back, and Karl decides to take advantage of his apparent good humour.

"So listen, Manny. Apparently there's something in the rumour mill about downsizing next weekend. I know, it sounds crazy coming so soon after –"

"God damn!" Lakeman doubles over, scratching at toes that

have become inflamed and painful. "I hate this! What is it with body hair?"

"I really don't . . . I'd have to give that more thought, Manny. But as I'm saying, about these layoffs. I was just wondering if you might have a little more information. Or maybe even some influence –"

"Armpits! Bellies! Balls! You know, lately . . . lately," he continues, lowering his voice, "I've been finding hair in the strangest places."

"Ah . . . I'm sure it's quite natural, Manny. Part of the aging process –"

"Yeah, yeah. Hey, what do you think of Judy?" Lakeman finishes half a beer in one pull and holds the bottle by the neck.

"Well – as you know, Judy and I don't always see eye to eye –"

"If I fucked her – she wants it, you said so yourself – but if I fucked her, you know, tonight, would there be howdoyousay repercussions later?"

Karl is a little surprised by how savagely the word "fuck" leaves Lakeman's mouth. "It, ah, well, it could be awkward, but you're not her employer so ethically I don't –"

"Yeah, you're right. I think I should fuck her." He tucks the bottle between his legs and twists it in his fist, looking at Karl in disgust. "Maybe I'll fuck you too."

Karl watches the man across from him, the logo on his T-shirt like a dark window into his chest. "If that's supposed to be funny –"

"Settle down, I'm just messing with you. Hey, Paco! Did you burn those Pacos yet? Those – ha, ha – tacos yet?"

But the patio doors soundproof the house and Gabriel doesn't hear. He's standing before the stove, gazing sadly at the ruined food. The scorched ground beef, the sauce boiled into thick paste, the tortillas charred into little black wings. The injustice of it makes him want to cry. And then he is crying. The fire alarm goes off and he turns to the portrait for help. It no longer looks so eerily like Consuela, but still calls her to mind.

"Aren't you taking it a bit hard, Gabe?" Judy says, having tracked her cousin down in the washroom. She knows that

Gabriel is an emotional drunk, and is not overly surprised or concerned by his present state. The alarm sputters and dies. "Let's go! Fireworks!"

Gabriel continues to sob, waving vaguely at the food, at the portrait.

Amelia, who has never seen a man weep so unabashedly before, stops to ask if he's okay.

"Suit yourselves!" Judy says, and leaves them behind. She's hitting her stride and catching her buzz. Outside, fanfare erupts from the radio, which Lakeman has turned up. She whoops and races over to him as white spears thrust into the sky and burst into red, white, and blue globes above the distant stadium. Lakeman dances her over to the wicker loveseat, swivelling it away from the table with his free hand. They sit down together, feet wrestling on the cedar boards.

Ahead, bright splashes of colour approximate the music, which somehow shifts cleanly from Beethoven into Neil Diamond's "Coming to America." Judy and Lakeman move progressively closer, while Karl sits alone behind them, talking about the origins of fireworks. Peripherally he watches Gabriel and Amelia through the patio doors, which have reversed their mirror in the transition from day to night.

Gabriel hasn't once mentioned his wife, Consuela. How he met and married her six months ago while visiting family in Mexico City. How, since then, immigration has kept her from entering the country. What he talks about is the El Condor apartment complex of his childhood, where he and his brothers slept five to a double bed, like cigars in a box. And the ten years he spent clawing up to where he is today. "Do you see?" he asks the girl. "Why I can't just quit and risk losing it all? Do you see?"

The girl says yes, she sees. It occurs to her that she's missing all the fireworks outside.

"Oh, those are new!" Judy says, pointing to the technological feat of U-S-A exploding repeatedly, followed by what look like Pepsi symbols. Lakeman's hand is on her naked back where the fabric dips, his uncallused fingers brushing lightly. Her own hand falls onto his thigh as the music softens to Tchaikovsky, then John Lennon. The lights reflect this change in tempo.

White fuses twist up, disappear, and burst into swarms of fireflies. The pop-pop-pops are restrained, working in countertempo to the occasional whump of larger spiders reaching down.

Karl has been silent too long. Judy and Lakeman – in his direct line of vision – seem oblivious to everything but each other and the light show ahead, but they must be as aware of his presence as he is of theirs. Their heads, bent together to the point of touching. His hand, locked around her neck. Her arm, out of sight, moving with a subtle, regular rhythm. Light blooms and spills all over the sky. Karl turns to the patio doors, also a stage: the girl nodding and frowning with the kind of sympathy one offers a raving harmless man. The raving harmless man reaching out to lay a hand on the girl's shoulder, a gesture misinterpreted by the girl as paternal and acceptable. This acceptance itself misunderstood by the raving harmless man, who takes a firmer hold and leans in, free hand swinging to her waist. His mouth covers her mouth, and then the girl is recoiling away from the raving harmless man. The blind mouth and the dark hands that won't let go.

Outside, the music has shifted into anthem-mode. The exclamation of cymbals and pounding of snare drums. Larger and larger fireworks jostle for attention in the sky, overlapping. "Ah, Judy?" Karl says, pleased to have a reason to interrupt. "I think you better rescue your cousin."

Judy's reaction is delayed, but when she turns to find Gabriel bent around her cousin in the attitude of a clumsy waltz, Amelia twisting and clearly protesting, she is up and running through the doors.

Lakeman breathes heavily, blood singing in his head. The lights stutter and smash against him in waves. Inside the house a wild-eyed banshee is shouting and gesticulating at a fat Mexican, while a skinny girl hangs off to one side. The females in the picture go soft focus, and then he can see only the Mexican, hands open on either side of his head, waving like maracas, mouth gasping like a fish on the deck of a boat.

Lakeman's toes burn.

"That's it," he says.

"She's really laying into him, isn't she?"

"That's it!" He pushes to his feet and lumbers into the house, heedless of the erection pressing at the fabric of his shorts, a lance swaying in front of the charging knight. The air conditioning and false daylight in the kitchen are starkly real. The three people standing on the linoleum are animals. Bleating animals. Furry, defecating animals, and that one, that one . . . He collides with Gabriel, grabbing his shirt with both hands, and hurls him across the room.

Gabriel does nothing to defend himself. None of this feels at all real to him. Lakeman's cartoonish rage. His eyes drift down to the absurd bulge in the man's shorts and he begins to laugh. Lakeman advances, swings, and connects. What Gabriel experiences is not pain exactly, but a kind of pulse, a jitter in consciousness. He is inside of his body looking out, watching this happen to someone else. He absorbs another blow, and hears words: "Stupid-wetback-spick-mother-fucker . . ."

Karl is standing by the patio doors, watching.

Goaded by Judy, he makes a half-hearted attempt to restrain Lakeman and catches an elbow in the forehead. He staggers back and falls heavily onto the sofa in the adjacent living room, where a big-screen television is projecting the very show going on outside the window. "Would you look at that," he says.

Judy yells at Lakeman, telling him to "Stop, stop, stop!"

Amelia is pinned against the wall, horrified. She's thinking about how she kissed back at first – and not just from pity. How helpless she felt when pushing away, as if caught inside a broken machine.

The racist tirade bleeds into Gabriel's head, and when it finally reaches his brain, he begins to bellow incoherently, fighting back with an intensity that shocks them all. Lakeman staggers and hits the floor, forearms locked into a defensive X. Gabriel's fists fall like clubs.

From the couch, Karl watches blood spread across Lakeman's face and wonders if the man's nose is broken. He broke a finger once, skiing in Vale, and remembers it hurting like hell.

Then Amelia is shrieking.

This is what finally stops Gabriel, the sudden violence of a girl's shuddering vocal cords. He sits on Lakeman for a moment, breathing hard, then stands and backs away. Judy rushes to the fallen man, still balled up like a beetle.

"He shouldn't –" Gabriel says, and vomits on the floor.

"SEA TO SHINING SEA!" belts from both the television and the deck. The camera has to pan back to catch all the light forming an immense cloud over the ballpark.

Judy alternately shrieks at Gabriel and tries to touch Lakeman, who shoves her away. After a few dry heaves, Gabriel makes for the front door without a word or a glance at anyone.

"Should I call an ambulance?" Amelia asks, embarrassed by a reaction that seems excessive in this relative calm.

"Nuh-no," Lakeman says, struggling to his knees then to his feet. Moths swoop in and batter the kitchen lights. Through the front door, which Gabriel left open, they hear his car tear out of the driveway and fade away.

"He's driving?" Amelia says.

Judy tries to approach Lakeman again and again he resists, slipping in spilt food. He's looking for something to wrap his nose in. She pulls at him, and he turns his dull eyes on her. "Fuck off."

"I'm just trying to –"

"Fuck off!"

Judy stands for a moment in the middle of the kitchen, hands frozen in a pantomime of catching, then her face closes and she walks quickly from the room, from the house. Amelia hesitates and follows, turning at the door to offer the men a polite "It was nice meeting you."

Lakeman, having found a towel, wraps his face in it and tilts his head back. The blood trickles down his throat.

"Well, that was exciting, wasn't it?" Karl says. "You gave me quite the knock on the head there."

Lakeman waves him aside and makes his way out to the deck, to the liquor. His face feels caved in and throbbing.

"Yes. Well, I suppose I should be –"

Lakeman rolls the patio door shut on Karl's ridiculous accent and kicks the squawking radio out of its socket. He tests and finds that the blood has stopped flowing, then pours himself a strong drink. The show is over. Only the smaller, backyard fireworks remain, continuing like echoes, involuntary spasms. In their glow he sees a tall column of smoke rising from somewhere near the ballpark. An errant spark must have touched off a fire. Even from this distance he can hear the sirens unravelling through the night, under a sky weak with stars.

LESLEY MILLARD

The Uses of the Neckerchief

Rob flexes the strip of cedar before he lays it back on the pile. It vibrates for a moment, like it's alivc. *Not today*, he thinks. *I can't start today.* Instead he takes another pull at his coffee. He slides open the window over the workbench, lights up a smoke. It's a walkout basement, with a nice view out the back – swamp and a little bush. He inhales deeply and blows a rich double stream out his nostrils, pursing his lips at the end to send up a forceful jet of smoke on an angle that intersects with the nostril streams and, in theory, sends the whole tangle out the window.

But today the air outside is as damp as you can get without feeling like spring is coming. The sky is low and dark and the wet wind just slaps the smoke back inside. He slides the window shut and takes another drag, holds it in, feels the little pleasure circuits firing off in his brain. As he exhales he hears that funny squeaking sound from his lungs. *Spring is coming. That will be a good time. I'll quit smoking in the spring.* He thumbs the butt into a half-empty beer bottle and hides it beneath the bench.

He's supposed to be working on the canoe. He told everyone he'd finish it, he told Nora he couldn't go to the mall because he had to work on the canoe. He wants to, it's half done, more than half. He's at the satisfying stage, the beauty part. The frame's done, snug as a cradle. Perfect lines, a skeleton ready to be clad in the creamy red-gold sheath of cedar that he ordered from B.C. a month or two after Toby got his discharge. Takes a while, the guy said. He picked it up at Love's Lumber the week before

Toby drove up to the lake and left his truck parked on the ice.

Toby said great when Rob called him with the news that the wood was in, but he'd quit going out of the house by then, and they both sort of knew it was too late.

He left the Forces – or they let him go, Rob's still not sure – a couple of years after he got back from Rwanda. Rob hadn't seen him for a while, hadn't really been close since they were teenagers. But when Toby came home they picked right up again. He seemed pretty normal, he still had his truck and he'd drive around town in it, run errands for his mother. He had a funny look and he was pretty quiet but people went easy on him, they knew he'd been through a lot.

Toby always got along great with Nora. That summer he'd often come out to their place for a barbecue on the weekends, or else he and Rob would go fishing and they'd bring the catch home and cook it with Nora and the boys. It was on one of those warm blue nights, drinking beer by the fire and eating planked trout, they got the idea for the canoe. Toby started it, telling Nora about the time they were going to blow up the Agent Orange plant.

That was 1970. Too big for their bikes, huge awkward hands dangling from their bony wrists, hair sprouting everywhere. B.O. They were best friends for the usual reasons – proximity more than anything else. But even then, where Rob was dogged and methodical, Toby had the vision, he came up with the plans. It worked well for them, they laughed a lot. They'd meet in the mornings in Toby's kitchen, his mother gone off early to work, light slanting through the windows and spilling onto big bowls of Special K which they would fill and eat and refill as they spun out plans. Sometimes they listened to the radio – "American Woman" was on a lot, there were casualty lists and hills with names and napalm. They followed the news from Vietnam with a funny mixture of eagerness and distaste. They were against it, but at the same time they were fascinated by the details. Blown-up bodies, what they would look like. Army surplus was the new thing, you could get camping gear and shirts and all kinds of weird shit at the store in Toronto. Everything was that olive green, the way he remembers it. Geophones, Toby was crazy excited when he heard about these gadgets, you laid them to the earth and you could listen for footsteps, worms, anything. You'd hear it. You'd hear them coming. Lie still.

They would eat, and play The Doors or Hendrix, turning up the volume a little each time they flipped the LP until they reached critical mass and burst out the bungalow door in their army shirts and ragged cutoffs and crusty, sockless Adidas, laughing, each of them swinging a canvas backpack from the army surplus and the dogs fanning out behind them.

All kinds of trouble they got into that summer, but one mess they didn't get into was blowing up the fertilizer plant, because Rob got Toby onto building a canoe instead.

It was the fishing made them notice. A trout stream cut across the back yard of Toby's house, brown and dimpled, shaded by willows and the odd tall elm. Buckthorn grew thickly along the edges and dogwood straggled up the steep slope to the yard, so you had the privacy. When they were younger, eight or nine, and learning to fish, it was the first place they were allowed to go on their own and they made the most of it. Booby traps, a fire pit.

And the fish, lord. Fat, brown, they lurked and flirted, rolled and disappeared with a silvery flick. Finally, sometimes, they offered themselves up from the dark cool world like a gift.

Even that summer, the summer they were fourteen and had the run of the town, they would end up by the creek a lot of times, lying on the fallen log talking, and peering into the brown pools. Where the sunlight fell on the water you should have been able to see trout below the surface, but that year there weren't any. Mid-July they noticed even the crayfish were gone, and the water had taken on a funny colour. And smell. Not just the smell of dead fish, though there was plenty of that. Something metallic.

After Toby got back from Rwanda and it was clear he was not right, and Rob came up with the idea of building a second canoe, he tried and tried to remember how he convinced Toby to concentrate on the first one.

But that summer was so long ago, and when he thinks back only certain details are there. He remembers it as though there were only one morning – or as though all the mornings were the same – and on that morning they burst through the green bungalow door with the teardrop window and uncoiled their men's bodies onto the landscape of their boys' life. They could do anything. It was here.

It must have been around the middle of summer that things sort of dwindled. Not the usual laziness of August, but a feeling of confinement, paralysis. Thunderstorms. A dark afternoon when the trout should have been leaping and biting like blackflies. They followed the creek, wearing sneakers to protect their feet from the cans and broken glass, soaking their shorts as they waded the pools. Upstream of the factory they started finding fish again.

"So, my good Doctor, what may we infer?" Toby smiled his Sherlock smile and his eyes glinted green through smudged glasses and tangled hair. When Rob didn't answer quickly enough, he smacked him up the side of the head and switched accents: "Fool! Vee haff zee culprits! Und now vee vill make zem pay."

For a couple of days after that it rained a hot sticky rain. Toby sank into a high-intensity brood. He stared at the horizon and wouldn't talk. He lay on the couch with the music turned up loud enough to rattle the windows. He ate Cap'n Crunch by the boxful while Rob danced frantic circles around him: Wanna build a go-kart? Wanna go see if *After the Gold Rush* is in? Wanna canoe down the Grand to the lake?

And that's when Toby came up with the bomb idea.

It's a fact that about 40 per cent of the Agent Orange used to defoliate Vietnam was produced by the fertilizer plant in their hometown, and it's another fact that there are still no trout in Kuepfer Creek. But then again, blowing up the factory would have been a stupid thing to do. That's a fact, too. Even if (as Toby figured out in a couple of days) it could be done with ammonium nitrate. Fertilizer. *Blow 'em up with their own shit, man.* And even though, if they shut down the plant, it might have saved the creek. Because nothing would have saved their sorry asses.

Rob likes facts, they've always been a comfort to him. He's like that, he accepts things as they are and doesn't get sucked in by the drama. Where Toby would have gone and found you another fact. The strategy has been useful, he's kept his head down and worked hard, built a lot of houses. Built his own house on these acres, raised his boys and kept his family safe. He's done no harm, he thinks he can say that. But what else can he say?

With the kids gone the place seems bigger. They rattle around, he and Nora. He loves his acres, but at the same time, he feels fenced in, somehow. Embattled, almost. As though these acres are the only acres left.

You hear so much on the news. Those high-tension wires. Anywhere you step there could be old benzine tanks, toxic sludge. And the aquifer, for instance, his well taps an aquifer that draws from the entire watershed. Sometimes he wonders about what he's done in the world, the work his hands have done. What difference will his strategy make, in the long run?

He saved Toby's ass that summer, that's one thing he can say. You don't really think, that age, how bad it could get. Protesters were getting killed, students were going to jail. Some people need to be saved from themselves.

Like those kids down in Colorado, shot up their school. It could have gone like that. They were such a puzzle to everyone. It's no big mystery really. In a way, he can sympathize. That's not really the word. But he thinks he knows what they were after. Because for about six months, at some point near the end of your childhood, *you know*. You know what it's about. Morality, convention, going through the motions. You can see through the teachers and the parents and all the righteous assholes with their flimsy pretexts for social control, you see the budding civic leaders and the soon-to-be deadbeats and the little trophy wives spreading their cheerleader skirts like wings. But you haven't bought it. You can see what's coming for you, but you haven't been fed into the machine, not yet. And you get the urge to do one last clean pure thing before you get sucked in. Sure it's twisted.

In the summer of 1970 he accepted the facts, he dangled the canoe like a stick in a retriever's face and got Toby dancing off down another track – even though their hair hung ragged to their shoulders and Morrison and Hendrix were both still alive and there were four dead in O-hi-o – and he's wished a million times he could remember how. Even now. Even with Toby gone. Because something has happened to Rob that's making it hard for him to get up in the morning. It's as though he's forgotten something, something he's always known, something so important that you never even think about it, you just take it for granted. Like breathing.

There's a picture of that first canoe hanging on the wall above the workbench. Nora dug it out – it's just a Polaroid and the colours look stoned but she had it blown up anyway, and she framed it herself. Toby's a blur in the foreground, half in the water and half in the canoe, which is swamped. His glasses glint in the sun, but that's about all you can see of him because the dogs are all around, jumping on him and licking his face – they'd be so relieved when he'd finally come back in to the shore. His mouth is open, laughing, and Rob remembers Smoky stuck his tongue into it about a second later.

Everything's fuzzy but the river looks like he remembers, you can see it curve away towards town and back again in the distance. The highway crosses it now, it's all different. In the foreground there's a tree branch in focus, but even that seems to tremble over the water – green water, lit from below by reflected light. Red of apples on it. So it was September at least. School would be started. A Saturday, then, and early because the light is so slanted. Yes, it was, and though it's February and he's forty-seven, he's flooded with the smell of the green water, the smell of the wet dogs, and he remembers the surprised looks of the cows in the bottomland pasture just there, as two boys paddled through with the mist burning off. The river, just the way he remembers it, just the way it will never be again.

Nora is stalled. One hand hovers over the kitchen sink like a bird riding a thermal, but really, there is nothing left for it to do. The counter is clean and the dishwasher hums reassuringly as it fills, but she gets no comfort from the sound, or from the feel of clean tiles under her bare feet. She loves that feeling, that lack of interference between foot and floor. Some people, hearing a noise in the night, will put their glasses on so they can hear better. But Nora's one to swing her legs over the side of the bed and place her feet on the floor, rub them a little against the surface.

She'd had it in mind that they would go and shop together, and talk, and look at some things for the boys and the house. Have lunch at the hotel on the way home. She'd had in mind the ride to town, sitting up high and safe beside him in the truck with the grey dormant fields blurring past outside. She wonders if she should go herself – there's still all the Easter shopping to do. But shopping is not the point.

Anyway, there's no one to be plaintive to. He's not himself. He's been fiddling around in the basement all morning, the sounds drifting up through the ductwork. She can track him by the sounds, if she concentrates. Shop to rec room to garage and back. Right now he's shifting boxes, it sounds like. A while ago she heard him slide shut the window over the workbench. He's started smoking again, she's pretty sure. There's a tempo, too. If he's got his boots on she can tell what mood he's in by the way he steps on the concrete. Socks, it's harder, but you get a feel by the amount of time it takes to get from one place to another, or by the volume – the force with which a door is closed, the tone of the occasional muffled curse. What tunes he puts on.

Today, though, it's a complete mystery, except that lately there have been so many mysterious Saturdays. Since Toby died, of course, but surely it had started before that. Maybe years ago, even. Ten minutes after he went down he came up for coffee and said he'd changed his mind, he wanted to work on the canoe. He didn't give her a chance to say *But*, just ducked his head that way he has, looking past her. Then a lot of industrious pounding for a while, moving things around, then silence. Not working silence, with occasional clatters or shuffles or cupboards opening. Slumped silence, brooding. The window sliding open, then shut.

She can't remember when he turned into such a lump, she can't remember when she started feeling like she was spying on him, like he was keeping something from her. Since Toby, yes, definitely since Toby it's gotten worse, but it began before that. And when you think about it, how well has she ever known him?

The problem, she thinks, the thing is, really, that men are like dogs. They romp along all happy and excited, but no solid idea of what's going on. Rabbit goes down the hole, boot gets thrown at them, they haven't a clue. They just keep sniffing around, all sad and hopeful looking. Best buddy kills himself? Build a friggin' canoe, it's the only way.

It's like they don't want to know it's happened, they don't want to know they're hurting, if they *do* something maybe it'll go away.

And another thing they do, like dogs, they don't want *you* to know they're hurting. Like maybe then they'd lose their place in the pecking order.

She doesn't know what Toby did in Rwanda that could make him commit suicide. She knows he shot a lot of dogs, that's all. They got into the bodies. She believes it, but she can't imagine it, him killing dogs. Toby, of all people.

Rob won't tell her – he reminds her how she listened to stuff that came out during the Bernardo trial – details – and then she couldn't sleep, or she'd wake up retching. And actually she's not even sure *he* knows what really happened. But he makes out like he can handle it, where she can't.

And that's another thing they do – here's where her brittle anger cracks and melts, here's the chink – any trouble, they run towards it. They like to keep their dog's body between you and it, they're happy to do that. They're happy to die doing that. It's the combination of arrogance and dumb loyalty that's got her fingers drumming on the table, that's got two bright spots of colour on her cheeks, as she hears her husband's step on the stairs.

Rob comes into the room on the balls of his feet. He looks half asleep, but he's one of those athletic men – coordinated, a little pigeon-toed – who are always ready to jump sideways with no warning if they need to. It was the first thing she loved about him.

"Hon," he says, standing close enough that she can smell the cigarettes, the bitterness of coffee. She imagines the astringent taste his tongue would have. "Have you seen that jacket of mine?"

Now which of the dozens of jackets that have come through the door in their twenty years would that be? Like she's a psychic or what? His eyes are so mournful and quizzical she has to laugh. "You look like a puppy, Rob." She doesn't mean anything by it, not really, but his mouth tightens and his gaze shifts to the window over the sink. From his look, from the day, from a half-dozen other clues she couldn't name, she realizes he's talking about the army jacket.

"Actually, in the hall closet? I think I threw it out."

"What?"

"I threw it out, it had a big rip, you didn't expect me to sew it, did you? The thing was falling apart." His face crumples like he can't believe she'd do this to him.

"Lord, no. I wouldn't expect you to sew for me." Ah, she thinks, we disappoint each other, don't we?

"What, did you leave a pack of smokes in it or something?" She's trying to make light of it but somehow the words escape harsh. She sees his face redden with anger or shame in the second before he turns away. In a flat voice he says, "I'd had it a long time, that's all." And he closes the door behind him and goes down the stairs so fast that for a second she thinks he's slipped, fallen.

Rob hates the way Nora looks at him these days. Disappointed. Like she's going to cry. Or else mocking, as though he's got food dribbled down his chin or something and she's not going to tell him. *If only she would tell him.* The thought creeps in from somewhere and he squashes it.

She'll probably call her sister now and they'll have a good cackle over this. He slips on the concrete at the foot of the stairs and nearly falls. "Fuck!" The loudness of his own voice surprises him, echoing through the still dark rooms. Why does it have to be like this? Why does *she* have to be like this? He wants to get in his truck and just drive. He knows it's stupid, he's too old to feel this way, but the truth is he wants to drive away and never see Nora again. He pulls on his parka and throws a few things into a milk crate. Grabs the smokes.

Upstairs, Nora smiles grimly as she hears the noise. Touched a nerve, did we? When she hears the truck start she goes to watch from the living room window. Sky and ground are the same unrelieved, washed-out grey, the buildings and trees carelessly etched in a flat pewter. He's pulled up to the shed and he's throwing all kinds of stuff into the pickup. Crowbars, tools, ladder. Last to go in is the kids' old toboggan, for god's sake. Oh, he's up to something now. There's so much crap in the truck bed that the toboggan sticks out a couple of feet over the tailgate, and for some reason he stands there in the slush for maybe a full minute, looking at it. Then he goes back in the shed and comes out with a red rag which he ties to the toboggan. That's the sort of thing he'll do, tie a rag on the end of the load. You don't see that any more.

His work boots leave deep divots in the slush as he circles the pickup once. Wherever he's going, he'll have wet feet all day. Then he climbs in, he doesn't look back, the pickup rattles down the laneway and disappears behind the poplars at the road.

The divots are still there, darkening as they fill. They make her remember the first walk she and Rob took out here, just after they signed the papers. They hadn't even moved in yet. It was warm for December, and the thick snowfall was the first they'd had that year. No wind, big fluffy flakes falling straight down, gentle as a blanket. He held her hand and the sky was purple, close. The snow lay thick and they left a trail of deep blue footprints that went around the perimeter of their fifteen acres, then threaded its way through the bush. She remembers slipping off her mitten to feel his hand better, him leading the way, him offering up the land, the trees, the night. They heard an owl hoot. When Rob let out a low, soft hoot it was answered – she didn't think they'd do that, she wouldn't have believed a human could fool an owl. And they saw the stubby silhouette fly low overhead, black against the purple, snow falling in their eyes. He called it twice more, and each time it answered them, circling. She stood open-mouthed, looking up, the snowflakes melting on her tongue, holding her husband's warm hand as he called down an owl from the sky.

Hot salty rivers well up from Nora's tear ducts, fill her eyes, course down her cheeks. She doesn't shake or sob, just sits like a stone by the window, her body spouting tears the way it grows hair or fingernails. After a while she gets up – her knees creak, so it *has* been a while – and pads barefoot into the bathroom to blow her nose. She likes the window in there, she likes the natural light, but it shows everything. Rosy pools have formed in the creases below her lashes and from there the liquid radiates –

it looks like a river delta in reverse, an estuary with the tide coming in. Tracking through the cracks and fissures around her eyes, finally spilling over the parched hills of her cheeks in warm little torrents.

Well, it can't be that bad if you can admire it in the mirror. She seems to hear her mother, and half smiles. Her smile has always been lopsided, higher on one side, and she watches the crazed tectonic tilt with detached interest as one of the little rivers is channelled into the deep groove connecting nose to mouth. Her tongue flicks out and tastes the salt. Surprise surprise. And thinking of her mother, she realizes that she will feel much better if she cleans the house. Particularly the floors.

Rovers, that was it. The canoe was for Rovers. It hits him as the truck rounds the crest of the last hill in the chain that lies between his house and the town, watching the red rag flap in the breeze. It's almost the same colour as the neckerchiefs they wore to Rovers that summer. He'll veer off south now, skirt the town, follow the edge of these rolling hills all the way down to the river. Eskers, he thinks they are – something ice age, anyway, some frozen ocean of gravel hills that runs on south and east till it laps against the escarpment.

They weren't technically old enough to move up from Scouts, but they were about ready to quit and Akela knew it, he let them go. Plus Jerry, the Rovers leader, used to buy Toby's homegrown once in a while so he didn't mind taking them on. What a summer. There was a moot coming up in September, where you host another troop, you camp out, you show off what you can do. And he and Toby decided to be the youngest Rovers to build the best canoe in the shortest time, ever. Toby decided. Rob's idea, but Toby ran with it, made it sing.

That's what he was like. Fishing, explosives, bike trips, it was all put aside and they dove headlong into Rovers stuff. Rob heaving a sigh of relief, delighted to be rolling along in Toby's wake again. He's a follower, he knows that about himself. Mostly they worked on the canoe in Toby's mother's garage, drinking lemonade, listening to AM radio. But there were other things as well. Rovers was different from Scouts – cooking badges were out the window, for instance. Sleepouts were accompanied by loud music nearly till dawn, sharing tokes with leaders barely older than yourself, going off to jump the cliffs at Elora. But Toby was always a good Scout. He studied the lore – he memorized the fifty uses of the Scout's neckerchief, he'd quote them at you. *Belt. Smoke mask for rescues. Water filter. Bandage. "And as any scout who has been in a burning stable knows, the neckerchief can be used to blindfold a panic-stricken horse and convince it to follow the scout to safety."*

Sometimes he'd make them up: *Rat hammock. Hippie headband. In case of nuclear attack, bend down with the neckerchief in place, draw the tails between your knees, pull hard. This will move your head into position between your legs so you can kiss your ass good-bye.*

On the canoe's maiden voyage they got south as far as Paris, where the bedrock rears up and the river cuts down through layers of soft gypsum, leaving high bluffs on either side. It wasn't a race, but he and Toby paddled like demons in the canoe they'd built with their hands. It was a hot day. He remembers he could see the sweat darkening Toby's T-shirt where he knelt in the prow. Smell it too, shit. And Toby's shape was different. Triangular. His shoulders were broad, angular planes folding down to narrow hips. A man's shoulders, slanting and bucking as he reached with the paddle. They pulled so hard they were way ahead, they had time to haul out and scamper up the bluff at Paris. At the top they sprawled, dead still, letting the high breezes cool them. Every now and then one or the other would grunt out a line of song. Something from the Stones.

Rob, nearly asleep on his stomach, hears Toby shift and rise. He rolls over and up, and there's Toby on the very brink of the cliff, windmilling his arms and humming, doing a little dance. It's code, he realizes. Semaphore: "S-A-T . . ." Down below on the river, the other canoes are floating lazily into view. Rob sings the chorus down to them, he yells it so they can hear. His voice slides up an octave on the "get" and he shrieks out the rest, and the two boys leap off the hilltop, scramble back down. Halfway they switch to bum-sliding, choking on dust and snorted, high-pitched giggles.

Once he's south of the highway he figures he can start angling toward the river, take the back roads all the way down to the quarry. He pulls over at the Tim Hortons just after the overpass to grab a coffee and check the map. He'll be following the river and he needs to cross it at some point. Paris looks good, actually. There's a bridge. Gypsum. Plaster of Paris. That's where it comes from, Toby said.

He roots around in the glove box for the cell phone – he should give Jeff a ring. It crosses his mind to call Nora as well but he thinks of the grilling he'll get and he slams down hard on the thought. Jeff works at the quarry, he's the one who told Toby about the calcite crystal hanging there in a crevice like a peach on the lip of the living rock. Teetering, as the glacial fill surrounding it loosens and washes away.

"It won't hang there forever," Toby told Rob the last time they saw each other. "It sounds neat. You should go down there and pry it out. I can't, I'm too busy right now."

Busy with the coltan campaign. Toby had a bug up his ass about the coltan mining back in Congo. Tantalite and niobium, but for some reason they call it coltan. Rob thinks that's why they made him leave the Forces. He started a one-man campaign – towards the end it was all he did. Come near him with anything electronic and he'd start sputtering about what your capacitor's made of, and big business and American foreign policy and videogame consoles and murder and child slave labour. You couldn't shut him up but you couldn't get any sense out of him either.

Anyway, the batteries are dead. Oh well, have to wing it. He thinks Jeff works Saturdays sometimes.

After he crosses the river the hills flatten out but the plane of the land itself surges up in a slow, steady rise. He doesn't like it – the fields look bald and poor, exposed. There's still plenty of woods but the trees are stunted, he has the impression they're only there because it's too much work to drain the land. Dark pools he sees, among the spindly trunks. Different bedrock, must be. Closer to the surface, anyway, or there'd be no quarry here, right? Then he remembers the steel plant, just to the south; that must be it. Mostly the quarry produces stone – the crystals he's looking for are incidental, what they call sub-economic. Crushed stone for road beds, lime for farming. Won't burn for shit, you can line furnaces with the stuff, but add magnetite and oh yeah, *whoosh*, you got klinker. Klinker for the steel plant down in Hamilton, that's where most of it goes. So that's why the quarry's here. Maybe. Toby'd know. He knew the place, he'd been down with Jeff a few times and he knew what you could find there.

Deep-circulating sea water carries magnesium into the porous rock, where it reacts with the calcium atoms, transforming the limestone into harder, darker dolostone. Where this transformation occurs, cracks or fissures form, providing the conditions of growth for sub-economic concentrations of sulphide minerals.

Rob remembers Toby chanting the names like a litany, some time or other: *marcasite, sphalerite, pyrite, galena*. Maybe it was the mineralogy badge.

There's no sign that he's approaching a quarry, just the rain needling down on a bit of a slant and smudgy clouds scudding across flat poor fields. But the road changes to pavement after he crosses the highway. It's still a back road but it's not pot-holed or anything, it's been patched over so many times it's smooth as a baby's bum. He imagines trucks full of stone rolling along all day. Rolling Stones.

Then there's the flashing light, which he knows to turn left at, and then he's on a smooth broad avenue. New asphalt, looks like some rich guy's laneway, it's been prettied up with lamp-posts and rows of trees and great honking chunks of dolostone. Except no rich guy would throw landscaping rock down like that – squarish hunks of rock, some of them big as his truck, are scattered helter-skelter along the groomed verge like discarded Lego blocks – some giant's toys left out in the rain.

The road runs straight nearly to the lip of the quarry, where it swerves and begins an arcing descent along an informal-looking ramp that seems to have been built with rubble scooped from the quarry floor. It's sturdy enough, that's not why he has to stop. It's the sheer size, and the scale of the place, that make him slow, then stop, then roll the window down.

He'd been thinking quarry. Like, swimming hole. Like sugary limestone rocks maybe fifteen or twenty feet high, fringed with cedar at the top and arranged in a circle around the old swimming hole. What he's looking at is a basin maybe a mile across surrounded by dark grey cliffs streaked with black. Dolostone. Dolorous stone.

Tectonic collision causes warm, metal-rich brines to flow through shales in the sedimentary sequence. As they flow they pick up hydrocarbons from the organic-rich dolomite of the Eramosa member. These hydrocarbons are seen as a black coating in some of the cavities and on bedding surfaces of the dolostone.

There seem to be gaps in the cliffs, bites taken out of the rock, through which he can glimpse farther bays with cliffs of their own. It's hard to tell how high the walls are, because nothing he can see looks familiar or human. There are some trucks parked at the bottom of the road, and from the size of them he guesses thirty feet or so for the walls, but once he gets to the quarry floor he has to revise that, because up close the tires on the trucks are twice his height. Just the tires. Next to a big hopper and weigh scale there's a tiny box which turns out to be the office. A brown man in a navy uniform peers out and Rob realizes he hasn't really thought about how he's going to get in if Jeff's not here. And it looks like nobody's working. And, in fact, what the hell *is* he doing here?

But in the event, it doesn't matter. The security guard just wants to know if he's with the teachers.

"Huh?"

"The teachers' group. Are you here with them?"

"Uh. Yeah. With the teachers." And the guy smiles and waves Rob across the valley floor to where some stick figures are clustered around a couple of cars. So. Easy-peasy. He dekes behind the big trucks when the guard goes back inside, then heads off in another direction, away from the teachers.

He drives around for a while, pretty aimless because he keeps stopping to gawk and also because the road is fairly aimless too; it tends to peter out when he's not watching it, or drop off sheer onto shards of fresh-blasted rock, sharp as glass. Mostly it's packed hard, he can drive where he wants, but there are deep puddles, some crusted with ice, and once he tries to drive over what he thinks is a pile of snow and nearly gets hung up by the bumper. He feels confused, morphed down to boy-size by the machinery, the high dark walls. Okay, two miles. Ninety-foot cliffs. Where the hell is north? The north end, Toby said, but there's no sun, the sky's gotten darker, the rain or maybe it's sleet is blowing almost horizontal. The road has a plan of its own, it feels like. It could lead him around a corner and anything might be there. A lake with no bottom; a sinewy bronze giant stripped to the waist, hammering away with a sledge the size of a house; a sheer wall and a pyramid of freshly blasted rock ready to be graded and loaded and shipped god-knows-where, god-knows-why. The route makes no sense, its twists and turns are dictated by a necessity Rob doesn't quite get. Mapped out by some guy in sunglasses and a loud shirt, typing into a laptop. Poolside, in Mauritius.

Things move him, things he doesn't understand. Like those cartoons – the guy on the conveyor belt, rolled and flattened and sorted and finally squished into the shape of the jar, and the lid screwed on tight. They move everybody, choose their jobs, form their tastes, determine the cost of housing and the price of video games. He knows it, but he doesn't like to think about it. He stops himself. He just wants a calcite crystal, a big fucking jewel. Buried treasure. A prospecting badge.

Mineralogy must have been the last badge Toby got, he must have never got one for the canoe, because by the end of that summer he'd lost interest in scouting altogether. All that follow-the-leader shit, he said. And they wouldn't have given out the badges until the fall.

Electronics was his big thing after that. And computers, Toby got into computers early, got himself an Apple II back when nobody'd heard of a PC, and after that he was kind of in his own world, all through high school.

Rob and he didn't hang out so much, but Rob remembers sitting with him one time at least, laughing, in the cafeteria. Toby was spitting bullets after that book came out about the founder, the original Scout, Lord Baden-Powell. How old B-P wasn't a special scout in Africa or a tracker or a spy or anything, just a two-bit administrator in the British empire who came up with a great scam for recruiting working-class boys in the war. Values, they needed. So they'd march off to the trenches while Akela sat snug in the bunker. Drown in the mud if their feet didn't rot off first. Follow the leader.

"Shit, man, it's mind control, pure and simple!" Toby had a poster of Che on his wall by this time, and a beard, and tiny John Lennon glasses. After graduation he drifted around out west for a while. Something happened out there, Rob's pretty sure, but he doesn't know what. Afterwards, Toby surprised everyone by signing up with the armed forces. What could happen, to make Toby fall into something like the military? Himself, sure, he falls into life – you could say he carries through, finishes what he starts, but it's a kind of laziness as much as anything else. Toby was different, he had vision. He made the connections and he didn't take the easy way. And when Rob knew him he never, ever, let anyone tell him what to do.

"They send you to university for free, man, then you have to stay on for three years afterward. But you get paid, you know? Or else you can just bow out and pay them back. No strings." Toby was delighted, like he'd put one over on the man. And then he did stay on, said it was like being in summer camp all the time – the travel, the easy friendships. They cooked for you, they did your laundry, "plus the technology's good, Rob, they keep updating." He went into telecommunications, with a degree in electrical engineering.

And, funny thing, he got back into scouting. Maybe that's it, maybe somehow that's the key. Because Toby was someone who managed to stay a kid – he could always play, always be interested in something new. Lighthearted in a way, even at the end. He nearly bounced off his chair when MP3s came out, he was always downloading weird new bands from the Internet and making Rob listen to them.

They ran a troop off the base, he and the buddy he was with in Rwanda. That Christmas, his last leave before they went overseas, he was in the front room at his mother's house, bean-pole arms and legs sprawled across the couch like a teenager, on a sunny December afternoon. His glasses seemed to shoot sparks in the precious slanted light as he lectured Rob on the need for scouting, and bragged about the kids in his troop, the things they could do.

"We need it, Rob, we need the focus, we need the discipline. We need to put the energy in a good place or we'll waste it, or lose it, or fuck something up."

His man's face was vibrant and sharp, eager as a pointer, and that's the way Rob wants to remember him. But the truth is, the most time he spent with Toby in the last twenty years was this winter, in that dark basement, the desk lamp just bright enough to make a halo around the curly head. Or worse yet, only the greenish light from the computer screen, intensifying Toby's paleness. In all that time he only noticed the look – the alive look is how he thinks of it – he only really saw that look once, and that was the time he realized for sure that Toby had flipped.

He'd always been skinny, but in those last weeks he was living on beer, as far as Rob could tell. About ten a day, that'd be a couple thousand calories or so. It kept him going and it kept him calm. Calm was good; the basement was good for that as well. At first it was only certain things that upset him – people yelling at their kids, loud noises. But it got worse, it got to the point where any noise at all could set him off – a car door, a kid crying. Dogs barking were really bad. And gradually it made sense to be in the basement more and more. His mother brought meals down on a tray and she'd sit with him there.

One day she got a call from the Sobey's. Toby was standing in front of that sign with the stork – the special parking spot for pregnant mothers that's close to the door – he'd been standing there for about an hour and he was crying, and the produce manager wondered could she maybe come and pick him up.

Rob would drop by once in a while, in the evenings after work. Toby had it set up nicely, he had his little cocoon in the rec room area beyond the pickle shelves. There was a carpet and a pullout couch and lots of tables covered with bits of wire and stacks of paper, which were arranged around the main desk where he sat at the computer. There was a modem with its own line and the stereo right there where he could reach it, and a tiny fridge underneath for the beer. It was one of those wheelie chairs – he could kick with his foot and coast along the concrete to get something off one of the tables anytime he wanted.

They wouldn't talk about much. Rob would bring beer and Toby would put some music on – old stuff that they both liked – and Rob would sit in the other wheelie chair because if he sat on the couch he couldn't see over the tables. Toby stayed in his command centre and he kept the overhead light off, but if Rob asked he would adjust the domed desk lamp so it wasn't shining in Rob's eyes, so it shed its light in a dusky, conversational pool on the table between them. The monitor beside Toby was always on, he surfed a lot, and he'd made a Web site for his coltan campaign. His eyes would drift to the screen while he talked, his fingers would stray over the keyboard, tippity-tap. He showed Rob how to look up useful stuff with thc search engines – like how exactly Janis Joplin died, or whatever happened to spring peepers, those frogs that you used to hear all the time. Sometimes he'd check his e-mail, or the Web site, to see how many hits there'd been.

One afternoon Rob crept down the stairs in his socks to find Toby bouncing around on his chair all excited, skating it back and forth between the computer desk and the stacks of notes on the table. "Satisfaction" was playing so loud Rob couldn't hear what he was saying. Toby had to turn it down so he could ask Rob for his credit card number.

"For what?"

"Geophones, man," like it was obvious. "Remember geophones? They're going for forty bucks right now on eBay! I can't believe I never thought of this before. We'll try a few different ones – I think I like the PSR-1 best but we'll try the other type as well, the ones you mount in a series which is irrelevant to us but it says here they're better at filtering out the extra noise, like the seismic stuff. And anyway you can get parts, you can calibrate either of them once you figure out the frequencies you're after."

His idea was that they'd order a bunch and start messing around with them right away, take them apart and modify them so they could detect the slightest movement in a shallow grave. They'd test them when the ground thawed, they'd get funding from some NGO, start mass-producing them for distribution to the poor nations of the world, the conflict areas. So you'd know where to start digging.

"You wouldn't need to wait for the U.N., man, fuck the U.N. You just go around and look for fresh earth, stick the probe in. Anybody still kicking, you'd find them. Here look at this, it's the simplest little gadget in the world . . ." And he was wheeling off to the computer, *zing*, bringing up screens of diagrams and photos, and Rob still standing there with his wallet out.

"But Toby, why?"

"What do you mean, why?" Rob knew the story, that's not what he meant.

By the time Toby got over there, the killing was pretty much done with, the mass killing at least. The country was breathtaking, green hill after green hill rising through the mist, farms and villages crowning the hills, flowers everywhere, birds singing. But hundreds of thousands of people – some said a million – had been killed in three months. The smell was everywhere. Bodies were everywhere – houses, fields, ditches. There were churches piled with bodies, sometimes a kid would crawl out from under a pile alive, missing only an ear or a finger.

Sometimes the killers would have tried to bury bodies – hide them at least – by digging a shallow grave, or throwing them into a pit latrine already dug, and filling it up with earth.

The soil is mostly laterite, a fragile tropical earth that leaches out organic material quickly. The minerals stay, that's what gives it the red colour, and the second you expose it to the air it starts to erode. One winter's rain, half a field could wash away. The roads look like scars, bright orangey on the green, and they turn to a sucking soup, a mud river, when they're wet. Dry, they're like iron, under a soft deep carpet of orange dust. You try to dig a hole when it's dry, it's like scraping on concrete – nobody does it. So you just don't see bare earth, that kind of land, unless something is wrong. Any time you found some soil turned over, you'd check for bodies.

At first, before they realized the scale of it, they would do proper exhumations. One guy did an autopsy early on – a kid they'd found in a mass grave, a latrine they'd found packed to the top with bodies and parts of bodies at all angles, all stages of decay. His mouth was open, the kid, and full of the red laterite soil they'd thrown on. So was his esophagus. And they realized he'd been alive when they filled in the pit, he'd struggled and probably yelled, and tried so hard to live that he'd sucked earth into his windpipe before he died.

It's not the worst thing Toby heard about, it's not even the worst thing he saw, but it's the detail that seems to have stuck with him – the child under the soil, surrounded by corpses. Maybe his family. Maybe he was faking it, lying still, waiting for the killers to leave. Maybe they did it on purpose, buried him alive for a joke – they did that sort of thing, Toby says.

"But Toby, it's over now," Rob said, as gently as he could. Toby glanced up. The idea was taking a while to sink in, Rob could see. Toby slowed down. Sank into his chair, put his feet up on the table, fiddled with the light. Finally he turned to Rob with an affectionate, exasperated look, because Rob has always been a little slow off the mark.

"No, but it might happen again, Rob. It could, easily, it probably will, and this time, we'll be prepared." He spread his fingers authoritatively, and they trembled in the golden light of the desk lamp. He seemed to drift for a moment, eyes glazed, and he ran the fingers of both hands through his hair. The curls had grown out nearly to his shoulders, though even in the dim light, Rob could see how the colour had faded from the bright chestnut he remembered. Then Toby snapped back.

"And that's not all, Rob. This field is huge, you know. Geophones are the tip of the iceberg. They're only the beginning.

"Take elephants. Any elephant can hear with its feet, I kid you not. Special receptors, those big soft feet. And special areas in the brain too, for processing the signals they pick up. Like seismic waves, other animals' footsteps – they can filter out the crap. They can stamp out messages to other elephants fifty miles away – call them, warn them, whatever. They send messages through the earth. They hear what's happening, other places. *Rob, they can hear rain falling a hundred miles away.*

"Or earthquakes, Rob. The Tokyo quake in '75 – remember that was the year we got an extra day of holidays at Easter because the river was over its banks and the bus couldn't get past the bridge? That quake, all kinds of animals knew it was coming – cats, rats, dogs, horses, birds, insects – they're freaking out, they're leaving town, and the scientists are like, huh? And twenty-four hours later they start getting tremors.

"All kinds of things you hear in geophones, Rob, and 99 per cent of it you can't interpret. It's there, you can plug into it, you know it's the earth talking, but you can't understand it. If we could translate it, we could prevent all kinds of tragedies. Unlock all kinds of mysteries.

"Don't you see, Rob? We could hear what the earth is saying."

Rob felt giddy, nearly carried away by Toby's enthusiasm. He looked alive again, he was himself again, everything was going to be all right.

That's how Rob knew for sure.

His foot is hovering over the brake as he sniffs his way around the corner of a high rock wall and into one of the little bays that ring the quarry. Smack in front of him is one of the pyramids of blasted rock that litter the valley floor like castles in a sandbox, and beyond that, halfway up the wall, is the fissure. It looks just like Toby said it would.

He eases the truck around the pyramid, but has to stop short of the cliff – the ground is strewn with boulders and loose shards of rock. He picks his way through the mounds for a hundred yards or so and stops at the foot of the cliff. Somebody – Jeff? – has left enough rubble lying in front that he can climb up almost to the fissure, which starts as a tiny crevice about halfway up the wall and widens into a jagged V as it rises. The glacial till that has washed out in the months since the fissure was uncovered by blasting has formed a fan-shaped cushion of sand and gravel and rounded ice-polished pebbles that leads up into the crack.

Loose gravel and silt were deposited by the Laurentide ice sheet in the fissures formed during dolomitization. The minerals themselves were formed much earlier, when brines interacted with surface waters, travelling along fissures in the rock.

And there, halfway to the top, only a dozen feet or so from his head, he sees the crystal. Stuck to the dark stone with a crust of some whitish mineral, it's been packed in tightly with the dirty-looking till for only a few thousand years. But it has hung here, waiting, for a hundred thousand centuries. Roughly globe-shaped, the whole bigger than he could embrace if he were standing next to it, the crystal is formed from multiple individual scalenohedra that lay themselves down side by side and end to end with the deft precision of a mathematical formula. Where the muddy till has washed away he can see the orange-pink calcite peeking through; translucent, milky, vitreous. Somehow feathery-looking. It's lovely, it's the loveliest thing he's ever seen.

Rob's body is stiff from sitting in the truck all this time, and even though he's had the heater on his feet are kind of cold. But he feels a little thrill, sizing up the job, and as he picks his way back to the truck he finds he can roll or shift enough of the big rocks out of the way to make a path for the toboggan. No way he's going to carry the sucker out of here, it must weigh three hundred pounds.

And the trick, he thinks, as he starts throwing stuff down from the truck bed, is not going to be prying it from the rock. The trick is going to be controlling the fall so that it lands on that soft fan of gravel instead of rolling straight down onto the rocks and breaking into a million pieces.

Calcite may be identified by checking the broken crystal for cleavage faces, or planes of weakness. It has perfect cleavage in three directions, so any calcite crystal may be broken into simple rhombohedral fragments – no matter how complex the original form.

By the time he's loaded up the toboggan and dragged it back to the fissure he's warmed up, even though the rain is driving down and the cold wind tugs at his parka. He's got a sheet of plywood on the truck bed and a couple of four-by-four posts, which he can use to make a little hoarding, a barrier he can plant, so when the calcite cluster drops it'll roll sideways down the soft stuff. He leaps from rock to rock back to the truck, sure-footed. Over the pile of rubble instead of around it, and at the top he pauses and sniffs, like a mountain goat.

He digs the plywood sheet in on a bit of a slant about six feet down the till slope from where he thinks the cluster will land. It'll hit dirt, slide, hit plywood, roll sideways to the gentle slope, and slither on down to the toboggan. In theory. As long as he can get it off the rock face without cracking it, as long as it survives that first twelve-foot drop to the till, he should be rolling along with a hunky-dory hunk o' burning love around four o'clock, a peach crystal. Rob and the Giant Peach. *Peachy keen.*

There's a bit of a snag when he tries to set up the ladder at the bottom of the fissure. Even setting the hoarding was tricky, because the till is full of clay and soaked with rain. It's slippery and dirty and gives way too easily when he steps on it. The posts he used to brace the hoarding had to be set on chunks of dolostone rubble so they wouldn't slip, and finally he's able to rig the ladder in a similar way, skittering up the edge of the till from rock to rock, trying to keep his boots out of the sucking mud. He sets the base of the ladder against a bulge in the dolostone on the opposite side of the cleft and wedges the top end between two smaller masses of tooth-shaped calcite that loom over the peach. *Dog's-tooth*, he hears Toby whisper, *It's called dog's-tooth calcite.*

He strips off the sodden parka – he'll need the movement – then swarms up the ladder light-footed. Up close the crystal is rough, dirty, smeared with clay, and he reaches out, gingerly, to pry away some of the dirt. It's a bit of a lean – he's had to place the ladder farther away than he wanted in order to get solid footing – and he sways, mid-air above the mud-covered nugget, sheer dark walls squeezing in around him. But the ladder holds nicely and he moves his feet apart as far as he can, braces his knees on the next rung, starts chipping away with the crowbar. Left hand guiding the tip, right hand thrusting the butt end. Hard work, the bar alone is pretty heavy, but he's well positioned after all, the bar gives him a long reach. And his arms have always been strong. There has never been a time he could not support his full weight with his arms, he thinks.

His mother tells a story about dropping him when he was a day old – he was her first and she was eager to bathe him, change him, do everything right. Then he was so slippery coming out of the bath – she was afraid to grab him by the head, worried about his neck, off-balance as she reached for the towel at the same time. He slipped right off her soapy hand and arm, he would have hit the cast-iron tub, she swears it, except that his unearthly seeking fingers shot out before her eyes and clamped themselves into the nubbly weave of her sweater, so he hung there by his fingertips. Monkey-boy, she marvelled. The doctor said it's a reflex, they grow out of it in forty-eight hours, so don't try it again. But she always called him Monkey-boy anyway.

The scabby crust is flying off in all directions. Big chunks drop off and slide away below him and soon the cluster of calcite is nearly freed. Rob's breathing hard but it's great, he's excited, it's what he's meant to do. The combination of excitement and exertion makes him want to shout, or laugh. He wishes Toby were here to crack a joke. Shake the ladder. "Whatcha figger, Scouter Rob? Just a cunt hair more, eh?"

Jimmy drove in from Downsview for the memorial, Jimmy who'd run the Scout troop with Toby, and been with him in Rwanda. He told Rob about their first day on the job, over there. It wasn't the job they were supposed to be doing, they were a communications unit. But they got there and everything had fallen apart, their equipment was a hundred miles away and there were no trucks to get it to them, there was food and medicine but no clean water. Survivors were starting to die of festering wounds, cholera.

"It was the bodies, see. They were everywhere and any water, any well or creek or lake, it would have bodies decomposing in it. The NGOs were all over the place but their mandates were for feel-good stuff, you know, like feed people, reunite families, open medical clinics. Nobody wanted to clean up the bodies, nobody could get permission from their organization. But with the water all contaminated they would just keep dying.

"So while we were waiting for the trucks our CO put us onto that. Find them, lay them out on plastic. And the only people he could get to help – it's dangerous, eh? because they're all rotted like? – the only helpers he could get were these kids, for chrissake, these little ten- and twelve-year-old boys. They spoke

French, you couldn't get much out of them but they were volunteers from over the border, Zaire, I think.

"Anyway it's just, you can't imagine what it's like, that kind of work. You'll do anything to cheer yourself up. So the kids are good, they're working away like beavers and singing. They're good singers, they know all these old songs like 'You Are My Sunshine' and 'Sur le Pont d'Avignon.' And Toby and me start in with jokes, it's Scouter this and Scouter that – you have to keep calling to each other, eh? So you don't get separated – and pretty soon it's 'Hey Akela, over here!' and 'Yo Baloo, send a bag down,' which, you know, those were our names on the base. And the little guys got right into it, they were calling us Baloo and Akela too, we never thought nothing of it. But the next day we get to the shed, right? where we keep the tarps and stuff, and they're all there and they line up and number off – you know how Scouts do it – and they do the salute, the two fingers. And they've got their neckerchiefs on."

He smiled at Rob, like this was the punchline.

"It's hard, that kind of duty. It's grotesque. We all threw up a few times, some guys passed out. You see things you couldn't have imagined. But that was the only time I saw Toby lose it. He tossed his cookies all over his shoes, he shook for half an hour, that morning we saw the kids with their neckerchiefs on."

Brittle shards still attach the crystal to the rock face, but he doesn't want to strike it. Holding his breath, he slips the bent end of the bar into the crack, gives it a deft wiggle, pries ever so gently. There's a tiny sound, a bit of grinding as the surfaces slip, then a *whoosh* as gravity does the rest. He's looking right at the thing but he doesn't see it fall, it's just gone, and he looks down and it's there, half buried in the till, sliding down the slope, bumping gently up against the plywood. Tickety-boo.

He's whistling under his breath as he scampers down the ladder for a look. He bounds down the till fan like it's a sand dune, giant steps that don't pause long enough for his boots to sink in, his seven-league boots. Then he's nudging the crystal along the plywood barrier, hands plunged into the cold grit, grappling for purchase on the glassy-jagged feathers.

He's thinking about Nora, what she'll say, the way she'll dimple up when she sees what he's brought home. He's imagining the look of her hands as she runs a finger along the rhythmic tracery of the scalenohedra and, particularly, he is trying to picture the exact colour her lips will be as her mouth opens up. That crooked smile. He is dwelling so deeply on the image of her face that he doesn't hear the sickening slip of twelve tons of rock letting go of the face behind him. But something – the look around her eyes maybe – makes him vault, up and forward, from his squat. He feels the slump, more than hears it, as he springs. Coming down on all fours, he hears the *whoosh* of something coming, and knows that it is close enough to take him. From the corner of his eye he sees the calcite cluster, rolling like a drunken snowball onto the jagged scree below, and then he falls headlong, because the wave of gravel and mud displaced by the fallen rock has caught his legs with a sound like a hiss, the last of its strength.

The noise is gone almost before it has come; if it weren't for the ringing in his ears he'd say it was a silent rockfall. He's had a few moments like this in his life – he knows everything should be moving in slow motion right now, but outside of the rain and a last pebble settling into place, it seems as though nothing is moving at all.

His hands are okay, his arms move without much trouble and he can lift his head and neck. Shoulders okay, spine ditto. In fact, he could lie here all day doing ladies' pushups if that would help, but the real problem is that there's about a ton of gravel and clay and rock pinning him down from belly to ankle. Okay, half a ton. A few hundred pounds. Enough. Not much of him is pinned, but he can't wiggle out of it, and every time he squirms it seems to get heavier. It's settling, that's what. The watery soup of clay is draining off, the rocks and pebbles are packing themselves in around him. It's like quicksand – the more you struggle.

So he quits struggling. He cups his chin in his hands and lies there for a while like he's watching TV. Farthest he can see is out the gap in the rock wall to the main quarry. The far lip of rock, the big sky darkening a little now and coming down to meet it. Nothing of interest, no trucks or people, and if they're not here

Saturday they're definitely not going to be here Sunday, so that's, say, thirty-nine or forty hours before they roll in Monday morning with their coffees and their hard hats and their blasting caps, and find some guy's parked his Tonka in their sandbox, by which time. You figure in the rain, it's not good. He's cold already, he's been cold all day, he thinks. Cold feet, that's it.

Then up close there are the walls of the bay he's in, closer still the pyramid of blasted rock, red hood of his truck peeking out from behind it. Cell phone in there, no batteries. A gulp or two of coffee in the Thermos, cigarettes on the seat. Heater.

Some tools are scattered on the rock floor in front of him, nothing he could reach. Except maybe the tail end of the toboggan. The ladder must be gone, and the crowbar's disappeared too, not surprising.

The view is getting a little boring.

Now he really wishes Toby were with him. What would Toby do? What's he thinking? Toby cracked up, Toby's gone.

Sometime in the middle of that last night before he disappeared, Toby called Rob on the phone. He sounded excited, like he'd had more than his ten beer. Except he wasn't slurring or anything. Maybe he'd gone off the meds again.

"The geophones came in, Rob. I've been listening all night. Sorry to wake you, but I thought you'd want to know. Because now I know what it is – I just needed to put all the pieces together, and now I know what I have to do.

"Because the clues are all there, you see. Niobium. You know Niobe, right? From the myth? Well, you can look it up if you don't believe me, but here's the thing. She was a giant or a titan, or something. Well, they all were back then. A god's daughter at least, and she had all these kids, and she loved them so much, and she bragged about them so much, that the gods – I mean the big ones – were jealous, and they killed them all. Seven sons and seven daughters. With golden arrows, it says here. And you know, she just cried and cried, she couldn't stop. And even after Zeus turned her into a stone to shut her up, she was so sad that she still couldn't stop, so the tears came out of the stone, they became a river. The Achelous. It's in Turkey, but who cares? The point is, Rob, niobium.

"You know that's the main ore in coltan, right? Tantalite and niobium. Coltan. They're very close, atomic-wise. Very tight, hard to separate. They grow together in these big pegmatites you get over there, very old, big honkin' black crystals. Heavy. They use kids to get the stuff, they carry it out on their backs, trail it through the bush. Somebody at the front with a machine gun, and another at the back. It all goes to this one guy in Kinshasa.

"Do you know what it's like mining coltan? Well, they don't really mine it any more, with the war on. Infrastructure's gone. They sort of gather it, from stream beds, say, that cut through a dike. Or old mines that were closed before the stuff started selling for the price of cocaine.

"But you know all this shit, right? Cave-ins, ambushes?"

Rob didn't know, or else he'd forgotten. During the coltan lectures, he'd always found himself distracted by insignificant details, like the flecks of foam that would gather at the corners of Toby's mouth. He felt a bit guilty and tried to listen, though he was half asleep.

"And you know they use kids – offer them a job, buy them, even raid the villages and steal them outright – and take them out in the jungle to gather the stuff, then carry it down to the river, the Congo. Meanwhile they're all spying on each other – the ones with the guns are – and trying to hijack each other's caravans, steal the ore, steal the equipment, steal each other's watches and machine guns and children. And once they get it to this Kinshasa guy, he sells it to the big companies for cell phone capacitors, gaming consoles – all that shit. You know that shit, I've told you, right?

"But Rob, get this, I betcha didn't know this about niobium." And he paused, like he was about to offer Rob a hockey card with Lemieux on it.

Rob made a noise in his throat that tried to be appreciative, alert. And in fact Toby was sounding pretty lucid.

"Resonant Mass Gravitational Wave Detector." He stopped. As though that would be enough.

"Huh?"

"Astrophysics, man! Heavy shit. That's the new thing with niobium – even now they can measure the height of a wave on the beach when they're ten miles inland. They're using niobium to build gravitational wave detectors all over the planet – in a big circle, like, so they can have a parallel series – and detect violent events in space."

It's still not enough for Rob. "Huh?"

"*Violent events.* Niobium. Don't you get it? Niobe, Rob. Niobe crying for her children. Looking for them. *Detecting violent events.* That's what niobium can do, that's why it has to be left there, in the earth, Rob, in the earth so it can do its job. It's bigger than big business, the waves are all around us. That's why it's got to stop. The mining, the whole thing. That's why we'll never have any peace until it stops."

Rob remembers he lay silent for some moments, convinced there was sense to be made of this. It's a measure of something – faith? Friendship? Maybe just the force of habit, but he was still lying there trying to think of something intelligent to say when Toby broke in again.

"It's worth a try, anyway. So, but Rob, sorry to wake you, I just thought you'd want to know. Anyway, I gotta go. Gimme a call tomorrow."

And that was it, he was gone. Whatever happened afterward caused Toby to leave the house before his mother got up at six, get in his truck, which he hadn't done since Christmas, and drive it to Kettle Point, where they used to go as kids, and park it near the shore. The crust of ice that day was two feet thick for the first hundred yards or so.

Rob didn't call back till morning. He didn't know how serious it was, he didn't want to wake Toby's mum. He was still half asleep. Whatever. Toby's gone now, Toby's no help.

•

The sun is definitely lower. It's slipped out from behind the high blanket of rain clouds – not into open sky, but it's clearing toward the west. The clouds are thinner there and the sun in behind is turning them rosy, warm-looking. The dark dolostone all around has gone kind of purple, velvety, and the only sounds are the trickle of rainwater, the occasional gentle *tock* of a stone settling. The weight on his back and legs is not so bad, it's almost like a blanket – he's always been one for a cold room and a heavy layer of quilts. It seems to him that he should be able to roll out – it can't be that much harder than six o'clock on a Monday morning – and by concentrating on moving only his right leg, by lifting with his left and sort of dragging himself by the propped-up elbows, he does move, a little. The rocks and pebbles are not so bad, he should be able to inch his way out. But now his left knee, the one he was pushing with, has sunk way down. The mucky clay below is so yielding that he won't be able to lever his way out – there's nothing to push against.

The boys' toboggan is just there, battered aluminum with a squashed prow and a frayed rope of yellow-and-blue twisted nylon. The red rag he tied on to mark the end of the load trails toward him through an icy puddle. It occurs to him that if he were lying on that toboggan under all this pile of suckmud it would be no problem to push out. It'd be like surfing.

He reaches awkwardly and a little frantically, so that his arm flaps. His fingers actually touch the rag, but it swishes away in the icy puddle and ends up farther than before. He curses his clumsiness. It occurs to him that everything counts.

He thinks of Nora, and their house, and the land, his acres. He sees her wandering around them without him, how lost she would be, and it's not funny any more or boring either. He strains, and reaches – deliberately, fingers spread this time, steady – with his right arm. His left arm is folded beneath him, pushing down and back. His arms have always been strong. He hears his shoulder crack, feels the rush of adrenalin. Everything counts.

But he's cold. His feet have been cold all day and now he's cold right through and tired and hungry and for some reason fucking Toby is in his head, he's reaching for the rag and he can hear Toby counting off the uses of the neckerchief:

"Signal flag, staff lashing for broken mast, blind-fold for blind-man's-bluff. Most importantly, the wearing of the neckerchief in itself indicates that its wearer is not a cadet, but a Scout." That's the ticket, Rob, that's the loophole, see. A cadet follows the leader. A Scout scouts. A Scout is not a cadet, Rob.

His fingertips touch the red rag and seize it with the ferocity of a newborn. He gives a little tug and the toboggan skitters to him eagerly, scraping lightly over the ice and rubble, wedging itself into the gap below his chest. He grasps the sides and pulls it under himself till he feels it catch his belt buckle, and nearly weeps because now he can get up on his elbows, on his little aluminum life raft. He humps and pulls to clear the buckle, then wiggles his ass for all it's worth. *Shake what your momma gave ya.* Soon he's clear – impossibly soon. The coldness is gone, but he's weeping with relief and shivering with excitement as he gathers what tools he can and throws them in the truck. He swallows what's left of the coffee, strips naked there in the wet wind and shrugs into the dry coveralls he keeps behind the seat. Then he puts his boots back on but he can't do up the laces. He stumbles back to the crevice foot and does not pause to examine the house-sized pile of freshly fallen rock – doesn't even look sideways at it – as he grasps the blue-and-yellow cord and pulls the toboggan over to downslope of where the crystal lies. He heaves it on, then wads up what's left of his parka around the base to keep it from sliding off. Lucky it's downhill to the truck – in the end the hardest part is levering the sucker onto the bed without snapping the tailgate. But he manages.

Then he's in the cab and rolling past the gate house with the heater on and Neil Young singing high and sweet about silver spaceships and a queen. He doesn't care who sees him leave, he doesn't care how cold he is. The heater's on. And anyway, he's not cold, it's excitement that's making him shiver. All he wants is Nora. He's burning to get home, to see Nora, to show her what he's found.

He'll stop at the power wash on Highway 8, get that crust of clay off in about two minutes. There's a Tim's there as well. He's hungry, he wants a double-double, thick and sweet. He wants an apple fritter, soft and plump and sticky as Nora's thighs.

It's nearly dusk when Nora sees the headlights turn off the road, and a minute or two more until she sees the truck pull into the yard and roll to a stop by the shed. It's riding awfully low in the back. Rob slides out and slams the door and walks around, lowers the tailgate. That ready, athlete's walk. Like a cat. He looks up, straight at her, and smiles. He waves, as though she weren't hiding behind the living room curtain. He's got something around his neck. He's got that red rag tied round his neck like some kind of crazed cowboy, but at least it brings the colour up in his face. He's got that kind of skin, the kind that looks good with red. And the dark hair, curling now in the humidity. She waves back. She'll go down and meet him.

She's got the lights off, and the bathroom is quite dark, but she doesn't flick the switch as she glides bare feet over the slate. She loves that slate, still slick from washing but never slippery – not like the crap they sell at Home Depot. She turns the tap on and cups water in her hands, splashes it over her face. It's getting to be a craggy face, she knows. Maybe she should pluck her eyebrows or something. Halite crystals have lingered in rough, powdery patches on her cheeks all afternoon while she cleaned. Now they dissolve into solution, swirl around the sink and down into the drain, the weeping bed, the subsoil. They'll settle out on bedrock, once they hit the aquifer.

She strips off the track pants and the T-shirt that says *Because I'm the Mom that's why* and leaves them in a pile. She goes through to the bedroom. It's truly dark in here because it's on the north side of the house, but she walks straight to the closet and lets her fingers run across the dresses, stroking gently, till they find the one she wants. It's cotton, a soft open weave. Plain, green, with a long skirt and a snug waist, the way he likes.

ANAR ALI

Baby Khaki's Wings

Baby Khaki was born with a set of transparent wings which lay flat against her back, camouflaged against her dark brown skin.

If you inspected the baby closely enough, picked her up, laid her across your lap, perhaps ran your finger along the outline of her back, then maybe, just maybe, you might be able to feel a thin pipe – the frame of her wings. But even then it was most difficult, as it was easy to confuse this piping as a bulbous vein – ready to burst if the skin were slightly punctured. Across the width of Baby Khaki's back, between her shoulders, there was a thin slit – a pouch – a place to tuck the wings in. The tip of the right wing turned up toward the sky, but only ever-so-slightly, as if it were ready to be peeled or picked off like a raw scab or the soft-shell of an overcooked egg. No one ever learned about Baby Khaki's ability to fly until much, much later.

Thankfully, the secret of her wings was guarded by her *ayah*, Aisha.

With most Business People (and other Very Important People) in Tanganyika, it was customary to hire an *ayah* for each child – not because it was always necessary but because *ayahs* were quite an affordable luxury, so much so that they became a reasonable and expected expense line in many household budgets. Plus, many men reasoned, the presence of an *ayah* would not only ensure that each of their children received abundant care, but it would also free their wives to focus on other extremely important duties: those of properly taking care of their husbands.

The Khakis of Arusha had not been able to find a good *ayah* and Baby Khaki was due to arrive any day now. When Mr. Khaki told his brother in Zanzibar about their difficulty, his brother promptly offered to send their *ayah*, Aisha, to Arusha – as a loan of sorts. Mr. Khaki accepted and thanked his brother for what seemed, at the time, like a very generous gesture, especially since he knew that his brother and sister-in-law had hired Aisha with the hope of having a child themselves – but after months of trying, his brother's wife had been unable to conceive.

Before leaving for Arusha, Aisha overheard the Khakis of Zanzibar discussing the lack of children in their household over tea on the verandah. They had tried all sorts of remedies to counter such bad luck – they even left sacrifices for the spirits on the roof of the house, but nothing seemed to work. After some deliberation, they became convinced that Aisha was the source of their bad luck. After they hired her, hadn't their business taken a turn for the worse? Hadn't Mrs. Khaki fallen down the stairs and broken her ankle? (Poor thing!) And how about the time Mr. Khaki became very ill with some unknown plague (and he had been unable to go to the shop for almost a fortnight!)? And once, Mrs. Khaki had seen the ghost of a little child partially surface from the kitchen wall and then sink back into the plaster, as if she were caught between two worlds. It must have been Aisha – undoubtedly – who ordered an *uganga* on them, bringing them such bad luck and rendering them childless. On top of it all, they had also heard from several neighbours that Aisha had been seen returning from the bush late at night, and really, what kind of girl does that? Only a whore or someone up to no-good. Worse yet, there had been many rumours lately about the increasing activities of the Wachawi. What if Aisha hadn't just ordered the spell, but belonged to this secret sect and possessed the powers to evoke strong *juju* herself? They had to do something quickly. Otherwise their fates would be sealed!

They decided to test their suspicions by sending Aisha to Arusha. If their suspicions proved correct, then it would serve as a double blessing: a child in their home and a slip in fortune for the Khakis of Arusha – rectifying a lifetime of misalignment of the stars, favouring one brother over another.

Soon after Aisha left Zanzibar, Mrs. Khaki of Zanzibar conceived – trapping Aisha in Arusha. If she so much as placed her toe outside the prescribed path, the Khakis of Arusha would be sure to send her back home to Zanzibar straight away, where the stories about her ominous powers would have seeped and slithered their way into the gardens of the Very Important People. None of them would dare hire her again, not only in Stone Town, but in all of Zanzibar, and then what would she do? Aisha had no family, no husband, and she would be thrown out on the street, alone once again. Before she was hired by the Khakis of Zanzibar (who prided themselves on their charitable nature), Aisha had lived between the streets and the bush, doing whatever was required to survive. Aisha's father had remarried soon after his wife ran away with a young man from Oman, and when his new wife gave birth to a child of her own, she absolutely refused to keep Aisha any longer. Aisha's father felt trapped between his affections for his new, growing family and his unwavering love for his first child – no matter that she reminded him of the terrible insult from his former marriage. His inability to choose drove his new wife mad, so that there were daily arguments in the house, making life almost unbearable. In the end, Aisha's father apologized to his daughter and told her that he loved her very much, but he had no choice – she would have to leave.

It was on the Thursday after the Khakis of Arusha brought their newborn daughter home from the hospital that Aisha discovered the perils of her new position. She walked into the baby's room to find Baby Khaki pushing her way up and out of her baby-hammock, wings unfurled, flapping vigorously, the baby sucking the air as if it were a flaccid breast, desperately trying to fill her belly.

At first Aisha smiled and shook her head as a mother would when she finds her child in harmless mischief. But as she reached up on her tiptoes and plucked Baby Khaki out of the air – saving the baby from smashing her head against the ceiling – Aisha realized that the baby's deformity would most definitely be blamed on her. The Khakis of Arusha would accuse her of casting an *uganga* on their daughter in the same way that the

Khakis of Zanzibar had blamed her for the lack of children in their household. Her heart shook against her ribcage.

Aisha held Baby Khaki close to her clattering heart, patted down the baby's wings, and tucked them into their pouch. Baby Khaki screamed and squirmed, throwing her head back and kicking Aisha in the stomach. Without meaning to, Aisha let out a loud cry.

Hearing the mixture of Baby Khaki in distress and the *ayah*'s scream, Mrs. Khaki rushed into the room. "*Kamanini sveze, bana, huh?*" Mrs. Khaki yelled, snatching Baby Khaki from Aisha. "What in God's name are you doing to my child?"

"Nothing, Mamma. I am doing nothing." Aisha twisted her hands in the pockets of her A-shaped frock.

"Then why the hell is she crying like this? And why were you screaming at her? She is a baby for God's sake, not an animal. Such a good baby. Never cries like this, never fusses." Mrs. Khaki looked down and stroked Baby Khaki's head, but she continued to cry. "*Bas, bheta, bas.* It's all over now. No one is going to hurt you, okay? Don't worry, *mitu*, Mummy is here."

Juggling the baby in one hand, Mrs. Khaki reached out and grabbed Aisha's arm, leaned in closer, and said, "If I ever, ever find out you have done anything to my child, anything, by God, somebody better help you."

Aisha stepped back, her heart jammed against her ribs. Mrs. Khaki pulled her arm with greater strength. "Count it your luck that this time I won't be telling Mr. Khaki. You think I'm upset – he wouldn't tolerate your *shenze-wara*, not for a second!" Mrs. Khaki dug her manicured nails into Aisha's arm before she flung it free from her grip.

Aisha's face felt hot. She wanted to yell and scream back, maybe even slap Mrs. Khaki hard across the face. Instead she cradled her strained arm across her body.

Mrs. Khaki reassured her baby once again and then handed her to Aisha. "Be careful! I don't want any more trouble." She checked her watch. "Feed her. It's time."

She walked out of the baby's room, turned the corner, and ran straight into Mr. Khaki, who had just returned home from working at his newest venture, Khaki Arms & Ammunition.

"*Arrey*, watch yourself!" Mr. Khaki wrapped his fingers around Mrs. Khaki's shoulder, pushed her aside, and then removed the rifle that swung from his shoulder and leaned it against the wall.

Mrs. Khaki nodded and apologized – she sensed right away that her husband was in a foul mood. Must be all the stress from the new shop. Can't be easy working with those unreasonable tourists. And now with the onslaught of so many American hunters, it can only be harder. Mrs. Khaki felt great sympathy for her husband. Yes, she was a very lucky woman indeed, so very lucky to have a husband like Mr. Khaki – unlike the many, many other women who just did not seem capable of attracting good men. Poor souls! If only those women would volunteer for the community or do other charitable work, then good fortune would certainly be theirs.

Having noted Mr. Khaki's mood, Mrs. Khaki quickly changed the subject to one of his favourite topics: his daughter. "The baby is well. Eating plenty, *pani-pesab* – all good."

Mr. Khaki broke into a smile. "Good, good. Let me take a look."

Mrs. Khaki was pleased that she was able to change his mood. She asked Aisha to bring the baby out. Mr. Khaki placed his rifle in a scabbard lashed to the hall chair and then held his daughter at arm's length, let his glasses slip down his nose, and inspected his child. He glanced at his wife, then back at his child. Yes, yes, the child will be as beautiful as her mother. Thank God! And in that moment, Mr. Khaki felt great admiration for his wife.

She was exquisite, wasn't she? He remembered how he had been overwhelmed by her beauty right from the very start. When he announced his marriage plans to his mother, she had screamed and yelled and told him that he was shameless for making marriage arrangements without consulting her first, and worse yet, he had chosen such an utterly lousy family. Bad enough the girl's father is in the lowly shoe business – this will bring nothing but bad luck, believe you me. And then to top it all off, their family is littered with so many imperfections – have you not noticed, son? Haven't you seen that cousin-brother with a clubfoot? Can't even walk. Or how about that auntie, you know, the fatty-fatty one – she has an extra pinky finger. Then there's that uncle's second wife, her child was fine and then one day, God knows why, stopped talking. Just like that. Stopped right in mid-sentence. This must be the work of the devil only. And don't forget the older sister, huh? She has skin the colour of *makara*. *Uh-ruh-ruh!* Are you mad, son? Please don't do it! I beg of you. You will only bring such bad, bad *bahati* into this good family of ours. It will make your poor dead father turn in his grave.

Mr. Khaki's mother's pleas were futile so she enlisted the help of others – cousins, uncles, and grandparents – to knock some sense into the boy. But nothing worked. Mr. Khaki ignored everybody's pleas; he didn't care one little bit what anybody said. All he knew is that he wanted this woman and he would have her. And as he stared at the beautiful baby his wife had produced for him, he was certain, absolutely certain, that he had made an excellent choice.

Mr. Khaki handed the baby back to Mrs. Khaki and asked her in Kutchi so that Aisha would not understand, "Everything good with the servant-girl?"

"Yes, yes. She's working out fine."

Mr. Khaki smiled, happy that his house was in order. In his head, he started to organize the tasks at hand for the afternoon: first and foremost, unpack the shipment of .500 rifles that had arrived from Germany, get the servant-boy to clean and hang them properly on the rack (good merchandising, that's what the Americans liked, he was told), and ah yes, don't forget to put the new licence rate-card up on the window. (Thank goodness Tanganyika Hunter had increased the General Game Licence cost to 100 shillings!) Yes, yes, business would surely be good with all those rich Americans in town, ready and eager to cross off all the animals on their lists. Mr. Khaki realized he had much to do before the Americans arrived and requested that his lunch be served right away. Mrs. Khaki nodded, passed the baby to Aisha, and rushed downstairs to the kitchen.

Later that afternoon, during Mrs. Khaki's nap, Aisha quietly searched the hall closet, and returned to the baby's room with needles and a spool of brown thread. She lifted the baby out from her hammock, laid her across her lap, and fingered some Vicks VapoRub onto the wing-pouch. Then she turned on the tape recorder, slipped in the newest collection of nursery rhymes, gently stuffed the baby's mouth with a small cloth, and dipped a needle into a bottle of Dettol.

Baby Khaki's pouch remained sewn shut for months, until one day Aisha returned to the garden with some toys to find Baby Khaki caught in the branches of a small *machungwa* tree. The baby hung there, sucking her thumb, as if she were a ripe fruit, ready to be picked. The weight of Aisha's spine pushed down into her legs. She scanned the courtyard to make sure the Khakis were still inside. She grabbed a chair, climbed on, and reached up toward Baby Khaki – but the baby was out of her grasp. In a panic, she jumped off the chair, took the footstool from under the garden table, and placed it on top of the chair. She mounted the two-storey ladder she had created and, wobbling on the uneven surface, rustled the branches until the baby tumbled out – breaking and bending a few branches so that leaves and even an orange hit Aisha below. Ouch! Aisha ignored the spray of foliage but as she seized the baby the stool slipped from under her and she lost her balance, tipped over the chair, and landed on the grass with a thud, with Baby Khaki on top of her. Aisha quickly got up, dusted the baby off, and crumpled the baby's wings. As she tucked them into the frayed pouch, Baby Khaki let out a wail.

"Shssh, shshh, *toto*. Everything is fine." Aisha patted the baby. "Please stop your crying." Baby Khaki continued. "Stop it!" Aisha squeezed the baby hard. She looked up and saw Mrs. Khaki opening the bedroom window.

Mrs. Khaki leaned out of the window, her voice hurled down into the garden and rolled into the wild bush trail leading out from behind the house to the base of Mt. Meru. "What's all the *kelele* about? What the hell are you doing down there?"

Aisha looked up, still holding the baby close, and rocked back and forth, almost losing her balance again. "Mamma, she is crying for food. Look, I am feeding her." She reached into her dress for her breast, cradled the baby closer, shoved the breast deep into the baby's mouth. The baby refused at first, continuing to cry.

"Don't make me come down there. You are paid very, very nicely – and what all for if I always have to keep on checking on you!"

Aisha pushed her breast harder into the baby's mouth and whispered, "Drink, child-of-Satan, drink!" Baby Khaki bit Aisha's nipple. Aisha held her breath. She knew this was the baby's sign that she would now start sucking. Baby Khaki wrapped her mouth around Aisha's breast and pulled her milk out.

"See, Mamma," Aisha said, half-smiling, pointing at the baby, "everything, it's *mzuri-sana*."

Mrs. Khaki shook her head, closed the window, and turned away.

Aisha was desperate to find a solution to stop Baby Khaki from flying. She had no choice – she had to cut the wings off entirely! Aisha sterilized a pair of scissors and then set about preparing the baby. She slipped her fingers into the wing-pouch and pulled each wing out. Some white fluff flew out. Aisha smoothed out the creases on the wings and laid them across the baby's back. Only then did she realize that the wings had changed – they were now lightly downed with golden-brown hair. Aisha stroked the wings – they were so soft! What a beautiful baby! She picked up Baby Khaki and tossed her up in the air. The baby cooed and floated back into Aisha's arms. Aisha laughed and kissed the baby all over her chubby cheeks. What a sweet, sweet child! Aisha threw the baby up again. Baby Khaki giggled, flapped her wings and flew directly toward the open window.

"Oh, *toto*!" Aisha ran after the baby, arms high above her. "Come back, *toto*. Come back!"

The baby was partly outside the window when Aisha reached out and caught her ankle and pulled, but a gust of wind sucked the baby out further. Aisha held on. She was determined to pull the baby back inside. Another gust of wind and Aisha was dragged out as well, but luckily her toes caught the inside ledge of the window. Together Aisha and the baby formed a straight line up. They looked like balloons aired up with a hand pump and tied to the house to mark some sort of celebration. Eventually the wind let up, releasing both of them. They tumbled downward and collapsed onto the bedroom floor.

As Aisha regained her composure and straightened herself out, she realized how foolish she had been: this devil-child was toying with her, trying to win the affections of her heart! No, she wouldn't have it any more. She wasn't that gullible! Aisha was even more determined to stop the baby from flying. This was too risky! She had to cut the baby's wings off *maramoja*!

Aisha laid the baby on the cot, lifted one wing off the baby's back, and carefully placed the tip of the scissors at the apex of the wings. Her hands trembled – this was no easy task, amputating a baby's wings. But she had to do this. She made the first tear and a watery substance oozed out from the wound, trickled down the baby's back, and dripped onto the cot. Aisha looked away. Please, God, save me. What am I doing? What has become of me that I can harm an innocent child? Aisha shook those thoughts out of her head and continued. More water gushed out as she made her way across the first wing.

No! No! *Hapana!* Aisha threw the scissors on the floor. No! She wouldn't do this! She couldn't do it. She wasn't a monster. Aisha licked her finger, applied it on the torn wing, and leaned down and kissed the wound. She would have to find another solution, one that was not as barbaric.

A few days later Aisha heard rumours that a Zanzibari witchdoctor had recently moved to Arusha, and she decided to investigate. She discovered that the witchdoctor, Mamma Zulekha, lived on Old Moshi Road just a few streets over. Maybe, just maybe, Aisha prayed, this *waganga* would help her. Aisha made arrangements to take the baby to Mamma Zulekha when the Khakis went to the *mukhi*'s house for their weekly game of *karata*.

Mamma Zulekha was an old, old woman with a small wrinkled face and bloodshot eyes. She wore a long white robe that was speckled with red dots. She welcomed Aisha and motioned for her to follow her to the *shamba* in the back and sit near a small fire. Aisha undressed the baby and placed her on Mamma Zulekha's lap. Mamma Zulekha rubbed her shaven head.

"Yes, yes, I have heard of this phenomenon before. She is like big insect, hanh?" She laughed as she picked at Baby Khaki's wings. "But *weh*, it is too unusual for such a little baby to have learned the craft *fatafut*, oh-so quickly – especially when it is landlocked. In Zanzibar or Pemba, I understand – the island winds can help the child on its first flight, carry it for miles upon miles until a messenger of *Shatan* claims it. But in this case, I don't understand." Mamma Zulekha paused. "Oh-yo, this can only mean that the baby has extra-special powers! I am certain of it – we must act very quickly. This *uganga* has been cast by a very strong *djinn*."

Aisha folded her arms and cupped her elbows in her palms. "Why, Mamma Zulekha, why must I endure so much suffering while others enjoy such worry-free lives? I have done nothing to deserve such a fate. Nothing at all. I am a God-fearing woman. I have had a difficult life, Mamma, but I have never complained. I have never asked for too much and yet this is what is served to me!"

Mamma Zulekha nodded her head. "Yes, my child, we all are deserving of a good life, but you must have done something to generate so much ill will."

Aisha hung her head. Mamma Zulekha reached across the fire and stroked her face.

"Perhaps it is a simple matter, child. It could be that somebody is jealous of your beauty and has ordered this curse."

Aisha pushed Mamma Zulekha's hand away. "Or it could be the mother's fault! She is the one who has not taken all the normal precautions of preventing such deformities. I watch her. She is very careless – clipping her nails after sundown, taking evening baths, walking under trees even when she has her monthlies! It is her stupidity that has invited *Shatan*'s congregation into their house. She is asking for trouble! Yet it is I, I who will end up paying for her actions!" Aisha pounded her fists on her thighs. "Please, Mamma Zulekha, I beg you. Please help me. You are the only one who knows about my troubles. I am new in this town and cannot afford for anyone, not anyone, to know my secret. I am willing to do whatever it takes to make this baby stop flying."

Mamma Zulekha paused. "Yes, anything is possible, child."

She rubbed her hands vigorously over the fire and placed her palms on her eyelids. Then she shrouded herself and the baby with a white sheet. At first, Mamma Zulekha rocked back and forth, but soon she began shaking uncontrollably and started speaking in an incomprehensible language. Aisha instinctively got up, ready to run. But then Mamma Zulekha bolted up and the sheet fell to one side. Sweat covered her brow and her face was contorted into a silent scream. Mamma Zulekha held Baby Khaki in outstretched hands.

"Yes, yes, I have a solution. I must see this baby daily for forty days in order to rid her of her ailment. This is the only way. The remedy will not work otherwise."

"Forty days, Mamma? Dear God, how will I do that? I cannot get away from the *bwana*'s house for forty days." Aisha wrung the fabric of her dress around her finger. "Can I not administer the remedy myself?"

Mamma Zulekha let out a belly laugh and shook her head.

Aisha slumped down to the ground. "I don't know what else to do, Mamma. My life depends on this."

Mamma Zulekha touched Aisha's head. "You can apply the medicine, but your touch may well take forty years. My mother was a witchdoctor, and her mother before that. Training is possible, but it can take years upon years. Such an intricate craft cannot just be learned overnight."

Aisha burst into tears. "I have no family, no husband. Where will I go when they throw me out on the street?"

"Calm down, child, calm down. Let me think for one moment."

Mamma Zulekha reached for a cup, took a long slurp, and closed her eyes. A few minutes later, she opened them.

"Okay, okay. This is what you will do. I will brew an extra-strong remedy for the child. There will be some risk – but it has to be strong-*kama*-strong to offset the weakness in your touch. It is not the prescribed remedy, but it seems there is no other way."

Aisha stood up and rushed to Mamma Zulekha. "We have a solution!"

"But I warn you," Mamma Zulekha wagged her finger, "the welfare of the child will be in your hands entirely."

"Yes, yes, Mamma, that is fine."

Mamma Zulekha nodded and walked to the lone baobab tree. The tree had hundreds of nails hammered into its trunk and even more shreds of cloth hanging from its branches. She asked Aisha to hold the baby against the trunk and then she pricked its foot and collected a few drops of blood on a silver tray. Strangely, the baby did not cry.

"The remedy will take some days to produce. I will come and apply the first round. You will see what I do and then follow this plan daily for forty days, at the prescribed hour – one hour before sundown."

"Yes! Yes! It will work, I know it." Aisha clapped her hands.

"Don't be so confident." Mamma Zulekha warned. "You will tempt *Shatan* to counter your strength."

"You are so wise. Of course. I will contain myself." Aisha hugged Mamma Zulekha.

Aisha paid Mamma Zulekha the pre-negotiated sum of money and they arranged a time for their next visit.

That evening, Aisha slipped a thin sisal cord around Baby Khaki's ankle and tied it to her own wrist. She would use this temporary solution until Mamma Zulekha's concoction started to work.

Mamma Zulekha arrived as planned on the following Friday when the Khakis were away at *jamatkhana*. She carried a large bowl and several small sacks.

"Come, Mamma, this way. We have to hurry, I don't want the neighbours to see." Aisha waved Mamma Zulekha through the garden gate. They rushed upstairs to the baby's room.

Aisha took Baby Khaki out of her hammock and placed her on the floor. The baby cooed. Aisha reached down and slipped the sisal cord off the baby's ankle but left it tied around her wrist, dangling there like a frayed umbilical cord.

Mamma Zulekha turned the baby to face east.

"Watch and listen carefully, my child."

Aisha knelt next to Mamma Zulekha. First, Mamma Zulekha performed a silent prayer, and then she touched the baby's head, then each hand, her stomach, and each foot. She lit some incense and waved it over the front of baby's body. She tapped several herbs onto a silver tray, reached into the top of her robe, and removed a vial containing the baby's blood. She mixed the blood and herbs together with her fingers, flipped the baby on her stomach, and daubed the medicine on the wings. She applied most of the remedy to the crux of the wings at the base of the baby's neck, just under the pouch where the wings were fastened to Baby Khaki's body. Mamma Zulekha recited a prayer five times and then called on the demons. "Do not be angry with us, we will do all we can. To those who belong to the house of God, may they have mercy on you by their favour, and we ask of your pardon. Have pity on us and remove our terrible suffering. Pity her in whom you are, and forgive her with all forgiveness, because those who forgive die pious. Forgive us our sins, forgive, forgive, in the name of all true believers." Mamma Zulekha then took a bottle of rose water, sprinkled it over the baby, and spread her palm across the middle of the baby's back. "These wings shall get softer and softer and fall off after forty days, God-willing."

Aisha heard the front gate opening and the familiar sound of the Khakis' white Peugeot. "Mamma, you must go. Hurry. They cannot find you here."

"Burn some incense or they will smell the remedy. And do not forget to put an offering on the roof each night. Now go take care of the baby. I know my way out." Mamma Zulekha cradled Aisha's head in her hands. "Many blessings. Let us pray that the demons co-operate."

"Thank you! Thank you." Aisha held Mamma Zulekha by the waist. "I am indebted to you forever."

Mamma Zulekha smiled. "No need to be so thankful. First, let us see if the altered remedy works – that is the important thing." She waved goodbye and quickly shuffled out the door.

Aisha lit some sandalwood incense and pushed the bowl and sacks of medicine under her cot. She picked up the baby, wrapped her in a blanket, and put her in the hammock, and then sat down on the stool next to the hammock and hummed a nursery rhyme as she swung the baby gently. She pinched the last remaining ray of light from the setting sun between her thumb and little finger and slipped it into her mouth, let it sit there trapped under her tongue. She laid her head back and curled her calves under the chair, letting her soft brown body ease into the chair.

That night, Aisha dreamt she was pregnant. A nightingale pecked her plump belly, trying to crack it open. The baby wailed inside her, aching, it seemed, to get out. But just before it popped its head out and took its first breath, Aisha bolted up in bed. When she calmed herself down and was about to fall back asleep, she heard what seemed like a bird flapping away through the open window.

Each evening, one hour before sunset, Aisha administered the remedy exactly as prescribed. After each application, she would poke at the baby's wings – testing them as if she were testing the flakiness of *mandazi*. Each night, the wings became visibly weaker so that they were quite limp – as if they had been soaked in a washtub overnight. By the ninth night, when Aisha prodded the wings, it created a puncture the size of her index finger. Aisha smiled as she peeled the skin of the baby's wing off her finger. Thank God, the prescription was working! Aisha would have to visit Mamma Zulekha soon to express her thanks. She felt a surge of confidence and could finally see the end was near. She would soon be released from the terrible burden of hiding these wings. This sudden sense of freedom made her laugh out loud. She had never been happier, never felt lighter in her life. Her laughter spread like a bush fire, shooting up through her throat, filling her mouth, and finally bursting through her lips. She laughed so intensely that she eventually collapsed to the floor, rolling all over the room, intoxicated by this new feeling of freedom inside her. When Aisha finally came to, she was completely exhausted and fell immediately asleep.

As she slept, she dreamt that she was walking in and out along the corridors of Stone Town, but strangely all the streets were deserted. The vendors had closed their shops, and there were no school children to be seen even though Aisha could hear the muffled voice of a child counting: *moja, mbili, tatu* – Ready or not, here I come! She could hear children scampering here and there, as if they were right next to her, but there was no one in sight – all of them, it seemed, were tucked into various *gulleys* and gutters of Stone Town. But Aisha could feel the children watching her. Aisha stopped and turned around quickly, hoping to catch a glimpse of one. But nothing. She was alone. She kneeled down and looked under the fish vendors' stalls, peered into the tailor's shop. Nothing. Where were they all? Just then, the muezzin's voice bellowed over a loudspeaker with the call for prayers and the sky opened its belly. Water gushed out and poured down on Zanzibar with such intensity that the island was lifted from the earth, eventually bobbing up and down in rainwater, just under the surface of the sky.

By the thirteenth night, to Aisha's horror, Baby Khaki's wings started getting harder, not softer! At first, Aisha ignored this change, chalking it up to the nuances of the prescription, but by the sixteenth night, Aisha became extremely worried and frustrated. Why wasn't this remedy working? What had gone wrong? She was following the prescription exactly as ordered. She decided that perhaps the solution was to apply more and more of the concoction to the wings. But it soon became apparent that the more she applied, the stronger the wings became, so that they even became harder and harder to fold and tuck into their pouch. Once, they just popped straight out of the pouch as if they were feet being pushed into shoes that were too small. Without meaning to, Aisha reached for the pair of scissors but the baby slipped out of her arms and flew around the room creating a grand ruckus as she hit the wall and the windows. Eventually, Aisha cornered the baby, placed her knee firmly on the small of the baby's back, and reached, once again, for the scissors. Aisha was so occupied with the baby that she did not hear Mrs. Khaki walking up the stairs toward the baby's room.

"What are you doing?" Mrs. Khaki screamed, rushing toward her baby.

Aisha stood up immediately. "Mamma?"

"Badru! Badru! Call the doctor!" Mrs. Khaki yelled at the top of her lungs. She held her baby across her body. Mrs. Khaki turned to Aisha. "You devil-woman! *Kumamayao!*" She slapped Aisha hard across her face.

"What have you done? What have you done to my baby?" Mrs. Khaki cried and screamed, tears rushing out, ruining her make-up. She continued inspecting her baby. "What is this? What is this?" She tentatively poked the baby's wings. "Answer me, *bhenchod*! What have you done to my baby?"

"Nothing, Mamma, nothing. The baby. She flies."

"What the hell are you talking about?" Mrs. Khaki laid the baby on the cot, her legs shaking under her maxi. She collapsed to the floor, patting the baby gently. "Badru," she whimpered. "Badru, please hurry up! The baby is hurt!"

Aisha grabbed the baby from Mrs. Khaki's grasp. She cupped Baby Khaki in her hands and held her up to the ceiling. "Look, Mamma, the baby, she flies." Aisha released he baby upward, blowing at her like an eyelash for a wish, but the baby just fluttered her wings briefly and then tumbled down onto the cot, exhausted, perhaps, from the earlier chase.

Mrs. Khaki grabbed her child and cupped her in her arms. "Have you gone mad?"

Just then Mr. Khaki walked into the room and discovered his wife and daughter in this terrible state.

"Look Badru, look at what the servant-girl has done to our child." Mrs. Khaki displayed the baby's back to him.

Mr. Khaki erupted with shock and anger. "*Pisha Mowla!* What in God's name has happened to my child?"

"This is the work of the devil!" Mrs. Khaki was barely able to lift her arm, but pointed to Aisha. "And she is the devil's messenger!"

Aisha felt limp with exhaustion – as if she had been purged of all her energy. "No, Mamma. I am a God-fearing woman. Please, spare me. I have done my best to take care of this child."

"You will pay for this!" Mr. Khaki told Aisha in an even but harsh tone. "You will never work anywhere in Tanganyika, or for that matter, Zanzibar! Nowhere. You will wish you were dead."

"Please, Bwana, please forgive me. I beg of you. Despite all my efforts, I was unable to ward off the spirits."

"So you admit it? You admit your liaison with *Shatan* himself?"

Aisha felt cornered. She had nothing and nobody to fall back on, and although she knew the purity of her actions, she felt she had no choice but to repent. Aisha looked down. "Yes, sir, I admit. Please have mercy on me!"

Mr. Khaki felt reasonably satisfied with the confession and delighted that he would now have considerably more negotiating power over her. "You will have to pay for your mistakes."

"Yes, sir, I will do anything you ask. Please, I only ask that you give me another chance."

Mr. Khaki looked at his wife to gauge her reaction, but she was still distraught, and had not absorbed any of the conversation. Mr. Khaki shook his head and wondered why it had taken her this long to discover that a terrible spell had been cast on their child. What the hell had she been doing with her time? He looked at Baby Khaki and noticed she wasn't even wearing *anjar* under her eyes. He turned the child's ear down. No *anjar* there either! For God's sake, his wife hadn't taken any of the normal precautions to ward off evil! Did she not possess any common sense? As he looked at Mrs. Khaki, still sitting on the floor with her head on the edge of the cot, hair dishevelled, face smudged with make-up, he wondered for the first time if he should not have listened to his mother's warning about the terrible luck in his wife's family. Yes, she was beautiful, but in the end, she had still produced a deformed child for him and no amount of beauty could outweigh this fact. Perhaps he should have considered other qualities when he was choosing a wife. Mr. Khaki walked over to Mrs. Khaki, leaned down, and slapped her. "Useless bitch."

Mrs. Khaki was in such a daze, she hardly even felt the sting across her face. It was as though this new knowledge about her life, the idea that something this terrible could happen to her, to her of all people, broke like a wooden spoon across a knee, and paralyzed her. Why me? Why me? was all she could utter.

Mr. Khaki turned his gaze to Aisha. "You will have to pay for the rest of your life – you understand?"

"Yes, sir. I understand."

Mr. Khaki explained to Aisha that from now on she would now have to report to him and that he would be the one who would give her instructions with regard to the baby's care. As well, he would make prompt arrangements for the surgical removal of Baby Khaki's wings.

Aisha felt great remorse for her earlier attempt at cutting the baby's wings off, and without thinking she said, "Bwana, please do not cut them off." Aisha picked up the baby and held it tight against her breast.

A flicker of heat shot through Mr. Khaki's body and flushed his face. His arms reached out and pried the baby away from Aisha. He doubled Baby Khaki over his arm like a sack of rice, folded a wing, and ripped if off then and there like a page in a book. How dare she give me instructions on how to run my house!

Aisha stretched out her arm, and let the amputated wing land like a feather on her palm.

Mr. Khaki held the baby toward Aisha, arms outstretched. "This, this is your bloody fault!"

The weight of the wing on Aisha's palm gave her a sudden conviction. She yelled loudly and clearly, "No! This is not my fault!" and then grabbed the baby and ran out of the room.

Mr. Khaki could not believe the audacity of this servant-girl! He ran straight after her, clear he would teach her a good lesson. He turned the corner and pursued her down the stairs, but then his eyes caught the scabbard lashed on the hall chair and he smiled, certain that no servant-girl would ever outsmart him. He returned to the bedroom, opened the window, and waited.

Mr. Khaki heard a door being inched open and, soon enough, Aisha ran across the garden, the baby tucked in a *kanga* wrapped across her body. Mr. Khaki pushed open the window completely and aimed. Aisha ducked behind the *machungwa* tree, waited a moment, and ran again. Another shot, and she jumped into the lavender bushes, then behind the bougainvillea, running and hiding, running and hiding, past anything and everything in her way, straight toward the bush trail to the mountain.

The baby's wing snapped out of the *kanga* like the sail of a dhow and as Aisha ran faster, the baby bobbed up and down, faster and faster, until both of them whirred like a motor and lifted off the ground, ascending slowly toward the sky. As they rose, the wind generated a new wing from the scar of the old. Baby Khaki flapped her wings with a new fervour and clawed her way out of the *kanga*. Mr. Khaki saw them emerge above the forest and promptly fired again and again until he exhausted all his bullets. He then watched, with great satisfaction, as Aisha fell, arms spread, gently striking the tops of several cedar trees and then disappearing into the dense bush below.

But Baby Khaki circled the trees, diving down like a duck into water. She resurfaced several times before they emerged together, Aisha folded in two, Baby Khaki mounted on her back, pulling her up toward the sky.

DANIEL GRIFFIN

Mercedes Buyer's Guide

Wayne Krause claimed to know nothing about the stuff in the trunk of the car. The car had been his mother's and Wayne said he hadn't been up to sorting through it after the funeral. He did say that he was pretty sure the microwave worked. When it turned out it didn't and the toaster wouldn't keep bread down and both casserole dishes were cracked, Harry Stouffer suspected that Wayne had piled all that junk in just to get rid of it. Harry set the kitchenware, the type-writer, the bags of old shoes, the twelve windshield wiper blades and everything else in the corner of his garage. He vacuumed, sprayed air freshener into the car and tried to forget about Wayne Krause. Things kept turning up in that car though, things that kept Wayne and his family at the front of Harry's mind.

The first time Harry adjusted the passenger's seat he found a letter caught in the shifting mechanism. It was dated 12 January 1969. He spent some time wondering how a 1969 letter might have wound up in a 1981 car. Equally strange, the letter was written as though it was midsummer. It complained of heat, drought and dust. Harry read it to himself three times before taking it inside, where he asked his wife to guess what he'd just found in the car. "Another microwave," she said. Her books were fanned out before her. Harry knew she didn't want to be disturbed. The kids were asleep. This was her study time. He read it aloud anyway. Along with talk of weather there was mention of Myrna's health, a planned trip to the seaside and a cancelled New Year's Eve party. "Isn't this neat?"

"Yeah," Colleen said. "Neat."

"I think it's from Australia." Harry refolded the letter, tapped it against his palm. Colleen marked her spot in one book, turned to read from another. It was still a couple of weeks before exams, but she'd been working like this every night for a month.

"On the radio this morning they said you remember most if you study before sleep," Harry said. "Turns out whatever you were last thinking goes round and round in your brain all night." He waited for a response. Colleen looked up, nodded. "Neat, eh?" She nodded again.

Every night of his life Harry had had a shower before bed. Imagine how much smarter he'd be if he'd read the paper or the encyclopedia. Of course the Stouffers didn't have an encyclopedia. But still.

A week after finding the letter, Harry found thirty-two hundred dollars in a yellow envelope in the trunk. It was tucked under the lining, hidden or lost. He found it while returning the spare tire to its well. But that was a week later. Before finding the money, before Harry had even looked at the spare, he took the Australian letter over to Wayne Krause's place. It was after work on a Tuesday. Harry parked out front and walked across a yard full of toys – a trike, wagon, small slide, a couple of Hula Hoops. Wayne lived in a cul-de-sac in the Garrison development, which meant his kids could leave things lying around like that. It also meant his kids could run around in the front yard without worry. If Harry's kids left something out after dark it would be gone by morning. And if they stepped off the sidewalk and into the street they'd be dead. A car would zip along and Bang. Harry didn't like to think about it. He didn't appreciate thoughts like this visiting him. It was true though. Zip, bang. Cars travelled way too fast on Bayshore. All the way down greens fell in line. If Colleen wanted to become an engineer, Harry was fine with that. For starters she could re-engineer the traffic lights on Bayshore.

Harry looked at his watch as he rang the bell. He'd have to make it quick. He hadn't told Col that he was stopping at Wayne's. He counted to ten, rang the bell again. Dum dee dum dee dum. A little girl opened the door. Harry crouched. "Hi kid, what's your name?"

"Lisa Krause." She was wearing a Barbie T-shirt.

"That's a sweet name," Harry said. "I'm Harry. Would you tell your Dad Harry's here?"

"Harry's here," she said, but she was still looking at Harry and hadn't raised her voice.

"Harry who?" Wayne yelled from somewhere inside.

"Harry Stouffer."

"Stouffer?"

"Like the frozen dinners." That brought no response. "Harry you sold the car to."

That did it. There was movement inside; then Wayne appeared, stomping down the hallway, feet, arms and belly all on the move. He looked like a boxer who'd been set loose on the world of doughnuts and fast food. "I don't know what's wrong with that car, but it was running when I sold it to you –"

"No, no, it's not about that –"

"As is, remember. That's what we said." Harry held up his hands, shook his head and looked at his feet. "What?" Wayne said after a pause. "What?"

"You have any family in Australia? Any close family friends or anything?" Wayne filled the door frame and the way he was looking at Harry right now made Harry worry about his size. A man that big could really inflict some pain. Harry's scalp warmed. "Anyone who lived in Australia in 1969?" Wayne kept looking at Harry in that peculiar way. Harry pulled out the letter. He said it had been under the passenger's seat.

Wayne stepped back into better light, read, flipped the letter over, read the reverse. "Helen," he said. The salutation was smudged but the letter had been clearly signed by Helen M. For a moment Wayne stood in silence, then he turned. "Hey, Mer," he yelled. "Get me the phone."

Lisa came out with it. Wayne dialled, stepped into the living room and beckoned Harry. It occurred to Harry just then that he didn't really want an answer. He hadn't spent enough time day-dreaming about the letter; he hadn't even shown it around work.

All day it had sat in the glove compartment. And now that it was in Wayne's big fist, Harry was unlikely to get it back.

"Impulse," Harry said out loud. Wayne turned to look at him, but just then someone picked up on the other end and Wayne spoke into the phone. Col often said that Harry had to stop letting impulse carry him away.

Wayne covered the receiver. "Could it be South Africa? It could be, right?" Harry nodded. Of course it could. That hadn't occurred to Harry. "Helen," Wayne said into the phone. "Helen M." Harry must have assumed Australia because he and Tim had watched a documentary about dingoes a couple of months ago, before the TV broke.

Wayne covered the phone again, yelled for someone to get him a map or an atlas or something. Eventually Lisa brought in a map of North America. Wayne unfolded it, turned it over. "Jesus weeps. A world map. A map with frigging Africa on it."

In the end they used a map on the inside cover of a dictionary. Wayne pointed to South Africa as though Harry might not have heard of it. "That's the spot. Right there." His finger covered half the country.

On the verandah Wayne said he was sorry about all the junk in the car. He waved one of his big hands. "I just didn't want to deal with it. My mother's stuff and all. I get emotional about these things." Wayne pinched the bridge of his nose, closed his eyes and gave his head a shake. It wasn't easy watching someone as big as Wayne get emotional. Harry turned away to give the man some privacy. As he stood gazing down the street, he pictured the collection of wiper blades that still sat in his garage. Who would even have a dozen wiper blades? The rest of the junk Harry sort of understood, but a dozen wipers? The screen door banged and Wayne was back inside. He hadn't even said goodbye.

When Harry got home, Tim was playing tennis against the wall in the living room and Sashi was bouncing on the sofa singing something from *The Lion King*. Harry leaned in. "You'll break the springs, Sashi." Thwack. The ball hit the wall only inches from Harry's face. "Cut that out." It rolled under the stereo, and

Harry headed down the hallway. Thwack. "Jesus weeps." Harry liked that curse. He thought he might start using it regularly. In the kitchen Colleen had her books out. Thwack. "Jesus weeps," Harry said again.

"What's that?"

"Why don't we just get a new TV? Something cheap."

"It'll rot their minds."

"It'll calm them down. They're tearing the house apart. Just go look at them." There was a thud that wasn't the tennis ball. Sashi came running into the kitchen and straight into Col's arms. From the living room Tim shouted, "Wasn't me, wasn't me." Col rocked Sashi a while, then returned one hand to working the calculator. Thwack. "Tim, do that somewhere else."

"Where?"

"Outside."

"I'm grounded."

"In the yard."

"It's dark." The boy thumped down the hallway, poked his head into the kitchen. "What's for supper?" Oh shit. Harry had forgotten it was his turn to cook tonight. He opened his mouth to suggest they order pizza, but he already knew what Col would say. He turned to the cupboards. "Let me think a sec."

"You didn't stop at the grocery?"

"Thought I'd just make something from what we have here." Sashi was calm now, but she still leaned into her mother, enjoying the attention. Harry wouldn't have minded some attention. He wouldn't have minded leaning into Col and having her run her hand through his hair. Maybe he should jump up and down and fall off the chesterfield even after someone's told him not to. Thwack. "Tim, for Christ's sakes."

Eggs. He'd make eggs.

Harry diced an onion, grated some cheese, sliced a tomato and set a pan on the stove. He cracked eight eggs, buttered bread, and then asked Colleen if she could please clear away her books.

When everyone was at the table, Sashi raised her milk. "It's my turn tonight," she announced. "And I want to make a toast to the Queen."

Tim said, "Boring," but it was Sashi's turn so they all raised their glasses. Harry kept his thoughts about this exercise to himself. With the others he said, "To the Queen."

At 10:47 on Saturday 25 April, Harry found thirty-two hundred dollars in the trunk of the car. The day before, he'd noticed that the rear tires didn't match and he'd wanted to check the spare, see if it was the missing mate. It wasn't and getting it back in proved a bugger. Harry ended up pulling the whole lining off. That's when he noticed the corner of the yellow envelope. Straight away he knew it was money. And straight away he knew that unless it was Canadian Tire money or something, he had his hands on a good chunk of change. He peeked in. Full of twenties. His legs went rubbery. He had to sit. He opened one of the lawn chairs, took a load off and began flipping through the wad. One hundred and sixty twenties made thirty-two hundred dollars. "Jesus weeps." He'd only paid nineteen hundred. And that was a deal. The car was nearly twenty years old and eaten by rust, but it was still a Mercedes.

Harry tapped the envelope against his thigh, money tight in his right hand. Thirty-two hundred dollars. Imagine the things you could do with thirty-two hundred dollars. Col would want to put it into savings or a mortgage payment or something. She might be okay spending some on the kids. Horse-riding lessons for Sashi. Tennis lessons for Tim. Although Tim didn't really like tennis. He just liked banging the ball against the wall. He liked comic books, but that would be a waste. What about a new television? The boy would love that. Everyone would. It could be a present for the whole family.

Colleen was on the back porch having her one cigarette of the day when Harry stepped out of the garage. At least Harry hoped it was her one cigarette of the day. He didn't want to ask in case she got upset. It was only eleven. It was early to be having her one cigarette. You could bet she'd be needing another by six. She'd be desperate by nine. Harry considered saying something like that, making it a joke, only then Col turned and noticed him. Instead Harry said, "Guess what I found in the car."

"I don't know. What?"

"Colleen," he said. "Look at me."

"I am looking at you."

Harry threw the money in the air. It took Col a moment to understand what it was, and then she seemed to melt. Harry watched her carefully. More than anything he'd wanted to see Col's reaction. Her eyes grew big and milky. "Harry," she said. "Harry." Her knees went soft, bent a moment. Bills fluttered everywhere. It was like hitting big cash in a game show. The air was money.

"Three thousand two hundred dollars," Harry said. Col brought her hands to her mouth. She ran on the spot, jumped up and down, dropped her cigarette. By now the money was blowing all over the muddy yard. They noticed this at the same time. Some bills were already near the fence. Harry chased after them while Colleen bent to gather what was on the porch. "Kids," she yelled. "Hey kids!"

Harry ran along the fence line scooping up bills. When he looked back, Tim and Sashi were standing at the door. "Help pick up all this money before it blows away." For a moment the kids stood watching their parents scramble about, then began chasing after bills themselves.

When they'd collected all of them, Colleen counted: 158. Two missing. Harry told Tim to hop into Mister Yee's yard, and Sashi crawled under the porch with a flashlight. After Tim found one of the missing bills they gave up. Harry felt a little bad about losing the other, but when he thought about Col's reaction, it had been worth twenty bucks. She'd melted. She really had.

Inside they had Cokes to celebrate. Colleen proposed a toast. "To thirty-two hundred dollars," she said. They tapped cans, drank. "To being rich," Tim said. They tapped cans again and Sashi said, "To being the richest." After the excitement had died a little, Harry called a family meeting. He'd never called one before. It had always been Col, but today he said they had to decide how to spend the dough.

"Har," Col said. "Har." She touched his shoulder. "Maybe we shouldn't talk about it like this. Maybe we should think about it a while, not do anything impulsive."

"We can discuss it though," Harry said. "No harm in talking, right? And I wasn't thinking we should spend it all, either. We should definitely put some aside for savings. More than some. A good chunk. Most of it. But I thought we could do something special with the rest. You've been complaining about having to take textbooks out of the library, so why not buy some? Sashi's been wanting riding lessons and Tim –"

"A TV," Tim said. He said it right on cue. It couldn't have been better if they'd planned it. Harry clapped his son on the back. "That's an idea." He couldn't remember when he'd been happier with something Tim had said. "A TV," the boy said again. It gave Harry a pinch of regret for having grounded him. He'd overreacted. He saw that now. The lamp had been old, worthless really.

"Maybe that could be the present to the whole family. The rest goes to savings or to the mortgage." Harry was trying to make it seem like he hadn't thought this through.

"Har." Col wasn't buying. She shook her head, but then Tim started chanting, "TV, TV." Sashi joined in and Harry couldn't help but grin. "Some textbooks too," he said, pointing at his wife.

"Everyone." Col raised her voice, but Tim and Sashi kept chanting and banging on the table. Harry took the money out, threw it in the air. It filled the room, rose to the lamp, fluttered groundward like dead leaves. Tim stood to bat at the bills. Sashi began running around the kitchen. Finally Colleen broke into a smile and started nodding. She scooped up some money, threw it in the air, scooped up more, threw it at Harry.

By 4:36 that afternoon they were all watching the new television. *Lassie* was on. Without cable there weren't many options. Harry couldn't find his glasses but the screen was big enough that he could do without. He was just thinking how he'd want them for the hockey tonight when it occurred to him that there might be more money in the car. Think of all the things they'd left in there. A microwave, a toaster, typewriter, shoes, an old letter and a wad of cash. Obviously not very careful people. Obviously not very well-organized. Not that Harry was either of these things, and not that he was complaining, but still.

"What if there's more money in there?" Harry said during the next commercial. "What if they were really rich and just had lots of cash lying here there and everywhere? They had a Mercedes after all. Plus at least thirty-two hundred in cash."

"We have a Mercedes and thirty-two hundred in cash," Tim said.

Harry patted him on the knee. "You're right there, son." And then Harry stood. "Who wants to help me search the car?" No one answered. Harry said, "Who wants more money?" and Tim's ears perked up. "If I find more money, who do you think should keep it?"

Tim stood. "Whoever wants some money had better come help." Good old Tim. It was nice to be getting along so well. They'd had a lot of fights recently, and that whole incident with Grandmother's lamp had cast a long shadow.

In the end they all went. Colleen put on rubber gloves, groped between the seats. She found some tissue, a pen, a pair of broken sunglasses and an unsigned birthday card for a ninety-five-year-old.

Tim searched the doors – their pockets, handles, trim panels, armrests and ashtrays. Harry gave Sashi the flashlight and coerced her into searching the trunk. He told everyone to keep an eye out for his glasses, then began removing the front seats. He knew this was taking things a bit far, but he wanted to be thorough. By the time he had the second one out, Col and Sashi had gone back inside. Tim was just watching. There was nothing of interest under either seat. Tim tried sitting in one. The springs gave an old man's sigh.

Harry crouched where the passenger seat had been, emptied the glove compartment. Stuck in a crevice was a driver's licence for Barbara Krause. She was pictured in the corner looking startled and pale. It had expired in 1988. Harry held it up to show Tim, but his son had left too.

Harry removed the dashboard cover. Beneath he poked about the instrument panel's wiring, the heater unit, the passages that led to the vents. He began on the steering column, then realized it was six o'clock. It was also a Saturday, which meant it was his turn to cook. He walked in whispering, "Pizza, pizza, pizza." Tim and Sashi screamed their approval but minutes later bickered over the toppings as they always did.

While tipping the deliveryman, Harry realized that the money hadn't been lost or misplaced. No one would misplace thirty-two hundred dollars. They'd hid it deliberately. Old people always hid money. They distrusted banks. And if the Krauses had hidden more, wouldn't it be somewhere unusual? He'd have to search the entire car. Every inch.

Harry didn't watch *Hockey Night in Canada*. Instead he removed the roof panelling, pulled up the carpeting and took the trim off the doors. He checked the rusty bumpers, the rusty wheel wells, looked over the whole rusty underbody. He removed one piece of the side moulding just to assure himself nothing could fit in it. He didn't give up until five past eleven, by which time half the car seemed to be strewn about the garage. Harry hadn't found a penny. He hadn't even found his glasses.

On 16 September 1980 a silver Mercedes 126-S rolled off the S-Class line at the Daimler-Benz plant in Sindelfingen, West Germany. It was near the end of the second shift. The red light had been on all day indicating the assembly line was behind quota. What was more, it was Torsten Fast's birthday and his family would soon be gathered and waiting for him. All the same, Torsten took his time on this last car, examined its heating and air conditioning systems, its instrument cluster and steering column; then he noticed a piece of paper lying on the floor. He bent, lifted it. "Gutten Geburtztag Schatz." Torsten looked about, smiled self-consciously, tucked the note into his pocket and turned fully around. No one was watching. He patted the car and moved on. Torsten gave every car he inspected a tap on the hood. He called it his *letzter Kuss*.

The car left the plant by train bound for the port of Bremerhaven and travelled to Montreal by container ship where it cleared customs and was inspected, tagged and transferred to an eighteen-wheeler at the Mercedes preparation centre. While driving it onto the trailer, Martin Roche brushed it against a concrete pillar. He'd been adjusting the radio so he could listen to something for the few seconds it took to move the car. The contact left a small scrape and a shallow dent, but Roche was the only person to notice. His palms grew damp and his stomach did somersaults until after the driver had signed for the cars and was headed for Markham. The moment the truck was out of the prep centre that scrape could have happened anywhere. Roche swore up and down that he'd be more careful. He'd only had the job two weeks and at this rate he wouldn't last long.

The silver 126-S arrived along with two C-class sedans and a station wagon at the Frank Cherry dealership next morning and Frank had a fit. He spotted the scrape straight off. He had an eye for that sort of thing. He said he'd send it back, said he'd send the whole load right back to fucking Germany. His son-in-law told him they could fix it, but Frank wasn't listening. He gripped his chest. Was someone trying to kill him? Didn't they know he had a heart condition? Frank was at the loading entrance, but customers could still hear. Barbara Krause blushed. The man had to be seventy and here he was carrying on like a twelve-year-old. She tried not to listen. On the way back into the showroom Frank Cherry said he wanted someone fired for this. His face was bright red. Cherry, Barbara thought.

Tuesday evening Harry remembered to stop at the grocery store. He picked up sausages, potatoes and a head of cabbage. The Garrison development was only a couple K away and Harry found himself turning towards Wayne's place. All the toys were still strewn across the front lawn. It had been a week but they seemed to be in exactly the same spots.

Lisa answered the door. Harry crouched. "Would you tell your dad that Harry's here?"

"Harry who?" Wayne called.

"Stouffer. Like the frozen dinners." Wayne stepped into the hall, wiped his mouth with a serviette. "I'm sorry." Harry stood. "Hope I'm not interrupting anything. Not eating are you?"

"No, no, come on in. Find any more letters?" Wayne chuckled. "My sister and I got a real kick out of that." The screen door banged behind Harry.

"I was just driving by and thought I'd. . . . I just wanted to know. I could have called for this but I lost your number. Hi, Lisa." Harry was having trouble getting to his question. He was no longer even sure what his question was. He wanted to know something. He wanted to know a lot of things. Things about the elderly parents who'd hidden money in their car, the great aunt living in South Africa, the startled face staring out of the driver's licence, the birthday card for a ninety-five-year-old, the windshield wiper blades and all the other junk in the car. He wanted to know about all of these things, but he didn't know how to begin. Wayne was still staring at him. Lisa was staring at him. Neither ever seemed to blink. Harry dug both hands into his jacket pockets, felt the taped arm of his second pair of specs. He shifted from foot to foot. How do you ask? Where do you start?

"Harry?" Wayne said, and Harry took a deep breath. "Something wrong, Harry?"

"I can't find my glasses. I didn't leave my glasses here did I?"

"He leave his glasses here?" Wayne called over his shoulder.

"No."

Harry nodded. He nodded as hard as he could and said he wouldn't bother them again. He waved to Lisa and waited for her to wave back. She didn't.

Ken Krause liked the idea of a scraped car. He liked the idea of saving a grand for a scrape and a dent which they could fix and make imperceptible. Plus there'd be no waiting list. It could be his today. Barbara wasn't so sure. Wouldn't it decrease the resale value? Wouldn't it rust? And didn't it seem strange to spend thirty thousand dollars for a damaged car? She didn't say all of this, at least not in so few words. She said she didn't like silver. Too flashy, too much glitter. And she spent a long time standing near the one she did like. It was deep green and in perfect condition. Eventually she pulled Ken aside and asked if they shouldn't at least look at some others.

"Lovey, I'm negotiating. Just let me take care of this. Please." But Barbara could see that the only thing Ken was taking care of was that silver car. They'd be stuck with it. She knew it.

In the lounge Barbara lit a cigarette. She shouldn't be upset. It was a brand new car except for the scrape. But it bothered her all the same. For one thing, Jeannie would notice no matter how they painted it. Remember last year when she spotted that mark on Eloise's gown? It was tiny and they'd all but removed it, but in the end Eloise was in tears blaming Barbara for spilling the mascara and ruining her wedding.

When Barbara returned to the showroom, Ken had the silver car on the street ready for a test drive. The two of them circled the nearby blocks, drove the highway a mile in each direction. Ken said it was an Arabian thoroughbred on wheels. Barbara said as little as possible. They parked in the lot. Ken went in for the paperwork. He asked if she wanted to join him. Barbara shook her head, lit a cigarette, switched on the radio. Ken was almost an hour in there, and when he came out he had a toothy, owner's grin. He raised the keys, suddenly a little boy holding the best present ever. It lit her heart a moment. At the car he offered her the keys. "Do the honours?" Barbara shook her head.

Ken pulled out of the lot, made a right onto Drummond Road. Barbara put a hand on his leg, let it lie there. She wanted to ask when they were going to fix the dent, but held back. Two blocks from the highway a snowball hit the windshield. A second hit the hood with a deep thud. Ken slammed his foot on the brakes, brought the car to an abrupt halt. Barbara wasn't wearing her seat belt. Her body hit the dash, her face hit the windscreen. Straining against his own belt, Ken lost his breath. His heart sputtered, clamoured against his rib cage. When the momentum was spent, Ken fell back against the seat and Barbara fell from the dash. She lifted a hand, groped at the arm rest and pulled herself up. "You all right?" Ken said in a whisper.

"Yes. I think." She didn't say anything else. She ran fingers across her body, brought them to her face and sat slumped in the passenger seat.

"Goddamn kids. Jesus." Ken unbuckled, climbed out of the car. He brought a hand to his chest. That had scared him. It really had. His knees trembled. All through his body he could feel it. Jesus, what a scare.

No one in sight. That was always the way. As soon as he drove away the little fuckers would be back. A car passed, horn blaring. Ken got back in, pulled over to the curb. Barbara lit a cigarette. "Give me one of those, will you?" Ken said. Barbara nodded, passed him hers and lit another. "Jesus." Ken banged a hand against the steering wheel and that too hurt.

When Harry got home that night the TV was on. Tim and Sashi were quiet in front of it, faces illuminated by the flashing screen. Down the hall Col was studying at the kitchen table. Harry set the grocery bag on the counter and said he was making bangers and mash. He put a pot on the stove, peeled the potatoes, cut them in half so they'd cook more quickly, then sliced the cabbage, tossed it in the frying pan with the sausage.

Barbara Krause's driver's licence lay on the counter. Harry lifted it as the kids came down the hall for supper. For a moment the sound of Col laying the cutlery evaporated and in that moment, Harry glimpsed beyond Barbara's startled face and into a sorrow that lay beneath. For an instant it could have been his own face in that licence, his wife's, even one of his kids'. It made Harry want to go back into the garage and sift through all those things which had cluttered the car, look for something he might have missed, not money, something more personal, something that would testify for Barbara: evidence she'd been here, engaged, participating.

When Harry turned, Col and the kids were seated and waiting. He set down the licence, walked to the table and raised his glass. "To life," he said. For a moment his children and his wife just looked at him. In all the weeks they'd been making toasts Harry had never offered one, but now he held steady with his glass in the air until one by one, the family raised their cups and toasted life. They drank, and when Harry sat, the family began to eat.

JENNIFER CLOUTER

Benny and the Jets

The lights in the house across the street began coming on. I had parked practically in front of the place, and sat up immediately. This address was proving a tough nut to crack – a tightly stitched Victorian house immaculately manicured, fenced and illuminated by motion-detecting lights. *No problem, Benny.* The problem was the curtains. The blinds. The fucking shutters. Always drawn and closed at the moment of dusk. Then the lights would come on, apricot and orange windows lit like lanterns containing the tantalizing, shadowy flashes of their occupants. Such careful people. I glance up and down the street without unrolling the window. My breath is fogging up the glass. No one around. That's good. I open the door of the car and get out, shutting it silently behind me. The asphalt shines, black and oily under the streetlights. The air is cold, thick with mist. Fluttering moths fall through it, eerily luminescent. They fall dead in white drifts against the curb. In the distance the foghorn lows and the shush of wet tires rises up from the street as a cop car slides past. I wait for it to move on before crossing. As I walk up the driveway, the car keys in my hand jingle. Tossing them jauntily in the air, I catch them overhand. I pretend I live here. The fine hair on the nape of my neck rises, and the slow prickle of it produces a shiver. I can feel my pupils dilate when I reach the shaded area beyond the cobblestone driveway. I'm an interested animal. Curious. Sniff the air. I smell the mulch of garden, the rot of wet leaves fallen for months. It's like fresh bread, crumbling.

It was summer. The summer I was four. I remember I was running, chasing someone. Something. I was in the vacant lot at the centre of our block, where the older kids hung out. Drug dealers, high-school dropouts. They smoked cigarettes in the stripped shell of a car that had been abandoned in the lot. It rested on its rims not far from Mrs. Cahill's house that burned down during the winter. All that was left was the black hole of the foundation. A dark pit in the centre of the lot, filled a foot deep with broken glass. Bake Parsons, Jonny Lalli, and Pills Murphy spent a lot of time there, drinking beer. Whenever they finished a bottle they'd spin the amber empty high into the air, to smash in the gaping hole the burned house left behind. The black hole filled steadily with brown glass as the summer warmed. I remember taking my shirt off that day in the sparkling light and running like the wind through suspended motes, over crumbled concrete, holding the shirt like a sail high over my head. Bake and Jonny calling out *Whaddaya at, Benny?* and *Runnin, are ya?* Bake lived next door; his real name was Wayne. Jonny Lalli and Pills lived a few doors down. I considered all of them my close and personal friends. They'd been sitting on nearby stoops, curbs, fenders and bumpers drinking beer and selling hash, for my entire life.

The thing I was chasing was a butterfly, now I remember. It fluttered erratically, great big velvety wings, brown and blue and white, just out of reach. I wanted to catch it, but the real unparalleled excitement I felt was of running fast, by myself, in front of Pills, Bake, and Jonny. Showing off. They were giants in flared jeans and platform boots. Their long greasy hair stank of smoke. I ran, arms outstretched, reaching for the butterfly, but really concentrating on my feet and the ground blurring past beneath them. A few trees overhead shed yellow green spring light. There seemed to be a million motes of dust, chaff and tiny bugs filling the air. Pills and Jonny laughing because now I was running in great looping circles. *Look at 'im go, Bake, Benny and the Jets or wha?* Breathing fast, running faster. Laughing because Pills and Jonny were laughing. Then, Bake running. The fastest I had ever seen him move. Yelling, maybe more like screaming. In the sunshiny haze, I tumbled end over end. A sudden unending fumble of sneakers and blood and screaming. Surprise black pit stitched with glass.

I came to as Bake yanked me up and into his arms. He stood in the pit, up to his ankles in broken glass, and I screamed and snotted and bled all over him. He was crying. Jonny and Pills looked over the charred edge of the foundation, all white eyes. *Jesus fucking Christ, Bake.* I screamed on and on in great whooping gulps. Black spots swarmed like bugs in front of my face, my throat became a thick purple constriction as I howled. The day shimmered. Heatwaves sent their invisible smoke up all around us. An ocean of amber glass, broken and sparking like fire. *Bake, he all right? Benny all right?* The mild heat of fresh blood cooled on my skin. Bake's dirty hands slipped in it feeling for broken bones. Hash oil sweat oozed from the back of his neck as I clung to him, howling, no longer a little boy, just a small animal. Fractured, this moment is stitched back together in my memory. Falling, a sea of broken glass. The liquid shimmer of summer drenching us.

Around back the sculpted garden is shrouded in mist. Secret scents lead me like an animal to the grey slate patio. There is a window, orange lit and full round like a harvest moon. This time I silence the faint domestic jingle of my car keys in the centre of my sweaty fist. Move like water, like darkness. Like oil. I watch for pit traps sunk in black corners, seek slices of darkness. Spin myself a shroud of wet scent and shadows. This place was light-tight by god and now, finally, the creamy smooth expanse of its arse end is lit up like a peep show.

Whadd'ja do that for, Benny? I'm eleven and seeing out of only one eye. The other is bandaged in clean white gauze, sealing in a moist soup of oozing fluid and ointment. There are angry red blisters covering my cheeks and chin. My older brother, Brent, is sitting on my bed squeezing a soccer ball between his knees. *I dunno.* I examine my hands – small wrists, chewed nails, a flock of small hooked scars. *Stupid.* Brent delivers this gem from under smirking brows. The ball pulses rhythmically between his knees. *I wanted to see what it would look like.* Brent lets the ball drop from between his knees and stops its bounce by stepping on it. *Mom's still crying ya know. Idiot.* I pick at the edge of my blanket. I can hear her in the kitchen, chopping things and washing things and crying away. Brent's eyes glimmer maliciously. *Retard.* He stands and with an expert toe flips the soccer ball up into his open hand. *You're never going to get laid.*

Attracted by the light from the window more late fall moths batter gently against the glass, ghostly white. Inside, a dining table. Mellow gleaming wood and a big stone fireplace. Great warm flames bounce and sputter inside, the whole room pulses with firelight, wavers with warmth. My breath is a shiver and it briefly fogs a grey circle on the cool glass. Too close, I back up a step and the dark night falls in on me, heavy. Someone has entered the room. My insides are water, a loose rush that leaches strength from my legs. In the same breath the prickle is back, up the length of my spine and stitching me back together. *There's no way she can see me, no way, Benny.* On her side the window is full of reflected flames from the fireplace. That's all she can see, the wall of fire between us.

We were camping in Bogwood Branch. Mom and Dad and Brent were roasting marshmallows over the roaring fire. In the shadow of brush nearby I could hear the snap and crackle of the flames, the occasional juicy *pop* as a bubble of sap in the green spruce boughs burst from the intense heat. Mom was shrieking and laughing, jumping away from showers of red flankers continually exploding in the damp branches. Dad slapping her butt and saying things like *Red-hot, Marsha!* Brent chasing her with his gooey marshmallow stick. The smell of wood smoke in everything, in my hair like hickory, like kippers. Nobody seemed to notice I was gone and it was unlikely anyone would look for matches either, because the fire was already lit. Dad had emptied the last of the kerosene onto the damp boughs and tossed in a single match. After slow smoking for a few seconds, the pile lit with an audible thump. Cool. I kept my eye on that can. Brent had it for a while, poked it full of holes with his pocket knife while I watched the fire. Sawing away at it with bullish intensity. His tongue stuck out wetly. *See anything green, snotface?* I shook my head. *Yeah, thought so.* A good bed of embers was building up. Ashy grey with red hot worms slithering across. Little worms eating fire.

Inside. There's a whole world of light sewn up in this dark Victorian house. White moths cling to the glass, powdery wings shivering in the escaping light. I can see their legs, serrated white, clinging to nothing. Lacy feelers trembling, twitching the night for the right female pheromones. About my feet their small white corpses disintegrate on the patio stones, worn from battering themselves so gently against the glass. The woman in that room is real, no mistake. She's no shadow puppet moving vaguely beyond stiffly drawn blinds. Like a match struck, her flame is suddenly the brightest thing anywhere and I have to step back. Breathing too hard. Gotta keep it under control. Believe the match of her won't go out. In the shadows I recede as she crosses the room to the kitchen counter, pouring herself a glass of wine from an open bottle there. She sips it standing at the counter as the firelight ripples across the room, streaming over the ceiling and down the walls like water.

Alone in the brush I gripped the empty stabbed kerosene can between my knees. Held my miniflashlight between my teeth and peered into the bottom. Brent's industrious destruction hadn't emptied the last drops; a thin sheen of fuel still shimmered in the very bottom of the can. A whole rainbow shining and trapped in there. Seemed prettier than it should have and I just breathed and squinted into the faint fumes. Thought about the *thump* when the pile of boughs caught fire. The delicate lace of flame crawling the branches and then suddenly exploding. Suddenly becoming *something*, a force to be reckoned with. I took the matches from my back pocket. There wasn't enough oil for a big thump, but maybe enough to burn low inside the can. Enough to be real cool. Brent had no idea what cool was, stabbing with his stupid knife, chasing with his stupid stick. I opened the box of matches. Only three left; had to be right on the mark with at least one. The first time I pressed too hard and the head of the struck match flamed off into the darkness. By the fire I could hear Mom and Dad singing one of their stupid songs and stupid Brent joining in. Well, I'd have my own fire. Maybe I'd bring it back with me to the campsite, a metal box filled with fire. With the holes Brent put in it, it would be like a really awesome flashlight. A caveman flashlight. The second match trembled out of my fingers before I could strike it, landing in the wet moss at my feet. Frig. I said a small prayer over the last one. *Please Holy God, I need to light this match.* Sulfur scraped sandpaper and a flame appeared like a small orange flower. *ThankyouGod.* Quickly, before the faint spruce-scented breeze could whiff it out, I dropped the small flickering thing into the narrow metal neck of the can and immediately glued my left eye to the opening. The match sputtered undramatically in the bottom of the can, almost going out and then suddenly shooting down the length of the small wooden stick. The metal inside the can shimmered brightly, first orange, then yellow. *Cool.* The smell of burning oil began to coat my nostrils, and my eye, pressed to the metal neck, began to water. With a sudden fluff the sheen of oil slicking the interior of the container ignited. Low blue flame stuttered inside, apricot tipped, liquid and rounded. Flowing like water. Slithering like a snake. With a low *punk* one of the many dents in the side of the can suddenly popped itself out with the heat of the fire. Then, racing up the inside of the can, red flame suddenly ravaging. A coughing roar as the fumes built up inside ignited and exploded. Landing on my back in the wet moss. Silence. Alone in the blackness except for the flaming wreckage of the can lying some feet beyond me. Dad yelling my name in some terrible way. I was falling through the woodsy night, alone again in the flashing red of skin and fire.

As I edge back to the pane glass window the wet cloak of fog thickens and damp moths fall around me, some clinging to my coat. Watching this big bay window I can understand why people like to watch TV. You know, so they can *watch*. Get right up close to the curved glass and look into the eyes of someone famous. Anyone. Try to see what makes them tick. In their small blue flickering boxes, they *want* to be watched. I don't care for TV myself. Hate watching people watching it, too. There's nothing worse than catching a glimpse of some cold blue room through a window. Some corpse slumped in front of it like a raw side of beef in some icy meat locker, trying to thaw itself with that constant cold blue flame. Not here though. This whole house is a lit lantern with a lucky cricket inside. So far so good. No rapid breathing yet, no panicked hyperventilation in the shadows. Legs still sturdy, heart rate only slightly elevated. The thump and pulse of my own fluids is only just beginning to sicken me. Those tides constantly churning inside made me throw up all the time in school. Sometimes even made me faint. I lean forward and peer inside, careful not to crush the moths fluttering at my feet.

I am sixteen. With some people, out at night. Teenagers running wild. Drinking in the graveyard. Brent is there, necking with one of the girls on top of a crypt. She's moaning. I'm still a virgin. The other two have crept off into the bushes for similar entertainment. Alone. I drink my beer and walk over the graves, headstones ghostly white and leaning against each other forever in the dark. I can hear faint giggles and the sudden smash of a beer bottle shattering on someone's tombstone. Dark in here. I try not to care that I don't have a girl, or that I'm walking by myself. I head for the old section of the cemetery, the fenced in part. Graves there so old they're almost invisible. Names and verses erased by wind, rain. I hate the tiny ones, the ones for kids and babies. Especially the ones where they make the iron fence look like a crib. A tiny, tiny crib holding a black infant corpse, a small pile of bones like birds. They don't mean anything any more. Fences around dirt, around stones. Tiny iron cribs tangled in the centre of rose bushes grown enormous and lush with abundant fertilizer.

The constant night runs on and on overhead, pricked by stars, cold and unyielding. Inside, the woman drinks her wine. Outside, my joints grind together in the damp dark and fluids percolate through my body. Brain fluid, spinal fluid, blood, bile, plasma, sweat and tears. All of it sloshes inside me like a skin full of wine. The thumping pressure of watching *is* starting to get to me. The orange pulse of light inside is becoming sickeningly liquid. The white flash of wings outside, shimmering white noise. Deafening. Only the steady thump of my body is keeping me warm.

My lucky cricket stretches her legs and paces her orange-shimmered aquarium. In front of the fire she warms her hands. She stands very still and dark hair falls to hide her face. The ceiling arches over her like the sky, her loneliness lights it up. She's crying. The small shake of her shoulders is like the trembling moths surrounding me on all sides.

I realize I want her to look up.

I'm standing at the base of the biggest tombstone in the cemetery. The night sky is wheeling overhead. In my beery haze it twists and turns, constellations like sinuous snakes, the edge of our galaxy like spilled milk across it. Brent is gettin it somewhere in the darkness. I can hear him and his girl grunting and cursing. I feel very alone and stupid. Sorry for myself in the black beery night. I want to see something. Anything. Things no one else can see. Everything. If I could just get up high enough. The tombstone in front of me is at least ten feet tall. A muscular angel with arching wings holds aloft an enormous cross. The angel's face is worn away, nothing but a smooth blank caul. Her empty eyes look right past me – I'll climb up, that's what I'll do. Right up over her rounded marble back. Grasping those magnificent wings for leverage, I monkey my way up the cross, skinning the palms of my hands and jabbing my crotch a good one on a marble wingtip. Then I'm at the top, legs hooked around the arms of the cross, arms wrapped around the top of the post. Whole graveyard spread before me and I'm at the centre, surrounded on all sides by angels, by corpses, by the beautiful night. I'm smiling up there. I can see Brent smoking a cigarette. His coat is wrapped around the girl and their heads are close together. He'll get a kick out of this.

As if she's heard me, the crying woman suddenly raises her head. She's listening, I can tell. Her face is still wet. I guess she's heard something. Maybe it's my heart she hears, one sick thump after another. I am my telltale heart. I am beating without a body. *I am one big eye.* Head cocked in my direction, she is one big ear. I am a whisper, she is the Bionic Woman. Turning, she faces the big window for the first time. For the first time, I don't shrink into the shadows.

Brent and his girl are holding hands. They're walking towards the gate. Leaving. Didn't even bother to call out to me. Who gives a fuck. They're going to walk past right underneath me. I won't make a sound. Serve them right, go home alone. But as soon as they're close enough I yell. Brent jumps, squeals like a little girl. He backs up quick and trips on a broken tombstone, falling right on his ass in someone's grave. I'm laughing hysterically, slapping the cross, nearly slipping off. Brent scrambles himself up, looking around wildly. His girl is crying about ten feet away. *Benny, you're a fucking cunt.* He's really mad, which makes it all pretty funny. *I'll fucking kill you.*

She doesn't see me, she sees the fire. I'm sure of it. Though she's looking right at me. Suddenly I really can't breathe. I'm drowning in my own bilious fluids, they're filling up my throat and I can't turn away. She walks toward the window slow, surely only seeing the reflection of the room behind her. Surely not seeing me, surely not seeing me at all. I am one big eye with no breath left, *I am one big eye filling up with blackness*. Everything disappears. Fluttering white moths on the fringe of my vision. Tiny beads of rain appearing on the glass between us, she reaches out her hand.

Brent is grabbing for my legs, trying to haul me down off the cross. I kick at him, catching him in the temple. This only infuriates him further, he's like a pit bull. I can't believe his stupid strength, his persistence – *Why don't you go fuck your girlfriend some more?* Brent's red, infuriated face hangs below me, mouth working copious spittle into frustrated rage. *You stupid fruit. You asshole. Grow up, Benny, just fucking* GROW UP. With that he delivers a solid soccer kick to the angel's head. A goddamn field goal. The faceless face crumbles; in three pieces it falls to the ground. The whole night sways around me. I thought I was getting sick but it was the marble cross swaying. Ten feet in the air, I feel it lose its anchor in the angel's back. Have to get off. It's going to fall. But my legs are hooked firmly around the arms and I can't untangle myself as the massive thing begins its monolithic backward swoon.

The woman inside is so close. I see her concerned blue eyes, unbrushed hair, both palms against the glass. She wants to see me. I want to be seen. *We want to be one big eye together.* I reach out and place the palm of my hand on the glass, over hers. The whole world begins to fade. It disappears. My head is an empty ringing and my legs give out, pitching me forward. Falling in the dark night, forever. Into the warm orange fire on the other side, I crash through the window in a splintered shower of glass, limp and blameless in a flutter of white moths and a single word of apology.

– *Sorry* –

I hit the ground on my back, legs pinned behind my ears by the huge marble cross. I'm definitely hurt. Bad I think. My head is spinning with the falling, the climbing, the watching. My back is a giant flame of pain. Brent stands over me. *Stupid fuck. Serves ya right.* I want him to help me, haul off the cross, free me. He stands over me, smirking. *One word, Benny. One word and I'll help you out. One little tiny word. Come on retard.* He places his sneakered foot on the crux of the cross and presses down. He is killing me, my breath is gone. The spinning sky is empty.

I'm so sorry . . .

MICHAEL V. SMITH

What We Wanted

Barry Somer's body went from screaming round the pool, rapping on foreheads, swinging from the shower rail, and flinging boogers to doing nothing at all, to disappearing, to dying. When he was eleven a dump truck flattened him against its grill and then the crumpled boy that was Barry Somer slipped under the truck and disappeared. That's when I looked away.

The crowd of neighbours that came out to help, or gawk, or bring their kids back into the house saw the smashed and tattered body that was Barry, but I didn't. I was the last to see Barry as Barry and not a broken mash of whatever bones and skin and hair death leaves behind. And if I'm right, I was the last thing he saw too.

They can say what they want, but I wasn't haunted by Barry's death. That was something of a relief. It was the living Barry that woke me up with night sweats and had me vomiting two out of three meals. I never told them. In the twenty years since, I have never told another living thing.

We were boys together. When my mother wanted me to join a sports team to impress my father – I was a miserably underweight gangle of arms and legs – she claimed all I needed was exercise to grow meat on my ribs. The weight sounded appealing. I picked swimming because it was the only non-contact sport we could agree on. We bought a pair of baggy green swim trunks at the Kmart and reserved a place for me over the phone. I was moderately excited. I had visions of myself heftier, doing elaborate dives that I would choreograph in my head in slow motion. I would touch my nose with my feet. I'd be amazing.

My first day of lessons started after supper on a Tuesday. Mom decided to make something light so I wouldn't get cramps, but the cold cuts and salad irritated my dad. They bickered until I told them swimming lessons weren't worth going to if it only made them fight. My mom looked at the digital clock on the microwave and packed up our plates. "We're late," she said.

As she turned into the parking lot for the community centre, halfway through a cigarette, Mom sighed, "You could help me out a little here. Is your father doing all this for nothing?" She gestured at the brick wall ahead of us. I shrugged and opened the car door.

She took a slow drag on the cigarette. "Sometimes, I don't think you like us," she added, chipping at her nail polish.

Unsure what she meant, I smiled nicely, trying to convince us it was a joke, and closed the door. I can see she thought I was cruel. Perhaps I was. I didn't like them much. I didn't like their drinking and the scenes my mother made. I didn't like the way they could bellow at each other and, mid-sentence, how my mother could pick up the ringing telephone and sound sweet as heaven. My life felt small and cramped. We were neither financially comfortable nor well adjusted. I hated my body. I invented friends at school whom my mother asked to meet. I told threatening classmates I had an older, bigger brother who went to a school across town. I lived a lie to protect myself from my parents and another to save me from kids at recess.

Walking into the community centre with my swim trunks and towel in a plastic grocery bag, I saw three boys in ball caps goofing around. We'd signed me up for an all-boys group because Dad said it would be more competitive, but, oddly, the swim instructor turned out to be a woman. Jenny was tall and lean, with unusually rough hands, and long chlorine-blonde hair around a tight little happy face. She was pretty enough, but more a failed movie-version of a lifeguard than an actual bombshell.

My mother came in after me and filled out the forms, signed her cheque, and said she'd be back for me. "Have fun," she coached, tousling my hair, which she'd never done before, in a move designed to make me look the part of a sporty kid.

I had never seen a public indoor pool. Dad didn't swim, which made paying for an hour at an indoor pool an unnecessary luxury. Swimming either involved a trip to the beach to wade in the river or a three-block walk to the local park's gated and crowded cement pool open for the height of summer. As the door to the change room closed behind me, I knew again that I had fooled myself into thinking things could change. I was sick with fear at what the next eight weeks held in store for me. We were sixteen prepubescent boys who already seemed to be grouping off into cool and uncool, in a cement room, without windows, with a large shower area, a row of freshly painted toilet stalls, and two sets of urinals, kid height and adult.

What I never realized until standing in that mess of boys was that we would all be taking our clothes off, unseen by the instructor. Already I was trying to devise ways to get out of swimming. Jenny could be dangerously careless or the pool water would burn my skin. I considered faking an accident, only I was fearful that I might drown for real.

Perhaps Barry noticed a look of dread on me right away. Perhaps he saw my doubts running across my face, but I didn't notice him when I came in. I have no idea where he was in the mix of boys pulling their shirts off. At that age, I tried not to look at boys. By comparison, my own skin felt softer, unconvincing, fake. I wasn't real like other kids were real. I didn't exist the way other boys made space for themselves in the world. It was – and is – a truth I stand by, that when boys take their clothes off, they *need* to be noticed and respected, which paradoxically makes them cruel. Watching them was both taboo and what they dared you to do.

I headed straight through the change room with barely a glance at anyone. I locked myself into a stall with a loud click of the deadbolt and slipped my trunks on.

When I came out, Barry Somer was waiting for me, holding up my pale blue briefs. He'd grabbed them from under the cubicle without my noticing. "Cute," he said, smiling. "They're like cotton candy."

He was a big kid, big in his hands and feet, with a thick neck, which made him seem more muscled than he was. He had clean hair that looked freshly cut. From first sight, I knew he wasn't menacing, not mean, but restless. He was a nice, attractive kid. It was just the two of us in the change room's white tiled bathroom area and he was smiling a killer smile at me.

"Where do you live? I'm across the street."

"On Carlisle."

"Which house?"

"It's yellow, why?"

He shrugged, and handed me my underwear, no jokes, no teasing, no humiliation, which dropped my heart to the lower depths of my stomach. With that bit of generosity, he was capable of convincing me to do just about anything. The look on his face said he knew it, and he couldn't wait.

I took my flimsy briefs from him and tucked them in a leg of my pants and rolled them up. Next week, I'd bring a knapsack with a zipper to keep a better hold on my stuff.

When my father asked me later that night as he turned the ground for my mother's flower bed how the "swim thing" went, I choked on my plan to get out of it.

"Great," I said.

"How many laps did you do?"

"We don't do laps."

He looked puzzled, not at me, but at the shovel sticking into the dirt. "What do you do?"

"We hold our breath. And dog-paddle. And the dead man's float." I thought he knew all this. "We're just learning. It's a beginner's class."

"But you can swim," he said. He looked me in the eye with a wrinkled brow.

"You have to do the first class," I lied, authoritatively, "before you start doing laps."

"Oh. So you'll do laps when you're done?"

"Next week," I lied again. There seemed no point trying to explain the organization of levels and testing and badges. "We'll do lots of laps," I said and he went back to gardening.

Perhaps I'm more like my father than I care to admit. I don't like children. When they begin to talk in full sentences, when school comes into their lives and they associate with each other, their minds change. I'm convinced they warp, betrayed by the trust they placed in their parents. How could we not resent being abandoned to a room of noisy spoiled strangers, each wanting to be cute and loved and necessary at the expense of every other demanding kid in the room? How to retaliate? How do we lose our fear to feel secure in our abandonment? We create roles for each other grounded in shame, guilt, humiliation, and fear. Those who invent the harshest situations for their peers are the ones who feel most secure.

Barry Somer had a talent for making himself feel better. Our first week there, he convinced a slim, hairy kid, Arvid, to hand over his case of retainers. Barry quickly slipped them on his own teeth and sang a poor, but effective, rendition of *Happy Birfday*. The jokes weren't particularly clever, but they came from nowhere. It was his spontaneity that fascinated, which saw us waiting for the next prank as we dreaded his attention.

For the third lesson, Barry and I were paired up as floating partners. Jenny showed the group of us how we were to support each other under the lower back as we tried to relax, with our eyes closed, and float face up. Holding her whistle, Jenny explained, "Now the person standing will lower his arms when the floater says, Okay, at which point the floater will be held on top of the water. It's real easy if you just relax."

My cousins had tried this trick with me a few times the previous summer. I wasn't expecting much.

"You ready?" Barry smiled at me. "You're first." His hand underwater absently toyed with the drawstring hanging out of his trunks.

Jenny walked towards us, stopping just to our left, checking to see if everyone was in place. "All set?" she asked, and blew her whistle.

As Barry extended his arms in front of him, I let my legs give way and was lifted into a cradled position next to his chest. He was warm. It wasn't what I expected it to be. It wasn't scary, it wasn't nerve-wracking, it wasn't exciting. With Barry's arms under me, I felt, oddly, safe. He was comfortable. I opened my eyes to see him looking at me, inches above my face.

"I got you," he said, so I closed them again, giving my okay and trusting my body to do what it had to. Barry let me go. My skin felt cold in two lines across my back where his arms had been.

The water gurgled in my ears and lapped loosely at my temples as my hair swirled about my head. The thick smell of chlorine settled in my nose. My arms and legs felt both heavy and light. The more I relaxed the muscles, the more I could feel my own weight held atop the water. If I needed him, Barry was there to catch me before I sank. With the dead man's float, you face down, like you've given up, but with my face to the ceiling, I felt hopeful, like I was waiting for something, like at any moment I might rise up out of the water and fly.

With a sudden bleat of Jenny's whistle, time was up. "Good!" she called. I stood, feeling a little disoriented, carrying my weight. "Now let's switch places. The rest of you float."

Barry punched my shoulder. "You did good. Don't drop me," he said, and jumped into my arms with a splash of water. He hitched his arms around my neck so that even if I let him go, I'd still be supporting us both, then he proceeded to bounce. "Am I heavy? Heavy? Can you hold me?"

"That's enough, Barry, get ready," Jenny said, the whistle between her teeth. As she travelled the width of the pool again to ensure we were all set up, Barry stretched himself out.

"Ahhh," he sighed, and then smiled at me. He was heavier in the water than I thought he'd be. I was wondering how heavy I had been and was hoping, secretly, that he wouldn't float at all, when he whispered, "You wearing your blue underwear?"

I squinted at him, confused. "Not under my bathing suit."

"No, today. I want to know if you got them here today?"

"What for?" I asked.

"I want to try them on," he said as the whistle blew. He closed his eyes, stretched himself out and said, "Okay." I let him go and stepped back. He floated butt-heavy at first, then managed to relax into it more, though he took his breath in rapid gulps.

When the lesson came to a close, I headed for the change room. Barry was right behind me. Inside, I took my bag off the bench and walked into the bathroom area. Another kid, Stevie, with acne, changed in a stall too, which made me feel less like a freak, though Stevie raced to be the first kid in and out of the room. When I arrived each week, he was already in the pool, or waiting on the tiled deck, his swim trunks on and a towel wrapped around his shoulders.

Stevie was in the stall at the far end of the room when I walked in. I could hear him bumping around. I chose a stall mid-way, pushed the door open and entered. By the time I turned around, Barry was there. I just looked at him, my heart doing laps in my chest. "No," I said, barely even whispering.

He glanced from the doorway to the last stall where Stevie was still shuffling, and mouthed, "Come on," like he was about to get seriously caught, so I stepped back, letting Barry in.

As he pulled cotton boxers from his bag and held them out, he motioned with his free hand for me to give up my briefs. What was I supposed to do with the boxers? I wasn't putting on someone else's underwear. Barry bugged his eyes out, making a frustrated face, to hurry me up. Both of us were dripping wet. He was nearly standing on top of me, a towel around his neck and mine about my waist. If I couldn't talk to him, I didn't know how to get him out of the stall without giving him my briefs. And, yes, I wanted to see him do it; I wanted to see Barry Somer in my underwear.

I handed them over. Without hesitating, he dropped his swimsuit and stepped out of the legs. I caught sight of his dink, redder than mine, when he hunched over and slipped his first foot through the leg. I could smell the chlorine in his hair. He didn't bother to dry off.

We heard a metal door squeak open and Stevie pad by, in too much of a rush to notice the number of feet in our stall. Barry winked at me, grinning. "I like them," he said. I grimaced like I didn't know what he was talking about. He looked down at himself, packed into my underwear, with wet marks spotting the cloth. I was excited, and thankful to have the towel around my waist.

Motioning to the boxers in my hand, he coaxed, "Put them on."

I frowned, shaking my head. For one, I had an erection. And we'd taken long enough changing as it was. My mother wasn't going to wait forever. Somewhat irrational though it may have been, I was terrified she'd see me.

"You gotta do it sometime," he said, and then with a click of the lock, he stepped out of the stall, snatched up his swim trunks, and added, "See ya next week." He towelled his hair, pushing the door closed in my face. A few seconds later, I heard him say as he entered the change room, "That was the longest dump of my life." Somebody laughed.

Meanwhile, I had Barry Somer's underwear in my hand and none of my own to put on. I was late. And felt freaked out. I stuffed his boxers in my bag, dried myself, and dressed, without underwear. I'd get a fresh pair when I got home.

Safely in my room, I closed the door, dropped the knapsack on my bed, and grabbed yesterday's briefs off the floor to put them on. I'd no sooner picked up my pants again when there was a knock-knock on the door and dad came directly in.

"Your mother wanted your wet things," he explained. He looked uncomfortable. I held my pants in front of me. "You forgot to drop them in the tub."

"I'll bring them," I said.

"Just give it here, I already made the trip," he answered, sounding like he wanted to be nice but was really feeling impatient. "Are they in here?" he asked. He took hold of my bag. "I've got them."

With that, Barry's grey cotton boxers left the safety of my bedroom. I whipped my pants on, visualizing my father holding up a foreign pair of boy's undies and asking me questions I couldn't answer. I had only been seconds behind him, but already Dad was in the bathroom with my mother. When I reached the door, he was just exiting.

The wet swim trunks dropped in the tub as I stepped around Dad. The towel was in Mom's hands, with the boxers lying plainly on top. "What's this?" she asked. She knew I only had briefs; she'd bought every pair I owned.

Dad turned around. I froze. Mom caught my terrified look and turned her back.

"Mom, I said I'll *do* it." I tried to sound thoughtfully exasperated.

"What's what?" Dad asked.

"His underwear's wet too, that's all." Mom hung them over the shower curtain rod, then threw the towel up too. She made a point of not looking at me.

"We were joking around in the change room," I said, trying to sound normal.

"And you got your clothes wet?" Dad asked.

I shrugged. "Boys were throwing water. I was getting dressed."

"Well, that's not such a big deal," he said. Then, as an afterthought, he asked, "How many laps did you do this week?"

I told him fifteen. Last week I'd said ten.

"Good," he said, and I followed him out. If Mom didn't get me alone right then, I was hoping she'd never come back to ask.

The next week I missed class because my dad had to drive to Caledon to help a guy from work fix his refrigerator. My mom wouldn't take me on the bus or let me go alone. I didn't think it was in my own best interests to debate; she hadn't confronted me about the boxers. I'd taken them down that night and hung them to dry on the door handle inside my closet, safely out of sight. For two weeks, they were stored between my mattress and box spring, except for the odd time when I took them out to look at. When the time came, I slipped the boxers inside my swim trunks and folded the whole thing over, just in case someone looked in my bag.

Though I insisted I could at least take the bus there, Mom was firmly determined to drive me. Since she'd decided to act like nothing was wrong, I had taken her lead, but the tension only made her petty.

Barry was waiting outside the community centre, doing his best to look nonchalant as he leaned against a concrete post, scratching a rock against the wall. Right away, Mom scowled. "Look at that kid. Be lucky you don't have his parents," she said, pulling our rusty Acadian up to the curb.

I jumped out immediately before Barry could make any move towards me. "Bye, see ya later," I said cheerily to my mother, then slammed the door shut and jogged past Barry to the entrance.

He followed me inside. Safely through the doors and out of sight of my mother, I turned to Barry. "Do you have them?" He smiled, patting the side of his leg. "Give them to me," I ordered, thinking they were in his pocket.

Taking me by the wrist, he led us across the hall into the girls' change room, which was empty, and into one of their bathroom stalls. There were two rows of them, instead of a wall of urinals. It was a weird feeling, like being in a world gone wrong. "How are we going to get out?" I asked.

Barry giggled. "Through the door."

"What about Jenny? She's gonna change here."

"She's in the pool already."

My stomach was in knots. Barry was breathing heavy enough for me to feel his warm air against my skin. He stood inches away from me. The girls' stalls, painted light green, had an extra dispenser on the wall beside the toilet paper. I felt crowded. "I brought yours," I said. "Let's trade."

As I pulled my bag open, Barry undid the button on his jeans and unzipped them. "What are you doing?" I asked.

"I have them on."

For a second, I had the impression he'd worn them the whole two weeks, but then realized he must not have wanted to carry an extra pair with him, which I thought was smart, though I wasn't able to put his pair on, even with my parents out of the house. "Okay," I said. I turned more towards the back of the stall to give him privacy. Though I wanted to see his dink again, I couldn't bring myself to look. There was some general shuffling. I could see him bend over in my peripheral vision and then he stood, silent. It occurred to me that now was the time to turn and hand him the boxers, giving me a chance to peek, but I couldn't bring myself to do it. My stomach roiled and burned in my belly. Taking his boxers, I held them out at my side, waiting. He didn't take them. There was a silence in the bathroom that made me crazy; only the low hum of the pool's filtering system travelled through the walls.

Then he touched me. He set a finger against my arm. I turned, with my heart pounding, afraid of what he might make me do. He was still in my briefs, with his pants on the floor beside him. "I like you," he said. There was an awkward smile on his face. As I stood there, unmoving, he played with his belly button. He was trying to explain something neither of us understood. "I think you're pretty," he continued. "My brother has a girlfriend and they make out. I kissed this girl on the bus once, with everyone watching. She gave me the tongue. She didn't really like me though. You have nice eyes. Sometimes my mother wears makeup on her eyes, but my dad doesn't like it. Do you have a brother? Or a sister?"

I couldn't stop myself from sounding belligerent. "No," I snapped, unnerving him.

And he said again, "You're pretty," which made me angry. We were eleven – we knew we could lie to each other to get what we wanted, but I didn't want to be talked into kissing him. I couldn't kiss a boy voluntarily. *Was he stupid?* I wondered. *Could he be that stupid?* I hated him offering me this in such a way that I wasn't allowed to accept. I hated the way he was so desperate to convince. Had he only humiliated me in private, had he insisted then, with force, with threatening intent, we'd have both been happy.

Three days later, with Barry's boxers out of my bedroom and my own underwear back in the dresser drawer – I hadn't put them in the wash, I couldn't yet – I felt my life was given back to me and I was safe. The only threat Barry posed was what trouble he might cause each Tuesday night and I intended to ignore him. I imagined how it would sting him, to see that I was uninterested. Done.

It was the weekend, late Friday afternoon. My mother had sent my Dad to buy two trees to plant along the back fence because she wanted something to look at from their bedroom window. Dad wanted dogwood he'd seen advertised in the paper, but Mom said no. When she heard the car pull up, the trunk door slam shut, and Dad didn't come in, she went to the window and called out, "What did you get?"

He said something that made her yell, "What the hell for?" and I heard him shout back, "They were on sale." That's when I figured I was better off at the park. I hung out on the monkey bars until some teenaged girls showed up with their boyfriends trailing behind.

I was gone an hour. When I got back, Mom was at the sink rinsing a shirt she'd stained at lunch. "Your friend was here on his bike," she said, very matter-of-fact.

I blinked. "Who?" I asked.

"That kid from swimming." Her tone said she wasn't impressed; it was obvious to her who was sending his underwear home with her son. "I told him you were at the park. He's coming back."

"He's not my friend," I said sourly.

Mom gave the shirt a twist and wrung out a stream of water. "Then how's he know where you live? You shouldn't tell just anybody our address. It isn't safe."

I shrugged.

"We're having supper in an hour; he's got to be gone by then," she said, turning on the tap to end the discussion.

Anxious, I decided to wait on the front lawn. He wasn't coming in my house. I wouldn't even let him on the property. When he pulled up on his bike, I'd tell him he had to go home because my grandmother was sick, or I hated him, or my parents didn't like me hanging out with losers. I was busy devising the fastest way to get rid of him as my stomach lurched with anticipation. Barry Somer came to see me. *Me.*

At the end of the block, a bicycle came round the corner. There he was, Barry Somer, in his blue-and-green-striped T-shirt and headphones stuck over his ears, biking down my street, passing along the sidewalk on the other side of the road. I called out to him, but he didn't hear me, so I waved. As he looked over, he grinned and my stomach clenched tighter.

Then, like careful planning, a dump truck turned the corner. Directly across from me, a moving van parked on the road at the Kennedy's blocked Barry's view of the street. And the thoughts ran through my head, the various feelings: this dump truck, that boy, this heartsickness, that bike, this hand of mine, that driver, that truck, that boy. I decided on impulse. If he made it across the road before the truck sped past, I would give in to what we wanted and be Barry's fair and hungry equal, or I could see it all go to pieces with one simple accident and never be plagued by Barry Somer again. I motioned him over.

For the split second of his impact, I froze, Barry and I both breathless. I didn't believe he'd be hit. I didn't believe it could happen until it did. For a second, he was a cartoon: arms splayed, his mouth a black spot, and one rubber leg swinging under the truck. The bike bent around the other leg.

Then, easily, Barry Somer was dead.

I bolted for the house just as my father raced out onto the porch. Behind me was the noise of squealing tires, the truck's horn, and scraping metal. In my few seconds to the door, I tried to gauge by Dad's manner if he had witnessed me with Barry or just Barry getting hit. Remembering back, all I see is a man who would betray nothing. He was a grim, stone-faced father, with hands that shook, racing to the road where a boy lay broken. I ran into the house, and my room, and dove under the bed in a sweat.

From that day forward, I disappeared. I was free. My parents forgot me, what they wanted from me and what they wished I was. So I come forward now because I can, to tell you, I killed a boy. I live with that, with perhaps less difficulty than you might expect, because it's prepared me, hasn't it, for the way we love one another?

KENNETH BONERT

Packers and Movers

Benji got his licence around the same time that Da called a family meeting and told them all they were going to leave the country. By the weekend there were boxes everywhere and a dense halo of sullen hell about Simon. What he probably felt in his heart was egregious loss plus a venomous sense of betrayal. Benji knew this because he understood just how deeply, how genuinely, how unchildishly, Simon had counted on the army. In his mind he'd already joined. All of his metaphors still leached quite naturally from this well-sunk vision of his martial destiny, so it didn't surprise Benji to be informed solemnly by his little brother that they, as a family unit, were now committing blatant cowardice in the face of the enemy, Under orders from General Da.

Benji said: "Don't talk kuk Simon. Da's not any *coward*."

"We're running away. The blacks are winning. If no one stays and fights they'll take over everything."

Ma remained as busily cheerful as ever. She hummed and bustled a great deal and repeated ad nauseam a line plucked from musty pirate books about them all "embarking on a grand adventure of exploration." Her constant whistling was becoming an irritant no one remarked on.

On the Saturday Da called the boys over to the far side of the garage by the orchard, where the flies zubbed softly in the broken entrails of fallen fruit on the sunlit concrete – the jammy blood-purple of spoiled mulberries, the beaded mucus of pomegranate guts, a paste of apricot rot, rancid plums. One sweet hovering stench.

"You listen properly to me now, both."

"Okay Da," said Benji.

Simon folded his arms.

"This is something big, oright, this is major big stuff."

"Okay Da."

"Hey Simon. I'm talking here."

Simon sniffed.

"Look at me boy. Don't start. Don't start the nonsense. You're ganna get my bladey back up all over again."

Simon said: "So?"

The breath began to whistle in Da's nostrils. He spoke through his teeth, "I'll give you such a wallop my boy. Don't get my temper going. I'll klup you such a backhand. I'll give you one frusk into next week. Bladey Christ." He grabbed Simon by his T-shirt front. He shook. Simon's head lolled and Benji saw moisture gleaming on the eyeballs. "He's sorry Da," he said quickly, "Simey's sorry."

Da was coated with an oil of his own dirty sweat. His hands were grease-blackened and a stained rag dangled from the back pocket of his work jeans. When he let go there were black fingers left on Simon's shirt.

"Oright now. Both a you bladey wake up now. You not playing some bladey nursery school joke with your little friends. You not on monkey play time anymore. Emigration – right? Hey?" He jabbed a stiff finger into their foreheads. "Get it through those thick kohps. Time to. Grow up." Then he brought his palms sharply together. "Now let's move it."

Da led them round into the tool shed. He unlocked the door with a key on a jingling ring from his pocket then locked it again behind them. He lifted aside a heavy tarpaulin. There were a variety of incongruous objects laid out on the ground beside a large chest: all kinds of glass shapes, several immense plastic jars of Black Cat peanut butter, golden coins on a tray.

Da glanced backwards. His cheek twitched. It was hot in the tin shed. He wiped sweat from the tip of his nose; the back of his hand left a grease smudge. "You keep your voices down while you in here. You tell no one what's doing, which includes Ma. This is secret. *Secret.* Oright?"

"Ja Da."

"Simon?"

Simon shrugged.

"*Simon.*"

"Oright, I got it."

"What I want you first both to do is take all that Lalique and wrap each piece nice and separate."

Simon said: "La what?"

"Aw Jesus Christ man," said Da. "Haven't you bladey learned one thing?"

Simon shrugged.

"It's all this glass stuff he means," said Benji.

Da picked up a pale blue punch bowl engraved with nude angels round the rim; their wings were smooth, frosted, delicate. "Have a look here. See the signature? Says, 'R. Lalique.' That's important, the 'R' makes it the real goods. The 'R' is how you know it's a proper old piece. None of the new factory chuzeruy has it. This one is the twennies – would bring in four, five thousand bucks on a Sotheby's auction. So don't you bladey drop it. And don't you dare chip it or I'll bladey chip *you*."

"Ja Da."

"Ja Da."

He showed the boys how to cushion the pieces in plenty of balled newspaper and where to pack them. Then he left, locking the door behind him. The boys got to work. They filled up the deep, iron-cornered wooden chest with the glassware. There were bowls and lamps and bookends and vases and ashtrays, all kinds of items.

When the chest was tightly packed and the lid closed, Benji prodded its side with his toes. "Yisluk but this is heavy as hell."

"Well *we* not ganna have to lift it."

"Wanoo bet?"

A key scratched in the tin lock. Da entered. He locked the door again. "There're some of those bladey loading shochs still wandering around outside on this side," he said. Then: "Let's see."

He lifted the pine chest's lid. "Good. Good boys." He lowered it and closed the latches then pulled a wad of plastic sandwich bags from his pocket. Simon tittered. "Lunch-time hey Da?"

Da glared at him. "What a comedian. I'm falling down dead on my back laughing." He shook his head. "Oright, now this is ganna sound little bit odd but never you mind. You take these Krugerrands four at a time and you stickem in one of these bags I'm giving you –"

Simon oohed breathily. "Are *those* Krugerrands Da? Like real ones hey?"

"Jesus Simon – can't you keep your beak closed and your ears open just for once? I'm just sick to here of your bladey chirping in all the time. I mean really man, really."

But Simon wasn't properly listening. Nor was Benji. Staring fixedly, the boys had begun to drift in toward the golden coins.

"Hey," said Da. "Hey! Look here."

"Sorry Da."

"Sorry Da."

"You take a sannich bag and you stick in the Krugerrands. No more than four per. Then you open up one of these peanut butters. Oright? Then you take the bag with the coins in with your hand just like this, and you shove it right down into the peanut butter, right deep down in."

"Ach sis," said Simon.

"*In* the peanut butter you mean Da?" said Benji.

"No I mean up your arse chewing grass. Obviously the peanut butter. You stick it in in in, right all the way down to your elbow, to the bottom, but make sure in the middle. And you do it nice and equal for each one until all the coins are finished."

Simon sank into a squat. He stroked the coins. They were very shiny even in the gloom of the shed. Benji followed suit. They were smooth and thick and cool. *Krugerrands,* he whispered.

"Ja, Krugerrands," said Da. "So don't go losing any, Don't go putting one in your pockets or anything stupid. That's an ounce of real proper gold, not play play. Get caught at the airport going through with one of these bugguhs there will be a lot of major big shit for all of us."

"Ja Da."

"Oright Da."

"And make sure the top of the peanut butter is nice and smooth before you fit that lid back on. Use the shmatas to wipe. Do it all nice, make it look brannew again. In case some chutus inspector decides and sticks his bladey nose in."

Da left. The boys worked. It was strange, gooey, sweaty work in the oven heat of that shed. The sickly peanut butter smell mixed with fertilizer reek and a sheen of lawnmower oil in their nostrils. At times Benji felt he was caught in a dream. They worked in silence, dripping. He couldn't tell what his brother was thinking, but he had an expression that was like disgust around his mouth all the time. Eventually Simon spoke. "Why do you scheme Da's doing this?"

"Ach you're such a dumbbell."

"Aw like you know."

"You're such a little doos. It's obvious he's shlepping the money out."

"Der hey. Derrr. Like I didn't know *that*."

"Oh ja, then what does it mean?"

"What?"

"What. *Shlepping*."

"It's means it's ganna be sent to Canada for us."

"See – you know nothing."

There was a pause in which they worked on at their hot, sticky labours.

"Okay, then what?" said Simon. "I mean why duzzen he just stick it in the bank like?"

"The guvmint don't let you, you stupid ox. They block your Rands. That's our wonderful chutus guvmint that you love so much. It's cos of them we here sticking our hands in all this bladey gunk kuk."

"Ja well, then what about the glass hey? Where's the glass stuff going?"

Benji shrugged.

Simon began to sing-song. "You don't know, you don't know-oh, you don't –"

"Ach shut your trap man."

Da returned. He inspected the vats of Black Cat peanut

butter. He opened each one and looked at the surface. He lifted them, hefted them. He grinned like a skull. "Good, good. Got you, you bustuds. Got you, you stuffing bustuds."

"Da?" said Simon.

"He means the guvmint, dumbbell," said Benji.

Da said: "Chutus is not taking what I worked my whole life for that's one thing for bladey damn well sure. Now what I want, you boys go wash all that moosh off by the tap behind the girl's room, while I bring the bakkie back here. Then we ganna get this kist all loaded up and nice."

"I told you," said Benji.

"What?" said Da.

"I told Simey we ganna have to lift it."

"I'll help. Meanwhile start taking the peanut butters. Stickem in the lift with everything else. Make sure you don't do anything stupid like try hide them away, okay, just put them with all the toilet paper and stuff, just like they normal, under by the couch there. Nice and in the open. Nothing wrong with shipping a little bita peanut butter, hardy har har."

"Okay Da."

"Ja oright Da."

They washed off then they carried the peanut butters to the main lift which was an orange cargo container mounted on a truck outside. The peanut butters were heavy with all the gold inside. Simon could handle only one at a time, Benji managed two. They both huffed and quivered. The loaders were on their lunch, sprawled down the garden in the shade by the bluegum trees. Only Snoopy came up to the ramp and sniffed, her tail buzzing fiercely.

When they were finished, Simon fell on his knees and said yes girl, yes my girl, yes girl, and kissed Snoopy's terrier snout. She writhed in delight. "Yes my girl," said Simon. "She's so nice. She's so good. She doesn't know she's about to lose her house and go to the SPCA kennels where they'll kill her with a sleep injection."

"Shut up dumbbell," said Benji.

"Snoopy doesn't speak English you know."

"You think you so bladey clever. You know nothing."

"Shut up you arse."

"You shut up. You're just a lightie. Supposed to be all seen-not-heard."

"Wanker."

"Shmock."

"Doos."

Simon lifted Snoopy's front paws and let her lick his face. Her stiff tail beat the air like a cane.

"You'll get worms again," said Benji. "Come on."

They heard a hooter. Da had backed the bakkie up to the shed and had started yelling. They ran.

"Where the hell you bladey boys been? Hey? Hey?"

"Sorry Da."

"Sorry Da."

"How many times must I tell you this isn't some stupid play play little game of yours. Both a you. You the older one Benji, I expect better."

Benji's face burned.

They moved the chest to the bakkie. It took all three of them, sweating and swearing. Da dropped the bakkie's rear flap that said TOYOTA in rusted letters. They then heaved all together and somehow slid it up onto the corrugated steel. Da secured it with yellow nylon rope and special knots. His sweat dripped on his hands but then he seemed suddenly merry. His moods were unpredictable. He grinned his skull grin. "This is real kaffir work hey boys. Just what you both need. When I was your age my daddy didn't come before me." This was a favourite saying of his. He grunted. Benji knew another saying was in the offing and could guess which. Da said: "We all need a little bit of a taste of Auschwitz every now and then." Benji nodded to himself. Right again.

Then Lena walked around from the kitchen side and Da's face darkened. "Shit a brick. The hell is the girl doing here now; the hell does *she* want?"

Lena said: "Master, master."

Da said: "Ja?"

"Master."

"*Ja.*"

"Madem say for you come for tea."

"Tell the madam not now. Later."

"For later?"

"Later! *Later!*" The veins in Da's neck sprang like cords taking strain.

Lena cringed and retreated, twisting her hands in the frilly apron of her overalls. "That bladey shiksa," said Da. "I've never liked her." Then to Benji: "Oright – I want youda drive this load out Northcliff way. That's your job I'm giving to you. There's a chutus there called Bezuidenhout. He's expecting this."

"Me?" said Benji.

"No the boy standing behind you. Of course you! Wake up here!"

"Sorry Da. I mean do you mean by myself?"

"Ja, I need Simon here still to hose the dog's drohlls in the yard. I'll give you directions for Bezuidenhout. All you do is you drive this to him. What you think your licence is for? But you be very bladey careful, boy. And use your own two eyes and make sure he gets it with his own two hands. If he's not there, you don't leave this with no one oright? Okay? Understand? And when you see him, also you . . . come here . . ."

Da stepped back behind the shed. The boys followed. Da went on in a softer voice. "You give him this hey Benji. You don't need anything back from him. Just give him the box. And this."

He drew a yellow package from his back pocket. It was an envelope, doubled over, sealed around with sticky tape and grubby with sweat and grease. Benji took it. Something thick and firm in there. "Okay Da."

All of a sudden Da grinned and winked. "Don't look so bladey worried there Benjamus. You're fine now with your licence. You don't need me. Doesn't that feel nice, isn't it nice to be independent and not need anyone?"

"Ja Da."

Simon sneered. "Don't go prang her straight into the back of a Putco bus hey Benji."

"What's wrong with you?" said Da. "What kind of a thing is that to say to your own brother?"

"I's only joking Da."

"He's only joking. Sure. Right. You always only joking these days. Simon, let me tell you one thing. I'll only be joking when I kick you over the garden wall. You been doing nothing all this week but getting on my bladey tits. I have bladey well had enough! I don't know what your bladey problem is boy!"

"No," said Simon. "I don't know what *your* problem is."

Benji hissed. "*Simon.*"

Da, suddenly quiet, said: "Don't backchat me boy, I'm warning you. All week you've been krepsuching around like a moping I-don't-know-what."

"Ja well maybe because I don't want to go away. Maybe because no one asked me."

"Grow up."

"I – I – I'm –"

"I – I – uh – uh – uh. You're a fourteen-year-old pisher."

"Fifteen! You don't even know!"

"Ach shoosh already. Pipe down."

Benji said: "Listen to Da okay Sime?"

Simon started crying. "Go to hell. I'm sick a this! I don't want to go!" Angry tears moved on his taut and livid face.

"Aw stop bawling," said Da.

Simon sniffled. His breath caught.

"Like a little girl, man," said Da. "Unbelievable."

"I'm not the little girl. I have got courage. You the one who's scared. You're the one who's making us run away."

"Ach go inside if you can't work with us, Simon. Go help your Ma."

"What I say is true. I want to fight for my country. You scared. You scared. You're –"

"Simon," said Benji.

"You're the coward."

Da said: "What did you say?"

"*Coward.*"

Da struck Simon an openhanded smack across the face. Simon went bodily sideways into the bakkie. His mouth was open and his face turned white as plain yogurt except for the print of Da's hand which glowed a rich and darkening pink. Simon lifted his cupped hands to this place, then bent slowly over.

"I don't know what's wrong with you," said Da. "I didn't bring you up to believe the chutus guvmint kuk what they feed us on the SABC every night. You must be the only Jewish boychik in the world I ever heard of who actually *wants* to fight for chutus."

Simon's breath hitched, his shoulders jerked but he kept hunched.

"Fine," said Da. "You want to stay, you want to stay for the revolution? You stay. Stay. Be my guest. We'll leave you behind. Stay and go fight in the army for chutus, get blown up on the border. Or wait here for the shochs to come and cut open your white throat with a panga. I'll –"

Simon fled.

Da shook his head. "That boet of yours."

"He's just young Da."

"Ja."

"He's just all tense and hassled and that. It's all been so quick."

"When I make a decision I make a decision."

"Absolutely, Da."

"You understand hey Benji."

"Course I do Da. Simon just doesn't get it. He's too young to know. I try explain him about the revolution coming and we've got to get out now and that, otherwise we not ganna be able . . ."

Da grunted.

"You doing the right thing for us, Da. We could get stuck."

Da wiped his greasy nose. "It's his fault. Boy won't listen. Boy can't see it's all for him."

"Ja," said Benji.

"Completely his fault," said Da. "He just knows how to gimme the needle. He could get a Ph.D. in giving the bladey needle, that kid. Here."

He threw the keys and Benji caught them.

"Drive careful," said Da. Then he gave Benji directions to Bezuidenhout.

At a robot on DF Malan Drive there were skinny boys nimbly jinking and whistling in the halted traffic, copies of the

Johannesburg Star held like planks across their chests, holes in their too-short trouser legs, their shirt-tails marrowed as cheesecloth. Benji chewed at his bottom lip. He kept both hands tight on the steering wheel. He told himself he was cool, it was easy, he was cool, everything would be fine. Cool, cool as a cu. Easy. The robot changed green. He inhaled. Clutch in. Into first. Give petrol. Ease out clutch. The traffic river gathered speed with him inside, keeping up and rigid. Second, now third. Fourth. He pressed the accelerator calmly but firmly, exhaled at last. The radio speakers, set to the 702 Top 40 Hit Parade, abruptly released the first spangling notes of the new Duran Duran, a number called "The Union of the Snake." Out of reflex Benji almost reached down to twist the volume up, then caught himself. Except to change gears he was resolved those hands were staying locked on that wheel like a pair of lug nuts. He did allow himself the right to whistle along, though in a second that had died away. A beige Mercedes was following too closely in the accelerating traffic. He went back to chewing his bottom lip, worrying. The Nazi grille loomed in the rearview. He could feel the weight of the load of precious glass behind him like a physical pressure on his shoulders and neck. Fresh sweat kept sprouting in his armpits, moving on his flanks.

He passed Melville Koppies, the Jewish cemetery, the Emmarentia rose gardens. Once in Northcliff he veered left, carefully. There was indeed a veritable cliff in Northcliff. The road mounted its lumpen red-quartzy face like an adder craftily ascending a tree trunk. He had to change down to second, nearly stalling letting the clutch out too fast. And he was just calling himself a stupid arsehole for that when – *shit!* – a sinister little Volksie came buzzing from the blind turn ahead at wasp speed, halfway over into his lane. He yanked the wheel over and yelped. He breathed the words *Shma Yisrael* and felt a slop of iced adrenalin lift like a backwash from the pulse of tingling shock in his sphincter and guts. The glass in the back. The glass. That was all he kept thinking. He wasn't praying for himself. He watched a flash of blonde hair and some long red fingernails fall away with the Volksie clatter; in a moment it had diminished to plain air.

He stayed pulled over and sweat-drenched with his pulses ticking in both ears for some time. The glass had no insurance on it.

The house, when he found it, was an obvious mistake. No chutus could afford a place like this. There was an intercom on a white plinth but the gate of theatrically curled ironwork was wide open so he went right on up. A man was standing on parted legs, in front of a four-vehicle garage. A white cubist structure like a beached luxury cruise liner rose vastly behind both man and garage. Benji parked downhill from him, with exceeding caution. He pulled up twice on the handbrake to make sure it wasn't about to pop down and let the bakkie roll back and gather speed and go sailing gently off the cliff edge where, in open whistling space, it would tip slowly over to point its cargo at the blurred uprushing glitter of the quartz earth a hundred and fifty metres below. Crump. Crunch. Tinkle tinkle. Four hundred thousand Rands worth of uninsured art glass. On second thought he went back and gave the handbrake a third yank then rammed the gear handle into first as well.

"You from Friedland?"

The man had walked up on him. Benji said: "I'm Lazer's boy."

"Ach is that a fact."

"Ja meneer."

"Is it now. You must be your ma's side then hey. You don't look any like your pa one liddel bit even."

Shaking hands, Benji felt he was thrusting his own to the wrist in a vat of red sucking clay, blood-hot and ready to pulp his fingers with a swirl. Of course he'd expected Bezuidenhout to be large: chutaysim were always large. The word "boer" meant "mass" to him. Afrikaner, chutaysim – these sounds made him think of immense buffalo, wild and snorting. Trampled-hoofed beasts. So yes, big was expected. By all means big. But this. Holy fuckerollee. *This.*

"How is your pa?"

"Fine thank you meneer thanks for asking."

Bezuidenhout pressed his horn-rimmed glasses back against his face. He had a face that seemed as wide as a phone book is long. His fingers, Benji thought, were each the fatness of a Goldenberg's kosher polony, easy. He had on the obligatory pale blue safari suit. His neck was like a tree stump sunk into the rest of him through a dense pack of sunburned muscle. The belly hung down, Sumo-fashion. Drawn up to the ruddy knees were knitted socks, in the rim of one of which a black plastic haircomb was stored – another obligatory item of chutus style. The thighs were like two separate men kneeling with folded arms beneath his mass. No doubt he'd been a rugby champion in his youth.

"Tell me, they pack up all your goods your way already?"

"At our house you mean meneer?"

"Ja."

"The loaders put the crate and that, but not all everything is in boxes yet."

"Hell." He shook his vast head. "Hell."

"Meneer?"

"Leaving hey. Actually taking the gap."

"Ja meneer."

"Hell. A helluva thing."

They stood there for a minute. Benji didn't know what to say. He rubbed his neck in a grown-up way. Bezuidenhout just stood there, shaking his jowls.

"I want to tell you," said Bezuidenhout, eventually. "From my hearts I want to tell you, really and truly man, your pa he is a king that man, you hear me?"

Benji looked down.

"He is one of the kerels that they just don't make them like that no more. Really truly man. Really . . . ach, I'm starting getting all emotioneral. It gets me in my hearts, this." He wandered around to the bakkie. "This the whole lot in one hey?"

"Yes. Oh, meneer. I've got this also for you . . ."

But Bezuidenhout was shaking his great head again, staring down at the chest. "If it's another man I'm going to open up take a look inside that box. Honestly, But your pa? No ways, not Friedland. Me and him we dun a handshake and that is all I need. You tell him what I saying. Tell him his handshake is like gold and so is mine own. If there is such a thing as more than one hunned per cent then Friedland is it. You tell him I sayed it."

"Oright meneer, I will."

"Really."

"Yes meneer. But I've got –"

Bezuidenhout turned, stabbed two of his kosher polony fingers into his mouth, then emitted two short loud blasts. Then he said: "Kom hier Ou Boy, kom hierdie kant."

A shadow prised itself from the side of a berry hedge. It was a human being. He had been so still and hunched over there against the hedge that Benji hadn't noticed him at all. In fact he was an old man in soiled overalls, extensively grizzled, with long grey whiskers on his chin and prune-wrinkled cheeks criss-crossed with the keloid scars of his clan's ritual markings. He smelled bad. Bezuidenhout repeated himself: Come here, Ou Boy, come this side. Then he told him to take in the chest: "Vat hierdie agter nou, Ou Boy."

The old man said something like sah-sah-sah. He was stooped over, watching the floor. He began to pick at the knots.

Benji said: "It's really heavy hey meneer."

Bezuidenhout sighed. "Ja-nee, your pa. I tell you. One of the clevermost operators what I knowed ever. You tell your pa from me –"

"Really heavy heavy box hey meneer," said Benji.

"– tell him I am very sorry but what I hope, I hope he bladey well starts freezing his arse off over there in blerry Canadia so bad he turn around and come straight right back."

"Meneer?"

"I'm sorry but I do. I hope his feet never blerry touch the blerry ice ground over there and he can see a big mistake. This is the best country in the world! And it will stay this way. I'm telling you. Duzzen matter even if we losing people like your pa left and right which I see it happening in mine own eyes all the time now, we still can come right and sort this all out. Yisluk, you know, sometime I also feel tired of it and my hearts is getting really sore for this country, but then I think no man, you just going soft. And I remember my oupa. That generation. Like rock. No, no ways. They can't do nothing to us. We're too strong and we never ganna give in . . ."

Benji kept straining to see around Bezuidenhout's mountainous shoulder. Ou Boy had dropped the bakkie's tail flap. He was labouring. The chest was larger than him. Without looking around, Bezuidenhout told him to pasop because there are breakables in that box, neh.

"Heavy hey meneer."

"Hey?"

"The box."

"What box?"

Benji pointed, tentatively. Bezuidenhout swung around. Ou Boy was bent double and had the chest squarely on his spine. He kept shuddering. There was a spritz of white foam on his lips and he shuffled forward one half-foot at a time.

"Is it really okay meneer? I mean can he manage all by himself like that?"

"Who?"

"Your garden boy."

"Oh *him* you mean. I thought we talking about your pa still." His moustache peeled away from his yellow teeth. "You don't have to worry about Ou Boy. You have no idea how blerry strong he is. Let me tell you. One time I hadda contractor, see, and this oke he wanted to Je – to rook me blind, and sayed to me sixteen boys he needed to dig out for the one swim pool. I said thank you very much goodbye. I gave Ou Boy a spade instead. Just one spade, just Ou Boy and one spade. I put him on that swim pool job, ja. Ja, so do you know in one week he himself digged out that whole bliksem of a swim pool all out himself. One week! Show you it inna back, you can see the size of the blerry thing for yourself. So don't you worry nothing about Ou Boy now. Ou Boy is strong's-an-ox."

Benji was watching wetness spread like unfurling wings on the flanks of Ou Boy's overalls. His pink tongue was out now, and his eyes were swollen and protuberant as boiled eggs in the sockets of his skull. He kept shuffling forward, shuffling forward.

"Come inside and have a lekker cooldrink," said Bezuidenhout. "Plus I think you got summin else for me, neh?"

"Hey? Oh. Oh ja. Ja I do meneer."
"So come on."

Benji's father had often said there may be lots of poor Jews in this world but you just try telling a chutus that. He will not believe you. A Jood without money? Never-ever. Impossible. No such animal. To a chutus, Da said, every Jew is a millionaire. Benji was now made to ponder that that observation had a not-so unspoken converse: that Jews thought of Afrikaners as all being blue-collar and poor – the postal carriers, railway workers, prison guards, the cops and soldiers and petty bureaucrats of the nation. If it weren't for the Nat government they'd all starve, for everyone knew the shochedikah could do those jobs just as well for one-tenth the pay.

Benji hadn't realized before how deeply this preconception went in himself. The reality of Bezuidenhout's splendid home kept butting up against entrenched notions of how he thought the world worked – a baffling dissonance that left him wordless and gaping, somewhat giddy inside.

The front parlour had a skylit dome above and a chandelier fat with an inverted forest of crystal teardrops. There were grand vaulted staircases, plush carpets, heavy pieces of stinkwood furniture and oil canvasses softly lit by tiny electric bulbs: scenes of ox wagons on the veldt, the profiles of noble Afrikaners gazing out over their fly-cast sjamboks, or else standing firm in their laager of outspanned wagons, braving the charge of the mad-eyed Zulu savages with cool-and-collected volleys of accurate Mauser fire, while in the centre the women and children knelt to pray from their massive black bibles . . .

"Ja, jiz look at them hey," said Bezuidenhout. "Look and understand that spirit. It will always be here. My people. Our land. You have your people and your ways but I say this and I have respect – your pa is making a mistake for his family. He'll come back, all of you people will. Me, us, we have to stay and win here. There is nowhere else for us. It *will* stand. You like these hey?"

"Ja meneer. Very nice."

"You can touch."

Benji tenderly fingered the sterling silver inlay on the custom Berettas in the shotgun rack. Then they passed through the billiards room, then the library with its three floors of oak shelving and balconies with copper railings which two maids in overalls and doeks were busily using rags and Brasso and elbow grease to shine.

"You want that cooldrink? How bout I'll give you a brandewyn and coke."

"Okay meneer."

Bezuidenhout roared. "You'll be fast asleep on the floor boy!"

Benji pressed out a stiff grin.

"What's your pa ganna say to me if I'm gonna send his boy back with a dop in him eleven o'clock the morning hey?"

"I knew you're just joking meneer."

They went into the kitchen. It was gleaming and science-fictiony. Benji was struck dumb when Bezuidenhout showed him the cooldrink nozzles. It was like a real restaurant: you pinched a plastic flap on a nozzle and ice-cold cooldrink squirted into your glass. All kinds of flavours. Of course Benji picked cream soda. He drank it down.

"Have another one," said Bezuidenhout. "Have strawberry fuzz, that's a lekker one, neh."

"No thank you meneer."

"Sure?"

"Yes meneer," said Benji, though he very badly wanted a few refills. The ginger ale. The sherbert. Indeed the strawberry fizz. He chulished for them all. But it was time to be hard-nosed and adult, a grown-up businessman, his father's rep. He set his glass down with a firm hand.

"Okay, so let's go on the backyard," said Bezuidenhout.

They passed an alcove in the wall in which there was a very large chess set on a table between two matching easy chairs.

"You play?"

"Little bit meneer."

"At one time I was the Central Transvaal Regional Chess Champion. I was self-teached. Never went past primary school. Played a lot of you peoples games."

"Mine meneer?"

He moved his eyebrows significantly.

"Oh. Ja."

"Had a little threepinny plastic set from Christmas when I was six or something. You could fold it. Could play draughts the other side. There were tiny-weeny magnets in the pieces." He touched the queen. "She's a handcarve now this one, custom job, a hunned per cent ivory pure . . ." He stared down at the board for quite a time, until Benji cleared his throat.

They went on. Yet another lounge. This one was furnished in sweet bright colours, chewing gum shades of purple, pink, yellow, lemon, scarlet, neon. The seats were all soft and close to the thick, spongy carpet on which there were woven images of dancing rabbits and crescent moons and twinkly stars. There was an enormous television with an Atari video game attached and game cartridges scattered about amongst other toys and game boards.

"I built this room special for my kinders."

"Wow," said Benji.

"They got their own maids too. When I grew up we had newspaper on the floor and zinc walls and no barf. That's true. I used to have to go knock on my neighbour Missus Van Rensburg if I wanted get a hot barf. She poured it down from a kettle. Not my kids, uh-uh, no blerry ways. I'm making sure they are getting but completely blerry spoiled."

"What can you do?" said Benji, shrugging with ironic gravity the way he knew adults shrugged. Cynical irony, that was the ticket, that was currency – the wavelength of the grown-up world; everything important ran on it. The Yiddish phrase for the sentiment in question was *bitteruh gelechtah*: bitter joke. You cried as you laughed. So the tears went either way, not even you quite knowing which.

After a moment Bezuidenhout roared again. He copied Benji's gesture. Each time he roared it hurt Benji's eardrums. "Exactly, my little friend, exactly. What can you do? They is mine kinders and that is that, end of story." He did the shrug again.

His jolly mimicry vindicated Benji's insight. You needed to tune yourself to dispense and receive just that right pitch of cynicism. That was the art of what people called growing up.

Bezuidenhout rested one of his mitts on Benji's scruff and steered him out onto a patio which was all white marble and cool shade, with a white silk-seeming hammock and chattering tropical birds – feathers as vivid as fresh arterial blood – vaulting and fluffing about in an atrium big enough to walk into. They had their own tree in there. There was white rattan furniture and marble tables, the same marble, not altogether perfectly white Benji now noticed, but swirled in the grain with a storm eye of lacy butterscotch, as that they trod on. Several large red short-haired dogs were curled into circles like fur tires on the adjoining lawn. There were little juvenile cries and splashes like the silverine peals from tiny crystal bells on the soft breeze from ahead and below where the land dropped off steeply then levelled then dropped again. These terraces were verdant and neat as bowling greens, though here and there modestly dotted with white neo-classical statuary. Benji stepped out and noted that the source of the noise was, unsurprisingly, a swimming pool, struck brilliant as a chlorinated gemstone by the yellow sun. There were white plications and limbs, bobbing, on its flatness. The whoops and laughter and splashing were faint and piping as sparrow calls in the morning air.

Bezuidenhout moved along and Benji stepped with him. "Now there was the other thing," he said, suddenly quieter.

"Meneer?"

"Diden your pa . . . ?"

"Oh ja, right. Of course. Ja." Benji fumbled in his jeans, twisted out the package and thrust it over. He was immediately unhappy with himself. Too rushed, too nervous. He'd blown his adult cover. Bezuidenhout took the package, rapped it against his fleshy knuckles, then said: "Tell your old man I mean it what I sayed. I do hope he freeze off his bladey arse and come right back, right back." As he spoke he was breaking open the sticky tape with his obese fingers, tearing the paper. "What is worse of all is the nice bright boys like you who is the next generation is also now going straight down the, scuse me, toilet. Ach. When I think of the future of this land, my country . . ." He was thumbing the coloured paper inside the envelope. Cash. Latkes, as Da would have called them: many many Rand notes.

He sighed. "Ja-Nee. Ons sal sien." He plucked out two pairs of pink fifties. "Here wah boy."

Benji's pulses beat hard in his neck. "No meneer, I don't think . . ."

"Take it. Between you and me. You don't have to tell your old man. Stop and jiz buy for yourself an ice cream on the way home. You deserved it, you done good."

"Well . . ."

He winked. "Go on. Your father will never know. I promise you."

"Thank you meneer."

"And maybe you'll remember how good it was here when you get over there and you'll want to turn round and come straight right back, hey? I think it will be so."

"Maybe meneer."

Down beside the wet chlorine gem the kids had settled into a placid lull. They lay on their stomachs on the bricks, like corpses. A fractured sunbeam facsimile of the waterline swayed on the mosaics, settling.

"Is that the pool your garden boy dug all by himself with one spade hey meneer?"

"Ja. He's the one."

"It is big hey meneer."

"Ja it is. Very."

In the kitchen Simon was eating koeksisters and drinking Oros. Lena was ironing. Ma was bustling.

Benji said: "Hey spastic. Where'd you get the koeksisters hey?"

Simon opened his mouth and extended his tongue, bearing a masticated chaw of mooshed koeksister.

"Ach grow up," said Benji.

Simon swallowed. "I'm the big man," he said, starting to swagger. "I'm such a heavy oke. My name is Benji. I'm the main mun round her. Mr. Big Shot Benji."

Benji whirled to scratch back, out of instinct, then stopped. He could see yellow skin on his brother's cheek – the place where the pink had been. It looked rancid now, like the crust of some inner rot, blue-green as cheese mould in spots.

"That's me," he said, and smiled, and there was something like a shine of fear in his brother's face as he turned away. He knew now where the koeksisters had come from. He was dizzy with maturity, the knowledge of his own noble adulthood sang in both his ears like a new movement of the blood. He was truly a businessman, an operator. A doer and constructor of his own deals. A muchuh. Truly. He leaned over and hung the car keys back up with a tidy flip, doing it just as Da did, adding the same weary sigh. The hunter returned from the fields. *I just did half a mill's worth business*, he wanted to say. *Look at me.*

Lena hummed and the iron thumped as she worked. Woree, woree, she sang. Ma came near, whistling unmelodiously. "Have a koeksister my bubsi-booksi. I went and bought them special. Take."

"Where's Da?"

"In the backyard."

Benji looked at the koeksisters on the styrofoam and walked past. They were his favourite, from George's cafi down the street, narrow tubes of sweet dough braided like a havdallah candle and fried in honey. Crackly skin, soft as marshmallow within. He went outside into the sun with a squared jaw and saliva roving loosely under his tongue. A man takes care of business first, sugary things, children's things, consolations, come way down the line after. He swallowed hard. He thought with sharp pride of Bezuidenhout's strawberry fizz, the way he'd thumped his glass down. No.

He found Da not in the backyard but on the front drive, under the Chev truck.

"Nu. How'd it go?"

"Well, Da, well."

"No problems?"

"Nooit, it was all oright. Hundred per cent. He took the kist and I gave him that other thing."

Da blinked in the sunlight, looking up, wiped his eyebrow with the inside of his wrist.

"He also said I must tell you your handshake is like gold and that."

"Hey?"

"He said I must say how he hopes we get so freezing cold in Canada we turn straight back because you such a top guy to lose and that. For the country like."

"He told *you* that?"

"Ja."

"Typical."

"He said it's a big shame for the coming generation and that."

"Typical. Bladey dirty shit."

"Da?"

"You shoulda turned round and told him it's none a his bladey business."

"Ach he was saying nice things about you Da. Said only you and him had gold handshakes that people could always trust."

Da spluttered. "What?"

"Only you and him –"

"Let me tell you something about Bezuidenhout. That chutus is a big fat gunuf, a bladey gunuf that's all. He still owes me for sixteen oak tables he hasn't paid a cent on and never will. These guys. These bladey guys. These guys with the big talk, they are the biggest bladey liars and ganovim there are. You think I haven't heard he's not already on the go trying to chup up my old customers away from Kahn? Bladey arsehole."

"He said he was a chess champion."

"Bet you he took the envelope though, very quickly, ja, I'll bet he chupped that very nicely and no questions asked, didn't he just."

"He opened it in front of me."

"So you saw."

"Ja."

"I'll tell you something, boychik. But this is between me, you and the garden wall."

"Ja Da."

"He's such a golden handshake, Bezuidenhout, tell me what's he doing busy chupping from his own brother-in-law?"

"Really?"

"This is what it all is. This's why I'm sending you over there on the quiet on a Saturday morning with those latkes for him. On this Lalique deal it's him who's running the fancy shops and it's the brother-in-law handling the financing. He's doing a shlenta on him, what do you think."

Benji blinked.

"Look, what he's done he's got me overinvoicing him and I'm giving him a percentage from the difference in latkes to take under the table for himself, wink wink."

Benji gave a stiff adult nod. His brain raced and failed.

"You understand?"

"Uhm . . . the brother-in-law's paying for the glass?"

Da's mouth twisted. "He comes to me right, and he tells me he can talk his brother-in-law into buying up all my Lalique for a price that is way over. Well and good. The brother-in-law has no clue the proper valuation. Only thing my guy wants from my end is to slip him back a cash kickback and not say one word. Simple."

Benji said: "But he's so rich, why does he need his –"

Da was shaking his head. "He's rich. Who says he's rich? How do you know he's got?"

"Cos I saw."

"Saw what?"

"Jeez Da, you should just see the size of that place. There's one whole lounge in there just for the kids. There's a pool like –"

"I know. I've seen. Now you pay attention. I'm ganna explain something very important you should learn for life, boyki. What you see, what a man shows, it means absolutely nothing. Remember that."

Benji sniffed.

"You doubting me."

"He had these like hoses specially just for cooldrink, in the kitchen Da."

"*Listen to me.* These guys that look like such big shots, you give these guys one squeeze and you'll find out they really got shit. Chaym loksh. Bupkes. Be with me on this, I know from long experience. When you young you get impressed by all the wrong things. It takes experience be able to see quality, what's really underneath. Believe me, the more fancy do they look the more you can rest assured they are really on the bones of their arse."

"Not Bezuidenhout."

"Yes Bezuidenhout! Am I talking Bantu here? You not with the man when he goes in to see his bank manager. You not looking at his bonds, his balance sheets. You don't have his leases, God forbid. With that chutus, you can rest assured he is just draying from one week to the next."

"Draying?"

"Just juggling. Borrow here, pay there, keep the bladey pot boiling, keep talking fast boy oh boy and la di lah with the fancy footwork. That is why I laugh when you say golden handshake and all that kuk."

"Oh."

"Another thing, if he could afford to, he'd be on the first plane out to Holland or wherever. Believe you me boy. The very first one out."

"He said we'll be coming back, Da, said nothing's going to change here. They going to stay and fight."

"What people say is what people say. You watch what actually happens."

"Yes Da."

"It's the same what I'm telling about money. The country *looks* strong. Chutus keeps talking talking a big fight. The mighty chutus. The big staunch chutus. You can never beat the mighty chutus, so says the mighty chutus. You wait. You see when the time comes that they got shit. With their big army and all the rest. Be with me. You will see. They will fold up and cry like children and that'll be that. All your mighty chutaysim, finished and klaar."

"Oh," said Benji.

He sniffed, glanced down. "But this money stuff now – private hey, between you and me hey Benj."

"I understand Da, of course."

"Not your boet or even Ma. Special not your boet. I don't know what goes on inside that head of his nowadays."

Benji pitched a semi-cynical shrug at his father; but he wasn't looking.

"When it comes to business Benjuluh, the first thing you have to learn is how to keep your mouth shtoom. Absolutely shtoom. Keep out of the spotlight. Keep a low profile. That's the most important."

"Yes Da."

He heard his Ma's voice, calling from the kitchen door, faint and feminine. He looked toward it but kept still. He felt Da's gaze on him, on his face, his profile, and he raised up the chin a little and squared off his shoulders. He waited with every muscle for Da to settle an arm around him, like a regal cloak. He had the cement of his secret through his chest, his bones. The thrum of new-found nobility in his own sense of himself, his own autonomous cleverness, his fluid maturity, moved like clean new electricity through his vessels, unhurriedly, closing off a calm arc, and Ma's thin cry faded off to nothing. He thrust his hand into his pocket. He could feel the brittle paper of his cash there. His cash. His own secret commission.

Years later it would come to him that he still had a memory-feeling of those four fifty-Rand notes touching his fingertips. From Bezuidenhout's hand. And the birds in the atrium. And the marble. And that shuddering gem of a swimming pool carved from the land by a lone toiling neo-slave and one shovel blade. Then he would abruptly realize that this memory-feeling, kept secreted and carried alive and resolutely undying within him, was the atavistic sensation behind all the other subsequent contraband flutterings. Rolling a joint or crumbling pills. Chopping coke with a razor. Forging signatures with a pen. Creeping down softly as insect legs to the pubic dip between a woman's thighs, unpopping the slick heat there with a tiny safecracker fidget. A movement to open secrets and clear perceptions. Taking those notes had started him on the road to making the world more plain for himself, delivered him his magic wand fingers. So it was more than memory, it had been really almost a physical acquisition, virtually anatomical. It was a new weight, new goods. Part of the load they call experience.

WILLIAM METCALFE

Nice Big Car, Rap Music Coming Out the Window

Some people were camped under those stairs between the streets where all that graffiti and garbage is. I was watching them and the cops came, two cops. They were taking down a tarp the campers had there. There was two guys and a girl – those hippie kind of people with dreads and drums and old worn-out clothes. The two guys were saying hey this is our human rights here man why don't you just let us live in peace instead of oppressing the poor hey watch out for my sleeping bag and stuff where are you going to take it? The cop says I wouldn't have to take it anyplace if you guys would just leave when I ask you. Well we were just sleeping here man what's the big crime – that was the big guy said that. There was one little serious guy and one big happy one. The big one's hair was really long like almost down to his waist and he smiled at the cops. The girl had a kind of scarf wrapped around her head, long red skirt to the ground. She kept moving around, walking around almost like she was a dancer. I got embarrassed thinking maybe I stared at her too much because she looked back at me like what are you looking at, and then she sort of smiled at me. Sometimes I just go different places and watch stuff. I do that all the time. This town is on a lake and you can't smell the ocean.

The little angry guy, he got really mad all of a sudden. He threw a sleeping bag at one of the cops. The bag went right across the face of the cop and tangled around him. The cop grabbed it like fighting it off. This is bullshit man says the little angry guy we were just sleeping we were just stepping lightly on the earth trying not to use up the earth we are pilgrims we are the children of the creator not like you messengers of death the death of the planet. . . . The guy tells the cop stuff like that for a while. He is shouting, standing with his legs apart like he is trying to keep his balance, like on my uncle's fish boat. My uncle, his name is Ronald, he took me out on that boat at Prince Rupert when my mom died. My mom was a white woman married to my dad but she was pretty much like an Indian and they adopted her. My uncle told me he was the family member going to look after me now. I went to his place on the reserve at Port McKenzie and I lived there with all his kids. They were all younger than me. I went on the fish boat to help him. Sometimes he got drunk and didn't go out, that was before he got saved by God. On the fish boat I liked it. I worked pretty hard and I got some muscles. My uncle teased me about that – you look like a boxer pretty soon he said. My uncle liked boxing. He taught me some punches. I like it when you are out there fishing and then you come back and when you are getting close to land you can smell the trees. Smells like cedar. I liked that. He paid me some money. I bought a Discman with it and sometimes when we were fishing I listened to rap music on it but I ran out of batteries and then I lost the Discman someplace, I don't know where.

Me and my uncle were at the wharf at Rupert one day and I saw this guy, a white man – he had a suit on – walking around. Just walking around like, looking at the boats. He walked up to my uncle and he says, brother I recognize you. What, my uncle says. I recognize you as a fellow child of God, says the guy. Child, my uncle says, do I look like a child and he laughs at the guy a bit, but not a nice laugh, like not friendly, he is hungover. Hallelujah says the guy. My uncle just walks away and me too. The guy comes along with us. I recognize you in the name of God he says. I know that you want to receive the word of the Lord and be free for eternity I know that you want to bow down and kiss the holy feet of Jesus I know you are wracked in your soul I know you suffer the burden of the world the burden of doubt not knowing which way to go how to live a righteous life. His suit is pressed, like ironed really good. The suit jacket is the same colour as the cop's uniform, I mean the cop who is listening to the guy who threw the sleeping bag at him. The guy is still talking, like we are the pure ones who will stop the raping of the earth and that's why we just sleep under here it's how we keep our sacred connection to the earth. He looks so angry but the big one, his friend there, apologizes to the cop about the sleeping bag. He tells the other guy come on let's get going, and the girl smiles at me again like to tell me something, but I didn't know what.

And how old is this young lady here says the cop. The little angry one says she's my sister. I am not your sister she says, and that's the first time she talked. Do you have any ID says the cop and the little guy says we do not recognize ID we threw it all away we live like the flowers on the earth do they need ID do the clouds need ID? People need ID says the cop, specially young girls under age hangin around with guys like you. How old are you he says to the girl. Fifteen she says. She's ageless says the little guy she is an ancient soul and we do not recognize age it is linear thinking which destroys the earth. OK says the cop to her, where are your parents. I have no parents, she says. The big guy the one with the long hair laughs and says she was born of immaculate conception like Jesus and Buddha and Bill Gates and he laughs again, mouth wide open. I have no parents because I have been reborn as a child of mother earth she says. What are you talking about says the cop. The girl is smiling like she thinks he's going to get it, like understand everything any second, but he doesn't. Then she smiles at me again and she points at me and says ancient wisdom the first peoples are the ones who should be deciding who needs ID and who can sleep under here because they are ones with the land. They all look at me. The preacher guy looks at me and my uncle and he says, you are the father of this young lad here and you probably have other children how many children do you have it is a burden to have to look after a family and go fishing every day and Jesus was a fisherman too a fisher of men. My uncle is still ignoring the guy and we are walking up toward the cars at the road.

I recognize you, the man says to my uncle again. God works through me to recognize lost souls crying to be born to be reborn in this instant not later on not tomorrow not next week not next month not next year not in the everlasting kingdom of heaven or in the dark depths of hell but now my brother now. My uncle stopped. He had tears in his eyes. I stared at him. I looked at the preacher guy. He was crying too. A police car came up with the lights flashing. A cop got out and grabbed the preacher guy by the arm and says OK Delbert we need to talk to you. The preacher didn't notice at all, he was just looking at my uncle. The cop pulls his elbow and the preacher says to my uncle I have to go now but I'll come back and see you. OK says my uncle. The preacher gets in the car and they turn off the flashing lights. I watch them in the car, they are talking to the preacher guy and one of the cops points at me. The girl is still pointing at me and talking about ancient wisdom of the land. She says we are trying to make it unfold again my friends and I we are trying to get closer to the earth. One of the cops was talking on his phone about a big car accident on the highway and then he says OK we have to leave just move along you can't sleep here maybe we'll charge you with assaulting a police officer. The other cop says we gotta quit wasting our time here let's go. Right on to that says the big guy you gotta keep your priorities straight as a police officer I guess, and he smiled at the cops. I thought I heard seagulls then but I looked around in the sky and there weren't any. This town is a long way from the ocean. I wished I could see my uncle coming down the stairs but I was alone, like every other day.

Next day I went by those stairs again and there was no one camping there but the girl was there, the one from the day before, the one that looked like a dancer and talked about ancient wisdom. She was sitting there eating an orange. Peeling it pretty slow and looking at it. I walked up there and stopped at the bottom of the steps because I didn't know what to do. She looked at me. She was wearing a black thing around her hair, and her hair was pulled back under it, and went down long at the back like before. She had that same long skirt. I saw some dancers once at K'san. My uncle took me there. This girl eating an orange moved her arms and hand when she talked the same as one of them dancers with the drums. My uncle told me these are different Indians, like they do different dances and they have different drums and stuff and a different language but they are still Indians like us, so we should respect them and that's why I am taking you to this place. We slept in his camper that night. That's still the Skeena, he said, just like at Rupert. The Bulkley River comes in there but that is not its Indian name. I watched the dancers. There was mostly white people there watching but they liked the dancers too. It smelled like wood, the dance was like trees dancing, like the forest talking to me. But I did not tell my uncle that. I kept that to myself because I have no mother and father no more so I have to wait. That's what I think. So they drove away with that Delbert, the preacher guy.

I went to my uncle's house next day. Delbert was there standing in the yard and my uncle was saying you better leave my place and never come back you better get outa here I don't want to see you again and he was yelling and standing firm in the yard saying this is my family here and this is where I live and you got no right coming around talking like that, and the preacher guy, Delbert, he says but Ronald it is only a matter of time and I will be around ready when it happens you will maybe need me to help you and because I am a messenger of God and your fate is to sit at God's table I will stick around for when you need me. Then he got into a little car he had there, a little old green Datsun, and drove away slowly in the mud. It was raining. Next day I come home and Delbert is sitting at the table with my uncle. They did not hear me or see me because I am usually pretty quiet, like I never slam doors or walk noisy or talk much. They were sitting there and my uncle was crying again. There was little kids, Jackson and Severin, out in the living room but they were just little and didn't notice – they were watching TV. They are my cousins. Delbert is saying, Ronald the Lord is here now. My uncle was trying to talk but he was crying so much he couldn't. Delbert says this is the Lord entering your life actually he was always there but you are just recognizing him now let it happen it will bring you joy. So I listened to them for a while and my uncle fell down on the floor off his chair and layed there on the floor like a little baby and cried. Delbert said your sins will be lifted off you and you can stand up a new man stand up a new man Ronald. Those kids Jackson and Severin didn't even notice this because they was watching TV. Delbert got up and went around to my uncle and put his hand down and my uncle took it. Delbert helped him stand up – he stood up like one of them dancers slow and like he's wondering if he's gonna make it, except after this my uncle would not take me to the dancers again, all he wanted was for me to go to church but I didn't want to. The girl stood up like one of them dancers. She said my name is Heartsong. She smiled at me. First time anybody smiled at me for a while.

You want an orange? I said sure, and I took one and peeled it. She looked right at me. Her face was very clean. I'm just walkin around down here I said, and she said maybe you came to see me. I didn't know you were gonna be here, I said and she said yes you did. Where is your home she asked me. Well it's here, this is where I'm stayin these days, I said. No I mean were you born here? No, I was born in Prince Rupert. Can you speak your native language? I said no. What's it called she said and I told her I don't know, my uncle can speak it though. Can I meet your uncle and I said no he's in Rupert or someplace. Do you know any shamans there? I said no. I didn't know what a shaman is but I didn't say nothing about that. What's your name she says and I told her and she told me she changed her name to Heartsong last week. What did it used to be I said. It does not matter now the old me is dead and I have started a new life. Where's your mom and dad I said and she said that doesn't matter either, my mother is the moon now and my father is the sun. She smiled at me.

Heartsong took me up into the forest where somebody had put big rocks in a circle. She said this is a sacred space me and my friends made it but you are a First Nations person and I need your blessing we need your permission to have this sacred space here and talk to our ancestors and to the people in the future would you like to smoke some weed it's like a spiritual thing not like partying. I said OK. We smoked it and sat down. We were in the forest and no one was there and it smelled like cedar and spruce. She opened her shirt so I could see her. She came close and she smelled like wood smoke and sweat and something else like maybe incense. I had my hands on them smooth as water when there's no ripples on the ocean and she said I want to feel how hard you are and she put both hands there and then she pulled her skirt up. She was above me slippery and wet and I guess I was pretty high because I was burning like the fire in the middle of the floor at K'san when my uncle and I saw the dancers there. I could see that fire and feel it inside the girl. When me and my uncle were in K'san it was fall time and the trees around there are all poplars and birches so the leaves were yellow and falling. Outside that K'san building it smelled like rotting wood and wet leaves – that was before my uncle started praying all the time and he started it when Delbert lifted him up off the floor that day.

Delbert lifted him up. He was crying with no sound. He had his eyes closed. I forgive you he said. I forgive you I forgive you. I don't know who he was forgiving and I never found out but I know he was not talking about Delbert, it was somebody else. You can forgive anyone said Delbert because the Lord forgives you. Then my uncle fell down again but he landed in the chair, sitting there like almost falling on the floor. I forgive you and God forgives me, he says, and starts to laugh. He laughs for a long time, like when you are a kid and get the giggles and can't stop. My cousin Severin comes to the kitchen door and looks in at my uncle for a minute, then he goes back into the other room. Daddy is laughing at a real big joke says Severin to Jackson, and then they watch TV again.

My uncle wanted me to go to church – it was Delbert's church and it was in somebody's house on the reserve that Delbert was using. My uncle told me the cops had some problem with Delbert and they were always talking to him but my uncle didn't tell me what it was. Maybe he didn't know. He was very quiet and kind but he never taught me any more boxing and he didn't tell me the Indian names for things any more, like the names of rivers. He said praise the Lord sometimes when we was fishing. At K'san there's this one place there where the dancers have a fire, a really hot fire in the dancing place. I had a steady hot fire in my body lying there with that girl. When I looked up at her and she looked at me, we both knew the same things. Her face was so clean and she smiled at me. One of your ancestors was a shaman she said I can feel him in you and maybe you will be a shaman too. I was still in her but we were just relaxing now and I just laughed. I was lying there on my back with the girl still above me, and I looked up like behind me and there was another girl standing there. You two were beautiful she said, so beautiful. I layed there and watched her upside down when she talked. She said she was watching us the whole time and that she was studying a book. I forget what she called it but it was a book about how to live a good life by eating just some green things and water, like clean out your body. My body is pretty cleaned out already right now I said and they both laughed, that girl Heartsong still lying on top of me. They talked about the book and the purity of pure water from mountain springs and the chemicals the society puts in the drinking water. She was lyin on me like she wanted to stay there. I didn't mind, she was light and friendly and she smelled like a fire, like there was still heat coming off her. We went to sleep there. I don't know what happened to the other girl – I never did see her right side up. I had a dream then and it was about a fire burnin down the house Delbert was staying in. I woke up and saw it was a dream, I felt the girl on me asleep and I could see the spruces swaying and a chipmunk running up a log. I stayed awake like that for a while and watched the chipmunk who ran around so quick. All of a sudden I got homesick for the Skeena and the ocean and I had sort of a half dream – I thought the girl on me was a boat and I was the Skeena and she was crossing the river. OK, I figured, if that's what's happening here, cool. My uncle used to have a boat with an outboard and we'd run it up the Skeena sometimes in the fall.

When my uncle started going to church he quit drinking for good this time, and all he cared about was church and fixin up his fish boat. He worked pretty hard. One day the house that was

Delbert's church burned down. My uncle was in there sleeping and he died. Delbert died too and some other people that were my cousins. I saw that fire roaring way up in the air. Lots of people was watching – it was early in the morning just getting light, and we were all standing out there looking and not saying nothing, everybody cold with no jackets on but we could feel the heat. I was standing by an old guy, and he said I seen lots of houses burn down and this one here is the fastest and the biggest flames and the noisiest. Then he didn't talk no more, he just watched the fire.

I'm out here hitchhiking on the road now. That girl wanted me to do shaman stuff with her but I didn't want to do that, I couldn't figure it out. I guess I have to get some kind of job and there's none in this town so I need to go to a bigger city maybe. I never had a job except fishing, don't know what I could do. My uncle told me to work. Heartsong told me I should come back and see her and I might do that someday. Most people do crazy things, but I'm not going to, no way, I'm waiting. That's why I left home. That guy slowed down but he's not gonna stop, too bad, nice big car, rap music coming out the window.

ELAINE McCLUSKEY

The Watermelon Social

My house makes me cry.

It is an *executive split* built during that collective lapse in taste known as the seventies. When we moved in one wall was covered with barnboards, swag lamps cast a queasy light. Everything was brown and cavernous, like a subterranean restaurant that specializes in wiener schnitzel and German plonk.

"It's splendid," declared my husband, who bought the house while I was postpartum, a free-running creature drifting in and out of phase with the natural world. "Look at all the space."

The original owners, the Sandersons, fled after a wife-swapping debacle that left grease on the walls and cigarette burns in the bedroom. A casualty of divorce, neglected during the final days, my house reeked of damaged children and Singapore Slings. Outraged, as though I had foregone the seventies, as though I had never worn hot pants or owned a Vega wagon, I cursed the Sandersons for their bad taste and cheap morals, which had contributed equally, I insisted, to *their* divorce and my home's fondue stains.

I go to the kitchen. There is no symmetry to a split, just a Surrealistic discord of stairs. My house has no windows on the side, just the front and back where the sun never hits. Why do you want side windows? asked my husband. Last winter, as days shortened and SAD set in, I painted two rooms hysterical yellow, thinking sunlight, but somehow the brown, like mildew or sadness, can never be covered.

My son appears in the doorway, collecting himself after preschool.

"John's mother brought his new baby to school this morning."

"Hmmmm. How was he?"

"I think he was fake."

"Really?"

"Hmmm." He nods seriously. "He didn't move, he just laid there."

"Maybe he was sleeping?"

"No, Mom, he was fake."

"OK." I shrug.

We look out a window at a grid of splits. When I moved in, I thought there was no one home, that everyone worked, but then I discovered the houses were full of women. Like the Borrowers, their motto was to never be seen. They stayed in until dusk, or slipped through remote-control garages, hiding from the street, a street owned by quiet, an oppressive dead that skews your senses and blows your circadian rhythm.

In two years, I have never heard a child cry or an adult laugh. I have never seen a tossed football or a game of tag. My children move in a world of whispers and nudges. I've never known a place with so much power, not a place this ordinary and unassuming. *Be quiet,* it orders. *You are making too much noise.* I try to explain this to my husband, but he can't understand.

"Let the kids make as much noise as they want. We pay taxes!"

"You don't *feel* it. It's like telling a joke at a funeral."

He looks at me like I am mad, one of those kooks who stared at a Tim Hortons wall in Cape Breton until they saw the Virgin Mary. I thought suburbia would be streets of laughing kids, racing bikes and backyards without fences, mothers trading recipes, car-pooling to soccer, commiserating over measles.

"Hurry up, Mom," my daughter urges. "The watermelon will be gone."

"What's the point of a watermelon social" – I find it excruciating to say those last two words; they stick in my mouth, like *domestic engineer* or *puppy love* – "if there's no watermelon?"

"C'MON, MOM. Hurry up!"

We enter Greendale Elementary, a stucco institution of high standards and three hundred students, a launch pad for science fairs and piano recitals. The air is smug and claustrophobic.

I hand a toonie to a woman in a denim dress, an impenetrable blue habit. Her name is Marilyn. She is a Volunteer, the über-mom, proud parent of Gregory, Aliysha and Devon, star Greendale grads, *and* the baby, Virginia. Brought out of retirement, propped up, properly medicated, she seems determined to last the evening. For The Volunteers, The Watermelon Social is a no-brainer. Even the old warhorses easing out to pasture with the fourth child, exhausted by fifteen years of do-erism, drained by field trips and croup, leave their dark houses for The Social. Two Social hours are worth thirty-eight weeks of toil in the computer lab, four months of library, eight batches of Harry Potter cupcakes. The Social Volunteers are thanked by name in the school newsletter, posted in the lobby. Everyone sees you in your alphabet sweater and your most beatific smile. It doesn't matter if it's your only appearance all year, if you have sunk into a menopausal abyss of gin and regrets, if you never wash your hair or sleep with your husband, if you make crank calls to your teenage son's girlfriend who is taking up all his time. It doesn't matter: it is The Social.

Down the hall, a buff woman admires a leaf collage. "Ahh," she exclaims theatrically. Her pale, bespectacled daughter sucks her fingers.

"Who's that woman with Meagen?" my daughter asks.

"That's her mother."

I have seen the mother running in a Spandex bra and shorts, a water bottle strapped to her back. A Just Do It ad, defying the code of stillness. A sallow man admires the mother, new to the neighbourhood, a non-Volunteer.

"Well, who is the woman I always see her with?" my daughter insists.

"That's the *baby-sitter*." I drag the word out like a threat.

The sallow man, I realize, is Marilyn's husband, an expert on plankton. His name is Gerald. In recent years, he has become invisible, a mute walker who ignores her histrionics and lives in a secret world of sci-fi novels and CNN. Gerald is a skinny man who has lost all pigment in his body. His hair is preternaturally white, his skin the colour of unbleached paper. He could be sold in an environmental store, underfed, uncoloured, placing no burden on the ecosystem. He rides a bicycle and probably doesn't sweat. She, on the other hand, is a tornado of angst, nearing the end of her run. Marilyn has spent twenty years courting teachers, typing projects, collecting Canadian Tire dollars for tambourines, always checking her progress against others, always needing to EXCEL.

We enter the gym, a pastiche of preening parents and darting kids. The motto disingenuously announces: Greendale Elementary Is A Place for Friends to Help. The dozen teachers are spread about like eggs in a scavenger hunt.

"AHHHHHHHH. This is refreshing!" A sweater-vested man grins as watermelon juice drips into his beard. He spits seeds into a paper napkin, keeping one eye on a teacher, ready to pounce.

"It used to be an ice-cream social," a stout Volunteer named Sally explains, "but we switched to watermelon."

"Uh huh?"

"Lactose intolerance."

Sally is wearing a sleeveless top and a white skirt that exposes her legs, purple stumps covered, like lichen, with broken veins and stretch marks. Her stomach bulges against the distended skirt, sweat drips from her armpits like battery acid. When she smiles maniacally, her face cracks like a ventriloquist's dummy and my son grabs my hand.

"That's prudent." The man nods, and just then, just as he takes his eye off the teacher, Sally shoots in to fill the void. "I'm Dylan's mom," she exhales. "Surprise!"

Outmanoeuvred, distracted by the small talk, the man swallows a seed. For a bulb-shaped woman with the flush of high blood-pressure, Sally is uncommonly swift. "Dylan LOOOOOOVVVVVES Grade 3. He and Warren live for dioramas."

On Sally's shoulders rests a huge pumpkin. Her eyes are slits carved into the fleshy pulp, her mouth is a gigantic slash, a canyon of teeth and gums that opens so wide you can see desperation. Sally's husband, Warren, is a gym teacher who earns as much as a postal worker and sweats through each round of layoffs. He and the girls are monochromatic, brown and dull as dried leaves. I wonder if they ever had life, laughter or chlorophyll running through their veins. Sally is a school fixture, the mini-Marilyn, making paper, Ukrainian eggs, origami frogs and all of the scenery for the Grade 6 production of Sleeping Beauty. Last year, Dylan, "a special learner," killed the Grade 2 hamster.

"Dioramas are lovely," says Mrs. Green, the teacher.

Sally laughs maniacally. Ha ha ha. Mouth open, she throws back the huge head. Ha ha ha. The laughter pushes up against the teacher like a barroom drunk, a sodden hooligan, and Mrs. Green nervously laughs with her.

I am not listening; I am looking at Sally pumpkin head. Something odd is happening to women my age, a genetic fluke like the preponderance of six-foot girls and the birth of quads, an insidious trend that goes unobserved until you look up and notice that every single girl in The Gap towers over you.

Women MY age are sprouting beards. Sally's starts at one ear and trails to her double chin, where it culminates in three witches' hairs. Despite her girth, she can't be over forty, I think, and the beard is BLONDE. Aren't beards and moustaches the domain of swarthy Italians and stout Lebanese, dark women who celebrate our Lady of Fatima and dutifully clean the church for Father O'Flynn? Nana's cleaning lady, Maria, who wore red sneakers, complained of chest pains and stashed away enough unreported income to buy a retirement villa in Portugal. Did blonde women in their forties really grow beards?

"OH NO!!!" someone screams. "OH NO."

"The watermelon."

"DANIEL!"

A shriek splits the air like a thunderclap and a boy runs through the gym, waving his arms. Ducking parents, a woman in a corduroy jumper gives chase, face frozen into a blank mask of paralyzed emotions, too potent to release.

"That's Daniel," says my daughter.

"Ohh." I follow the woman with my eyes.

Behind us, the principal is righting the toppled table. "It's no problem," he says too loudly. Watermelon seeds glisten like shiny black bugs and juice dribbles onto the hardwood floor that pleads for NO BLACK-SOLED SHOES. Split open, the red fleshy fruit looks obscene.

Where is Mr. Tarnapolski, the school custodian who ran a marathon last spring, and is often called upon to chase down Daniel when his inner voices say, *Bolt*, and he dashes from the classroom, through the fingers of his Designated Helper and out the door? Can somebody find Mr. Tarnapolski? Can somebody PLEASE find him? I see Sally shake her head *back and forth, back and forth.*

"Do you work outside the home?" Gerald asks me.

I'm telling you all this because it's important.

My husband is a photographer, which means he is never home for Watermelon Socials. He follows the news to strange and mundane locations, where he meets pros and wannabes like *Jimmy Belliveau Freelance Fire Photographer*, whose card reads: *Find 'em Hot and Leave 'em Dripping.*

Today my husband is home and cranky. The Office phoned at two a.m., scaring my son. One of the conceits of the news photographer is that he is always ready, poised to drop everything for The Next Big Story. To facilitate this, he must be kept aware of news, where and when it is breaking. Editors who have been chewed out for failing to stir the sleeping photog, deskbound drones counting the days until retirement, have a way of getting even. They phone for nothing.

"Ah sorry, Dan, but I see a note saying the premier is having a newser tomorrow on recycling. Gee, you weren't asleep were you?"

"Ahhhhh no."

"Ohhh Geez. It IS two o'clock isn't it? I've been so busy I didn't notice."

As my husband makes a coffee, he scans the paper for play. I try to tell him about Gerald and the Watermelon Social but he sighs and wonders why I "would even care about those people."

Oh, he mentions absently at the sports section, I ran into Gerry Webb at the rare wine store, where Gerry was buying a great Australian that he tried last month in blah blah blah. "He asked how you were and I told him you were writing a book."

I look up, stunned. "WRITING A BOOK!"

"I didn't want him thinking you were just at home."

"Well I am. When would I . . . ?"

"I just," he sighs. "*Those* people don't understand."

"What happens if he asks me about my book?"

He sighs again. "You're right, I'm sorry."

"The book that never gets published."

"He won't ask."

"Of course he will."

"How many first novels are published anyway?"

I look in the mirror, practising my encounter with Gerry, a binge drinker who once fired a starter's pistol in the newsroom where we worked. A forty-five-year-old woman in sweats attempts a knowing smirk: "A book? Yeah, it's a tell-all, Gerry, you better be worried." Gerry mutters something about rehab; I smirk again and wonder why I look so stupid.

In my mind's eye, I am tall, lean, bare to life's emotions. Being raw-boned implies an elegance that can carry jeans and sneakers. Raw-boned doesn't need the camouflage of high heels, big hair or shoulder pads; it screams bohemian indifference. I have always loved stripped-down men, angular, long-haired. In grad school, I met a six-foot-three swimmer with an impossible waist, who held me close over the flame of our overwrought poems, squeezed my torso and whispered, *Oh, oh,* at the inch of offending flesh. The inch has always been there and always will be. I have never looked like I was suffering for art or love. Always, I longed to be spare and free, unencumbered, a twig drifting downstream, a modernist beach house with bare windows and wooden beams. To sit on the floor and cross my legs, yoga style, or wear my hair straight and flat, maybe in a chignon.

I married a sapling with straight hair and a delicate neck. We met at an all-night Fassbinder fest, where he raved about the director's use of mirrors, curtains and shadows. For a while, he smoked Russian cigarettes and argued that *Veronika Voss* was more succinctly ironic than *The Marriage of Maria Braun*. I thought he would never grow fat, just lean and tired from the burden of his emotions. To my surprise, he developed a beer belly but stayed as melodramatic as his cinematic hero. My husband's neck stiffens as he opens the fridge; he grimaces: Miracle Whip instead of mayo. Didn't I know the mustard had to be Dijon, the sliced ham black and smoked?

"The kids like Miracle Whip," I explain, trying to shed light on my world.

"That's because that's all they have tried."

"No, they like Miracle Whip."

"Whatever," he sighs.

Outside, thc sun is shining. The mound of snow by the driveway has vanished, exposing twelve timid crocuses. Small rocks and gravel have appeared from nowhere, like coins in the back of a couch. They cover the bleached grass, the driveway; they stick to my shoes and hitch rides inside.

My son sits at the kitchen table, excited. It is career week at preschool and one of the fathers visited this morning. He was a helicopter pilot, my son explains, and he brought in a ceremonial sword, which the children touched.

"I think it was real gold," he says.

"He wasn't a pilot, he was a navigator," my daughter interrupts. How would she know this? She wasn't even there.

"It WAS real gold," my son decides. He picks up a slice of apple.

"Did anyone ask any questions?" I inquire, and think about the sunshine. Fat-breasted robins have filled the trees; the spiky heads of the crocuses remind me of a punk haircut. My kitchen is now the colour of a Granny Smith apple, a tart shade that covers the Sandersons' sins.

"One boy asked, 'Who is your best friend at work?'"

"Really?"

"He asked everyone the same question all week."

"Do you think he will ask Daddy when he comes in?"

He shrugs his shoulders, and he smells like love. I touch his soft blond head and I ache with the fragility of life. Unlike my daughter, he is shy, a watcher. My heart breaks with his doubts and I want to make them vanish, I want to make him strong. I know I fear too much, but they are a mother's fears, a mother's love, a mother's curse that even little boys as precious as him come without guarantees.

"It was HIM, Mom," my daughter says loudly, pointing at my son. "Sarah Mosher told me. HE asked them all."

The store feels like an underground bunker, a survivalist camp of cheap CDs and polypropylene pants. The metal racks around us groan, overloaded with no-name jeans from China and women's tops that soar to an Oversize 24.

"I know it's here somewhere," I mutter, peering around a stack of plastic sandals. "I saw it in the flyer."

"Can we go see the goldfish?" my son asks.

"Hmmm?"

"THE GOLDFISH in the tanks."

"They killed them all," my daughter whispers. *"Remember."*

When I look at my son, his hair is olive. The fluorescent lights are so powerful they make you squint; magically, they turn everything green. Lime-coloured and overexposed, we march on, looking for muffin tins, past the $19.99 comforters that scratch like horsehair and the blankets that come in an incongruous square: four feet by four.

We stop in an opening in the racks. The air smells like new tires, a ripe odour that overpowers the gift soaps and seeps into Ladies Wear. My son is thinking about the fish, I can tell, my daughter is explaining filters.

Before us, in a wasteland of scorched plastic, lies an oasis of six tables and lukewarm tea. Under the merciless lights, I can see a buffet of sealed sandwiches and Jello dotted with Reddi-Whip. The food looks like the rubber hamburgers I used to buy my dog, petrified food to masticate and maul. The cafeteria has no business being here, I think, in a place this overexposed, a place that smells like tires. Eight girls are gathered at two tables for what appears to be a birthday party, a stagnant, lonely scene that reminds me of an Edward Hopper painting.

A worn woman is passing gifts to the birthday girl, who is

wearing a Britney Spears belly top. A disconnected guest picks stuffing from her chair.

"Let's go," I order, running from the sight. Before we can be gobbled up by hopelessness, we rush to check out, clutching peanuts. Our line is stalled. A woman has lost her Frequent Shopper card and wants to give the bonus points to her friend. "They are not transferable," the clerk declares sternly, like she is ruling on something important, like bone marrow or a liver.

I look to the next lane, pretending not to hear, and see a clerk scanning a licence plate. "That's wrong," her customer insists. "I KNOW it's on for two-ninety-nine." The clerk drops the *Sexy Mama* plate and lifts a microphone for price check. Her voice cracks, unaccustomed to the mike. "Lane 6. I need a price check on novelties," she says, and I stare at her loose jaw and grey hair, trying to bring her into focus. I close one eye, the other; I read the tag on the Cheap N Easy smock. It is Marilyn, doyenne of the Home and School, proud mother of Gregory, Devon, Aliysha, and the baby, Virginia. What is she doing here, in this paranoid bunker of canned beans and Bingo markers? She has at least one degree in pharmacy, she worked in the Main Street Complex before she met Gerald at a computer workshop, got married and raised four perfect kids. "Would you be interested," she asks the Sexy Mama, "in the family portrait special?"

My daughter comes home from school with a papier mâché puppet and a notice on lice. That Volunteer, the one named Sally, was in her class this morning. In a loud voice, she asked Virginia, "Does your mother have a job?" "Don't tell anyone Mom," my daughter whispers. "Virginia said her brother lost all the family's money in the stockmarket."

"What?" I scoff. Gregory is Marilyn's validation, a pre-med student, a Big Brother who made the Dean's List. "How could he get all their money?"

"I don't know. That's what Virginia said."

The news spreads through the neighbourhood, through the petrified streets and motionless houses; it bounces off fireplaces and creeps into bedrooms. I can hear the sharp intake of breath. I can see Sally charging into school, nostrils flared, mouth twisted to a sneer. All the bones in her face have dissolved, as if dipped in a vat of venom, and all that remain are fat and jowls and blind retribution. Last month, just before Valentine's, just before her long-service award at the Home and School, just before Devon's violin solo at the Metro Music Festival, just before Dr. Zimmer changed her estrogen prescription, Gerald turned to Marilyn and said: "After twenty-two years, the free lunch is over."

I am sitting in a plastic chair, poolside. My husband is in Florida and we have checked into a motel with a sunlamp and a waterslide. I try not to imagine Marilyn scanning novelty plates, tables turned by the treacherous Gerald, uncoloured, underfed, but no longer mute. I try not to think about life and choices and risks.

Near the entrance, next to the towels, is a water cooler with paper glasses. Over and over, a human yo-yo, my son drains a cone-shaped glass, drops it in the garbage and springs back for more. "I'm thirsty," he says when I tell him he may pee his pants. My daughter is swimming, synchro-style, one hand over her head, up and down the ten-metre pool, keeping her glass dry.

I think about how the peace can be punctured. Last week, the kids were playing library, my son methodically checking out my daughter's selections. He had a stamp pad and a card for each borrowed book.

"I'd like something on cats," my daughter announced.

"Cats?" he mused, scanning his shelves. "Ummmmm. We have this – *Puss N Boots* –" followed by *Garfield's Christmas*. I could feel his sense of quiet accomplishment as he stamped the card. All went smoothly, until there was a flap over something and my daughter slammed down a copy of *The Secret Garden*.

"You are a terrible librarian," she barked. "You don't even help your customers." I wanted to laugh at the foolishness of the charge, but when I looked across the room, my son was crying, big hard tears that he tried to hide by burying his face in his chest, heartbroken tears that cut to his soul.

Now, he is smiling so I leave him to his water. I leave him, calm and protected, to his task.

About the Authors

Anar Ali is a graduate of the M.F.A. in Creative Writing program at the University of British Columbia, where she was also a member of the editorial board of *PRISM international.* Her stories have been published in *filling Station* and *Event.* "Baby Khaki's Wings" is from a recently completed collection of short stories entitled *Safari,* which spans a fifty-year period and is set in East Africa and Alberta. She has lived in many places, but now makes Toronto her home.

Kenneth Bonert is currently at work on a novel. "Packers and Movers," his first published fiction, has also received an honourable mention at the National Magazine Awards. His novella, *A Spy in the Valley,* was recently first runner-up in The Inconundrum Press's Melville Novella Contest. Born in 1972 in South Africa, he is now a freelance writer based in Toronto.

Jennifer Clouter is currently an English Honours student at Memorial University of Newfoundland and Labrador. Her poetry and short stories have been published in *TickleAce* and *Pottersfield Portfolio,* and in *The Backyards of Heaven,* an anthology of Irish and Newfoundland poetry. In 2002, she received top prize in the Senior Poetry Division of the annual Newfoundland and Labrador Arts and Letters Awards, and, in 2003, she won the Writers' Federation of Nova Scotia's Frog Hollow Books Poetry Prize. Her ultimate goal is to find enough time and money to pursue writing full time. She lives in St. John's, Newfoundland, with her husband and her brand-new son.

Daniel Griffin is from Kingston, Ontario. He has recently returned to Canada after several years living abroad. He currently makes his home in Toronto with his wife, two daughters, and their cat. You can read more of his work at www.danielgriffin.ca.

Michael Kissinger grew up in Nanaimo and now lives in Vancouver, where he recently received an M.F.A. in Creative Writing from the University of British Columbia. His writing has appeared in *Saturday Night*, *Prairie Fire*, *subTerrain*, and *Event*, among others. "Invest in the North" is from a collection of short stories tentatively titled *Thousands of Tiny Humiliations*.

Devin Krukoff was born and raised in Regina and now lives in Victoria, where he is pursuing graduate studies in Creative Writing. He is a current member of *The Malahat Review*'s editorial board, and is at work on a collection of short fiction. "The Last Spark" is his first publication.

Elaine McCluskey lives in Dartmouth, Nova Scotia. She is a former Bureau Chief for The Canadian Press news agency. She has had short stories published in *The Antigonish Review*, *The Gaspereau Review*, and *Pottersfield Portfolio*, which named her story "Bad Boys" the winner of the sixth annual *Pottersfield Portfolio* compact fiction contest. She is currently working on a story collection set in Atlantic Canada. In 1998, her novel *Going Fast* won the Bill Percy Award in the Writers' Federation of Nova Scotia's contest for unpublished manuscripts. She is a former tutor at the University of King's College in Halifax, and a graduate of Dalhousie University and the University of Western Ontario.

William Metcalfe's previous fiction publication was in Montreal's *Edge* in 1969. He has resumed writing fiction after a thirty-two-year break. He lives in Nelson, British Columbia, where he works as a radio station manager and a public affairs show host.

Lesley Millard won Honourable Mention in *The Fiddlehead*'s 2002 fiction contest, and first and third prizes in *Prairie Fire*'s 2003 fiction competition. "The Uses of the Neckerchief," first published in *Prairie Fire*, was also shortlisted for a Western Magazine Award and received an honourable mention at the National Magazine Awards. As well, she has published two stories in *The New Quarterly*, and is presently at work on a longer piece of fiction. She is grateful to the members of the

Kitchener-Waterloo Gem and Mineral Club, who introduced her to the Lafarge Quarry at Dundas.

Adam Lewis Schroeder holds an M.F.A. in Creative Writing from the University of British Columbia. His fiction collection, *Kingdom of Monkeys*, was published by Raincoast Books in 2001, and he is currently at work on a Second World War novel, a collection of ghost stories, and a one-man show about a guy in a loincloth. He, his wife, and their dog live in Penticton, British Columbia, in a rented house. It has three sheds.

Michael V. Smith's novel, *Cumberland* (Cormorant Books), was shortlisted for the Amazon.ca/Books in Canada First Novel Award. "What We Wanted" won the Western Magazine Award for Fiction. Not your usual writer, he also performs a popular stand-up and improv audience-participation act as Miss Cookie LaWhore. A poet, zinester, comedian, filmmaker, sex artist, and occasional clown, Smith is a graduate of the University of British Columbia's M.F.A in Creative Writing program. Find out more at www.michaelvsmith.com.

Neil Smith has published in several literary journals. "Isolettes" also won an honourable mention at the National Magazine Awards and will appear in *Coming Attractions 04* (Oberon Press), along with two of his other stories. He is working on a collection called *Bang Crunch*, whose title story will be published in *The Fiddlehead*. Another story in the collection was shortlisted for The Journey Prize in 2003.

Patricia Rose Young has published eight collections of poetry, two of which have been shortlisted for the Governor General's Award for Poetry. She has also won the Dorothy Livesay Poetry Prize, the B.C. Book Prize for Poetry, the Pat Lowther Award, the League of Canadian Poets' National Poetry Competition, and the National Magazine Award for Poetry. She began writing fiction a few years ago and is a member of lfc, a women's writing group. Her first collection of short stories will be published by Raincoast Books.

About the Contributing Journals

For more information about all the journals that submitted stories to this year's anthology, please consult *The Journey Prize Stories* Web site: www.mcclelland.com/jps

The Antigonish Review is a creative literary quarterly that publishes poetry, fiction, critical articles, and reviews. We consider stories, poetry, and essays from anywhere – original or in translation – but we consider it our mandate to encourage and publish new and emerging Canadian writers, with special consideration for those writers from the Atlantic region who might otherwise go unrecognized. Submissions and correspondence: *The Antigonish Review*, P.O. Box 5000, St. Francis Xavier University, Antigonish, Nova Scotia, B2G 2W5. Web site: www.antigonishreview.com

The Dalhousie Review has been in operation since 1921 and aspires to be a forum in which seriousness of purpose and playfulness of mind can coexist in meaningful dialogue. The journal publishes new fiction and poetry in every issue and welcomes submissions from authors around the world. Editor: Robert M. Martin. Submissions and correspondence: *The Dalhousie Review*, Dalhousie University, Halifax, Nova Scotia, B3H 4R2. E-mail: dalhousie.review@dal.ca Web site: www.dal.ca/~dalrev

filling Station, which has just celebrated its tenth anniversary, is a non-profit volunteer-run literary magazine based in Calgary. The *filling Station* editorial collective endeavours to strike a balance among new, emerging, and established writers, and among local, national, and international writers. *filling Station* encourages submission of all forms of contemporary writing (poetry, fiction, one-act plays, essays, and book reviews). All submissions must be original and previously unpublished; simultaneous submissions are acceptable. Submission deadlines are March 15, July 15, and November 15 of each year. Managing Editor: Natalie Simpson. Submissions and correspondence: *filling Station*, Box 22135, Bankers Hall, Calgary, Alberta, T2P 4J5. E-mail: editor@fillingstation.ca Web site: www.fillingstation.ca

Grain magazine provides readers with fine, fresh writing by new and established writers of poetry and prose four times a year. Published by the Saskatchewan Writers Guild, *Grain* has earned national and international recognition for its distinctive literary content. Editor: Kent Bruyneel. Fiction Editor: Joanne Gerber. Poetry Editor: Gerald Hill. Submissions and correspondence: *Grain*, P.O. Box 67, Saskatoon, Saskatchewan, S7K 3K1. E-mail: grainmag@sasktel.net Web site: www.grainmagazine.ca

The Malahat Review is a quarterly journal of contemporary poetry and fiction by both new and celebrated writers. Summer issues feature the winners of *Malahat*'s Novella and Long Poem prizes, held in alternate years; all issues feature covers by noted Canadian visual artists and include reviews of Canadian books. Editor: John Barton. Assistant Editor: Lucy Bashford. Submissions and correspondence: *The Malahat Review*, University of Victoria, P.O. Box 1700, Station CSC, Victoria, British Columbia, V8W 2Y2. Web site: www.malahatreview.ca

Prairie Fire is a quarterly magazine of contemporary Canadian writing which publishes stories, poems, and literary non-fiction by both emerging and established writers. *Prairie Fire*'s editorial mix also occasionally features critical or personal essays and interviews with authors. *Prairie Fire* publishes a fiction issue every summer. Stories published in *Prairie Fire* have won awards at the National Magazine Awards and the Western Magazine Awards. *Prairie Fire* publishes writing from, and has readers in, all parts of Canada. Editor: Andris Taskans. Fiction Editors: Heidi Harms and Susan Rempel Letkemann. Submissions and correspondence: *Prairie Fire*, Room 423–100 Arthur Street, Winnipeg, Manitoba, R3B 1H3. E-mail: prfire@mts.net Web site: www.prairiefire.mb.ca

PRISM international, the oldest literary magazine in Western Canada, was established in 1959 by a group of Vancouver writers. Published four times a year, *PRISM* features short fiction, poetry, drama, creative non-fiction, and translations by both new and established writers from Canada and from around the world. The only criteria are originality and quality. *PRISM* holds three exemplary competitions: the Annual Short Fiction Contest, the Earle Birney Prize for Poetry, and the Rogers Communications Contest for Literary Non-fiction. Executive Editor: Brenda Leifso. Fiction Editor: Catharine Chen. Poetry Editor: Amanda Lamarche. Submissions and correspondence: *PRISM international*, Creative Writing Program, The University of British Columbia, Buchanan E-462, 1866 Main Mall, Vancouver, British Columbia, V6T 1Z1. E-mail (for queries only): prism@interchange.ubc.ca Web site: www.prism.arts.ubc.ca

Room of One's Own is Canada's oldest feminist literary journal. In recent years we have broadened the scope of the magazine to encompass the entire female perspective. *Room* publishes fiction, poetry, and art by established and emerging women writers and artists, with an emphasis on Canadians. The magazine is unique in that its editorial staff is comprised solely of volunteers. Submissions and correspondence: *Room of One's Own*, Box 46160, Station D, Vancouver, British Columbia, V6J 5G5. Web site: www.roommagazine.com

This Magazine is one of Canada's longest-publishing magazines of politics, culture, and the arts. Over the years, *This Magazine* has introduced the early work of some of Canada's most notable writers, poets, and critics, including Margaret Atwood, Naomi Klein, Dennis Lee, Lillian Allen, Tomson Highway, Evelyn Lau, Dionne Brand, Michael Ondaatje, Mark Kingwell, Lynn Crosbie, Lynn Coady, and Jason Sherman. *This Magazine* publishes new fiction in every issue, and poetry three times a year, as well as an annual literary supplement. The magazine does not accept unsolicited submissions of fiction, poetry, or drama, but new writers are encouraged to enter the magazine's annual contest, The Great Canadian Literary Hunt. Editor: Patricia D'Souza. Submissions and correspondence: *This Magazine*, 401 Richmond St. W. #396, Toronto, Ontario, M5V 3A8. Web site: www.thismagazine.ca

TickleAce is a semi-annual literary journal that publishes fiction, poetry, book reviews, interviews, and visual art. Now in its twenty-seventh year, the award-winning magazine focuses on the words and images of contributors from its home province of Newfoundland and Labrador but includes as well a fine selection of pieces from across Canada and beyond. Decidedly eclectic in subject, form, and flavour, *TickleAce* offerings include pieces by the internationally renowned, the emerging talent, and the talented first-timer. Editor: Bruce Porter. Submissions and correspondence: *TickleAce*, P.O. Box 5353, St. John's, Newfoundland, A1C 5W2. E-mail: tickleace@nfld.com

Submissions were also received from the following journals:

Broken Pencil
(Toronto, Ont.)

The Claremont Review
(Victoria, B.C.)

Descant
(Toronto, Ont.)

Event
(New Westminster, B.C.)

Exile
(Toronto, Ont.)

The Fiddlehead
(Fredericton, N.B.)

Geist
(Vancouver, B.C.)

Green's Magazine
(Regina, Sask.)

lichen
(Whitby, Ont.)

The New Orphic Review
(Nelson, B.C.)

The New Quarterly
(Waterloo, Ont.)

Other Voices
(Edmonton, Alta.)

Pagitica in Toronto
(Toronto, Ont.)

Parchment
(Toronto, Ont.)

Pottersfield Portfolio
(Sydney, N.S.)

Prairie Journal
(Calgary, Alta.)

Queen's Quarterly
(Kingston, Ont.)

Storyteller
(Ottawa, Ont.)

subTerrain Magazine
(Vancouver, B.C.)

Taddle Creek
(Toronto, Ont.)

The Windsor Review
(Windsor, Ont.)

The Journey Prize Stories
List of Previous Contributing Authors

* Winners of the $10,000 Journey Prize
** Co-winners of the $10,000 Journey Prize

1
1989
SELECTED WITH ALISTAIR MACLEOD

Ven Begamudré, "Word Games"
David Bergen, "Where You're From"
Lois Braun, "The Pumpkin-Eaters"
Constance Buchanan, "Man with Flying Genitals"
Ann Copeland, "Obedience"
Marion Douglas, "Flags"
Frances Itani, "An Evening in the Café"
Diane Keating, "The Crying Out"
Thomas King, "One Good Story, That One"
Holley Rubinsky, "Rapid Transits"*
Jean Rysstad, "Winter Baby"
Kevin Van Tighem, "Whoopers"
M.G. Vassanji, "In the Quiet of a Sunday Afternoon"
Bronwen Wallace, "Chicken 'N' Ribs"
Armin Wiebe, "Mouse Lake"
Budge Wilson, "Waiting"

2
1990
SELECTED WITH LEON ROOKE; GUY VANDERHAEGHE

André Alexis, "Despair: Five Stories of Ottawa"
Glen Allen, "The Hua Guofeng Memorial Warehouse"
Marusia Bociurkiw, "Mama, Donya"
Virgil Burnett, "Billfrith the Dreamer"
Margaret Dyment, "Sacred Trust"

Cynthia Flood, "My Father Took a Cake to France"*
Douglas Glover, "Story Carved in Stone"
Terry Griggs, "Man with the Axe"
Rick Hillis, "Limbo River"
Thomas King, "The Dog I Wish I Had, I Would Call It Helen"
K.D. Miller, "Sunrise Till Dark"
Jennifer Mitton, "Let Them Say"
Lawrence O'Toole, "Goin' to Town with Katie Ann"
Kenneth Radu, "A Change of Heart"
Jenifer Sutherland, "Table Talk"
Wayne Tefs, "Red Rock and After"

3
1991
SELECTED WITH JANE URQUHART

Donald Aker, "The Invitation"
Anton Baer, "Yukon"
Allan Barr, "A Visit from Lloyd"
David Bergen, "The Fall"
Rai Berzins, "Common Sense"
Diana Hartog, "Theories of Grief"
Diane Keating, "The Salem Letters"
Yann Martel, "The Facts Behind the Helsinki Roccamatios"*
Jennifer Mitton, "Polaroid"
Sheldon Oberman, "This Business with Elijah"
Lynn Podgurny, "Till Tomorrow, Maple Leaf Mills"
James Riseborough, "She Is Not His Mother"
Patricia Stone, "Living on the Lake"

4
1992
SELECTED WITH SANDRA BIRDSELL

David Bergen, "The Bottom of the Glass"
Maria A. Billion, "No Miracles Sweet Jesus"
Judith Cowan, "By the Big River"
Steven Heighton, "A Man Away from Home Has No Neighbours"
Steven Heighton, "How Beautiful upon the Mountains"
L. Rex Kay, "Travelling"

Rozena Maart, "No Rosa, No District Six"*
Guy Malet De Carteret, "Rainy Day"
Carmelita McGrath, "Silence"
Michael Mirolla, "A Theory of Discontinuous Existence"
Diane Juttner Perreault, "Bella's Story"
Eden Robinson, "Traplines"

5
1993
SELECTED WITH GUY VANDERHAEGHE

Caroline Adderson, "Oil and Dread"
David Bergen, "La Rue Prevette"
Marina Endicott, "With the Band"
Dayv James-French, "Cervine"
Michael Kenyon, "Durable Tumblers"
K.D. Miller, "A Litany in Time of Plague"
Robert Mullen, "Flotsam"
Gayla Reid, "Sister Doyle's Men"*
Oakland Ross, "Bang-bang"
Robert Sherrin, "Technical Battle for Trial Machine"
Carol Windley, "The Etruscans"

6
1994
SELECTED WITH DOUGLAS GLOVER;
JUDITH CHANT (CHAPTERS)

Anne Carson, "Water Margins: An Essay on Swimming by My Brother"
Richard Cumyn, "The Sound He Made"
Genni Gunn, "Versions"
Melissa Hardy, "Long Man the River"*
Robert Mullen, "Anomie"
Vivian Payne, "Free Falls"
Jim Reil, "Dry"
Robyn Sarah, "Accept My Story"
Joan Skogan, "Landfall"
Dorothy Speak, "Relatives in Florida"
Alison Wearing, "Notes from Under Water"

7

1995

SELECTED WITH M.G. VASSANJI;
RICHARD BACHMANN (A DIFFERENT DRUMMER BOOKS)

Michelle Alfano, "Opera"
Mary Borsky, "Maps of the Known World"
Gabriella Goliger, "Song of Ascent"
Elizabeth Hay, "Hand Games"
Shaena Lambert, "The Falling Woman"
Elise Levine, "Boy"
Roger Burford Mason, "The Rat-Catcher's Kiss"
Antanas Sileika, "Going Native"
Kathryn Woodward, "Of Marranos and Gilded Angels"*

8

1996

SELECTED WITH OLIVE SENIOR;
BEN MCNALLY (NICHOLAS HOARE LTD.)

Rick Bowers, "Dental Bytes"
David Elias, "How I Crossed Over"
Elyse Gasco, "Can You Wave Bye Bye, Baby?"*
Danuta Gleed, "Bones"
Elizabeth Hay, "The Friend"
Linda Holeman, "Turning the Worm"
Elaine Littman, "The Winner's Circle"
Murray Logan, "Steam"
Rick Maddocks, "Lessons from the Sputnik Diner"
K.D. Miller, "Egypt Land"
Gregor Robinson, "Monster Gaps"
Alma Subasic, "Dust"

9

1997

SELECTED WITH NINO RICCI;
NICHOLAS PASHLEY (UNIVERSITY OF TORONTO BOOKSTORE)

Brian Bartlett, "Thomas, Naked"
Dennis Bock, "Olympia"

Kristen den Hartog, "Wave"
Gabriella Goliger, "Maladies of the Inner Ear" **
Terry Griggs, "Momma Had a Baby"
Mark Anthony Jarman, "Righteous Speedboat"
Judith Kalman, "Not for Me a Crown of Thorns"
Andrew Mullins, "The World of Science"
Sasenarine Persaud, "Canada Geese and Apple Chatney"
Anne Simpson, "Dreaming Snow"**
Sarah Withrow, "Ollie"
Terence Young, "The Berlin Wall"

10

1998

SELECTED BY PETER BUITENHUIS; HOLLEY RUBINSKY;
CELIA DUTHIE (DUTHIE BOOKS LTD.)

John Brooke, "The Finer Points of Apples"*
Ian Colford, "The Reason for the Dream"
Libby Creelman, "Cruelty"
Michael Crummey, "Serendipity"
Stephen Guppy, "Downwind"
Jane Eaton Hamilton, "Graduation"
Elise Levine, "You Are You Because Your Little Dog Loves You"
Jean McNeil, "Bethlehem"
Liz Moore, "Eight-Day Clock"
Edward O'Connor, "The Beatrice of Victoria College"
Tim Rogers, "Scars and Other Presents"
Denise Ryan, "Marginals, Vivisections, and Dreams"
Madeleine Thien, "Simple Recipes"
Cheryl Tibbetts, "Flowers of Africville"

11

1999

SELECTED BY LESLEY CHOYCE; SHELDON CURRIE;
MARY-JO ANDERSON (FROG HOLLOW BOOKS)

Mike Barnes, "In Florida"
Libby Creelman, "Sunken Island"
Mike Finigan, "Passion Sunday"

Jane Eaton Hamilton, "Territory"
Mark Anthony Jarman, "Travels into Several Remote Nations of the World"
Barbara Lambert, "Where the Bodies Are Kept"
Linda Little, "The Still"
Larry Lynch, "The Sitter"
Sandra Sabatini, "The One With the News"
Sharon Steams, "Brothers"
Mary Walters, "Show Jumping"
Alissa York, "The Back of the Bear's Mouth"*

12
2000
SELECTED BY CATHERINE BUSH; HAL NIEDZVIECKI; MARC GLASSMAN (PAGES BOOKS AND MAGAZINES)

Andrew Gray, "The Heart of the Land"
Lee Henderson, "Sheep Dub"
Jessica Johnson, "We Move Slowly"
John Lavery, "The Premier's New Pyjamas"
J.A. McCormack, "Hearsay"
Nancy Richler, "Your Mouth Is Lovely"
Andrew Smith, "Sightseeing"
Karen Solie, "Onion Calendar"
Timothy Taylor, "Doves of Townsend"*
Timothy Taylor, "Pope's Own"
Timothy Taylor, "Silent Cruise"
R.M. Vaughan, "Swan Street"

13
2001
SELECTED BY ELYSE GASCO; MICHAEL HELM; MICHAEL NICHOLSON (INDIGO BOOKS & MUSIC INC.)

Kevin Armstrong, "The Cane Field"*
Mike Barnes, "Karaoke Mon Amour"
Heather Birrell, "Machaya"
Heather Birrell, "The Present Perfect"
Craig Boyko, "The Gun"

Vivette J. Kady, "Anything That Wiggles"
Billie Livingston, "You're Taking All the Fun Out of It"
Annabel Lyon, "Fishes"
Lisa Moore, "The Way the Light Is"
Heather O'Neill, "Little Suitcase"
Susan Rendell, "In the Chambers of the Sea"
Tim Rogers, "Watch"
Margrith Schraner, "Dream Dig"

14
2002
SELECTED BY ANDRÉ ALEXIS;
DEREK MCCORMACK; DIANE SCHOEMPERLEN

Mike Barnes, "Cogagwee"
Geoffrey Brown, "Listen"
Jocelyn Brown, "Miss Canada"*
Emma Donoghue, "What Remains"
Jonathan Goldstein, "You Are a Spaceman With Your Head Under the Bathroom Stall Door"
Robert McGill, "Confidence Men"
Robert McGill, "The Stars Are Falling"
Nick Melling, "Philemon"
Robert Mullen, "Alex the God"
Karen Munro, "The Pool"
Leah Postman, "Being Famous"
Neil Smith, "Green Fluorescent Protein"

15
2003
SELECTED BY MICHELLE BERRY;
TIMOTHY TAYLOR; MICHAEL WINTER

Rosaria Campbell, "Reaching"
Hilary Dean, "The Lemon Stories"
Dawn Rae Downton, "Hansel and Gretel"
Anne Fleming, "Gay Dwarves of America"
Elyse Friedman, "Truth"
Charlotte Gill, "Hush"

Jessica Grant, "My Husband's Jump"*
Jacqueline Honnet, "Conversion Classes"
S.K. Johannesen, "Resurrection"
Avner Mandelman, "Cuckoo"
Tim Mitchell, "Night Finds Us"
Heather O'Neill, "The Difference Between Me and Goldstein"